THE JOHNNY TAGGETT SERIES

JOHNNY TAGGETT
THE KILLING SOUND

WILLIAM D. HOY

Copyright © 2024 William D. Hoy
The Johnny Taggett Series

ISBN:
978-1-966235-04-0 (paperback)
978-1-966235-05-7 (hardback)

All rights reserved.
No part of this publication may be reproduced, stored in a retrieval system, or transmitted in any form or by any means – electronic, mechanical, photocopy, recording, scanning, or other – except for brief quotations in critical reviews or articles, without the prior written permission of the publisher.

Published by:

OMNIBOOK Co.
99 Wall Street, Suite 118
New York, NY 10005 USA
+1-866-216-9965
www.omnibook.org

For e-book purchase: Kindle on Amazon, Barnes and Noble
Book purchase: Amazon.com, Barnes & Noble, and www.omnibook.org

Omnibook titles may be purchased in bulk for educational, business, fund-raising, or sales promotional use. For more information please e-mail admin@omnibook.org

CONTENTS

Chapter One 1
Chapter Two 7
Chapter Three 13
Chapter Four 19
Chapter Five 25
Chapter Six 31
Chapter Seven 37
Chapter Eight 43
Chapter Nine 49
Chapter Ten 55
Chapter Eleven 61
Chapter Twelve 67
Chapter Thirteen 73
Chapter Fourteen 79
Chapter Fifteen 87
Chapter Sixteen 93
Chapter Seventeen 99
Chapter Eighteen 105
Chapter Nineteen 111
Chapter Twenty 117
Chapter Twenty One 125

Chapter Twenty Two 131
Chapter Twenty Three 139
Chapter Twenty Four. 147
Chapter Twenty Five 155
Chapter Twenty Six 163
Chapter Twenty Seven 171
Chapter Twenty Eight 179
Chapter Twenty Nine 187
Chapter Thirty. 195
Chapter Thirty One. 203

CHAPTER ONE

So here's Johnny Taggett dreaming about the San Francisco night as it drifts around 3:30 in the morning somewhere in 1942. In his brain the darkness is covering the streets outside like a veil over a corpse's face. It's dripping down the walls of alleys where the winos are clutching their drained bottles and moaning along with the wind. It's filling in the windows of the whorehouses as they close down to give those storefronts the blank expressions of blind men. It drapes itself over countless rapes and murders and makes a soft blanket for the citizens who sleep with their eyes closed.

Johnny doesn't sleep so well. For a moment his eyes pop open to take in the darkness of his ratty little apartment, and then they slip closed again, and there he is walking his first beat back in New York City alongside old Sergeant Murphy. They're climbing up this rickety old staircase holding lanterns because it's all of a sudden sometime in the last century. The old wood creaks under their feet the way a cheap bed might creak under a big restless detective with bad dreams. Up they go through that darkness that keeps trying to press them back down. Murphy's muttering something as they climb; Taggett's not really paying attention because he's trying to figure out what the hell they're climbing toward. After a year or two of trudging through the stink of whatever ancient tenement they've been sent to, Murphy's grumble gets a little louder so Taggett can almost hear it. Whatever the old Sergeant's rambling sounds like the kind of story you might hear the grandfathers tell each other back in the villages, some kind of spiel about the creatures that live in the shadows and use their black teeth to tear apart the fools who aren't looking. That stairway's crowded with just the kind of shadows Murphy's describing through his clenched jaw. Suddenly the old man stops and thrusts his lantern in Taggett's face. Murphy's eyes are like pools of ink with the little reflections of the lantern's flame struggling not to drown in their centers. "Don't forget the sound," croaks the old Sergeant. For some reason he starts to stamp his foot on the rickety step they're standing on. "Don't forget the sound," he says again, his smoker's rattle fighting its way out of that whisper as he's stomping on that step a bull getting ready to charge. "The sound!" he shouts, and Taggett's sitting up in bed with the echo still in his mind and the banging from somewhere rattling his skull.

He's groaning, "Oh, what the hell," even as he's groping around the upside-down crate next to the creaky little cot he sleeps on for a cigarette and a match. Once he has the smoke lit, he looks around in that pale flicker at the shadows of his raggedy furniture. Naked, he sits there smoking for a moment and trying to figure out where the hell that pounding noise is still coming from. "What the fuck," he finally says to himself. "That's my front door. Who the hell would be trying to get me up at this time of night? Better keep my mouth shut in case it's some kind of bill collector." The match goes out, and Taggett sits there in the dark and listens to the hammering for a little while longer until it shuts up.

And then it starts up again, and Taggett moans, "Jesus, don't people sleep in this town?" He lights up another smoke and says to himself, "Wait a minute, maybe that's that tomato from last night. She was making noises about paying me a visit. Maybe she's got her panties in enough of a twist to finally come see me." He sits there in the dark trying to think of her name and wondering if he should get some pants on. He spits a crumb of tobacco down onto the invisible floor, letting the shadows swallow it up, and says to himself, "Nuts. That's not the way a little sweetie like that knocks on the door. Definitely bill collectors. I'll get in that fight later." He takes another drag and yells, "Scram! I'll pay up Tuesday!" The knocking stops.

For a few blinks of an eye the shadowy apartment fills up with silence, and then the little sounds of the city start to filter in. The wind rattles the windows that sit loosely in their frames. A truck growls past, and a can clatters to the pavement, and a hungry cat yells in the alley, yell turning to a screech as someone throws a shoe. Taggett sits there in the dark, smoking, listening, thinking. "No footsteps," he mutters to himself. "No one walking away. Someone waiting." The hum and buzz of the city keeps creeping around the apartment as Taggett ponders. "That dream. Murphy. Something about sound." He's keeping his deep voice down to a murmur as he goes over his memory, trying to grab on to what he needs from that dream.

In his memory, he's back there with Murphy on that staircase. Now that it's not a dream, they're not old-timey flatfoots carrying lanterns; they're going up fire stairs to get to some creep they need to bring in for questioning. Routine thing, but Taggett's new, so Murphy's filling him in. "You gotta be careful on these door jobs, son," the older man's whispering as they get to the floor below their destination. "I had a partner name of Williams back before you started sucking air, and he bought it exactly on one of these jobs. He didn't hear the killing sound."

"What's that?" says Taggett in his memory.

The sergeant takes a breath. "It's hard to describe, son. All I can tell you is that when some crazed fool decides to take you out, there's a noise. Sometimes it's the click of cocking gun, sometimes it's that little hiss of breath just before the knife pulls back. I heard that sound years ago with Williams in front of that door, and I ducked." Murphy's voice gets thick for a moment. "I ducked out of the way, and Williams took a full load of shot right in his face, right through the door. I had to put a foot on his body to steady myself so I could blast the son of a bitch who killed him back to hell. I tell you, son, it's nothing a man easily forgets."

In his bedroom, now, Taggett can't help chuckling a little. He knows by now that Murphy was wrong; Taggett's killed more creeps than he can remember. Back then, Taggett says to the sergeant, "What did you hear?"

"The tiniest thing," says Murphy. "Weird, it was like a little burst of silence, like the world just quit for a moment. Maybe like what you hear after you're dead, I don't know." Little Murphy looks up at Taggett, and the sergeant's eyes are glistening wet in the flickering light of Johnny's flash. "I heard that, or felt it, and I knew that would be it for me. So I ducked, and that was it for Williams." He falls silent for a second. The building creaks and breathes around them, and someone a few floors up is practicing violin at this time of night. "Anyway, I'm saying you gotta be careful and listen close."

Taggett sits there in the dark, listening close. His muscular body's shaking just a little as he pours all his concentration into his ears, so the BANG BANG BANG makes him jump and curse when it starts again. "These characters don't give up," he mutters. "Why the hell isn't someone out there trying to shut them up?" The noise is getting almost mechanical, regular, like someone's rigged up a jackhammer out in the hall to get Taggett's attention or get him to the door or something. He sits there naked, smoking, thinking.

The creep out there's hammering in threes. One. Two. Three. Pausing between each slam and a little longer after the third to start again. One. Two. Three. Not quite a rhythm, almost hypnotic. One. Two. Three. Taggett throws away his butt, glances at the little spark going out in the darkness. One. Two. Three. One. Two.

The quiet closes in again. "Someone playing games," Taggett tells himself. "Trying to rattle me. Well, let's see how he likes my game." He slowly swivels himself around, soft enough to keep the bedsprings from creaking under his weight, and just as carefully rises to his feet. Knots in the knitted rug push into the soles of his feet. He stands there for a full second, then he takes a step, and then another step, and then another, till he's off the rug and onto the cold tile of his cheap little rented room. In the quiet, as he tries to keep himself from giving away his motion, he can feel the sweat seeping out of his skin. The door's down a short hallway that leads to the bedroom he's feeling his way through right now. He's past where the streetlight filters into the window, so he's got his hands out to keep him from missing that hallway. He thinks he's almost to the wall when he hears something skitter on the other side of the door, so he freezes. A couple of heartbeats push against the inside of his chest, and then nothing happens, so he takes another step and then BANG BANG BANG freezes him again.

The creep out there's hitting that same crazy near-beat. Taggett takes advantage, creeping a little closer to that entry hall through the hammering, holding on the silences. He's looking down that dark little entrance hall. Even though he can't see it, he knows his side of the front door is covered with travel posters just slapped one over another by the nut that had the room before him. Taggett stares down that hall, waiting for the noise to start up again, wondering if the nut ever made it to Aspen or Tahiti or wherever. The racket starts up again; Taggett moves a little bit closer to that door and its invisible promises of escape and adventure.

He feels the floor change under his feet, smooth cool tile to rough wood: he's in the hall. He stretches out both arms and feels the walls against his fingertips. This close to the door it's like the noise is in his head, slamming his brain against the inside of his skull. He's ready to tear open the door and shove his .45 right down the neck of that—

The thought almost makes him fall down. "Goddamit," he grumbles in his throat. "How could I leave it next to the bed. Soft and sloppy, Taggett. Guess I'll just have to let my fists clue this creep in. Almost there." BANG BANG BANG. He inches forward. Silence. He stops. He reaches out with his left hand. His right's curled into a wrecking ball ready for whatever's on the other side of that banging. He can feel the air pressure pushing the noise into his ears.

And then silence. He feels the creak of the board under his foot. It's like the city's holding its breath.

That's when Johnny Taggett hears the killing sound.

CHAPTER TWO

Taggett hits the floor hard. The first blast punches a jagged hole in the door in front of where his face just was. The rounds burn the air above his back like a swarm of stinging bees as he squirms back around in the dark, the hall now just a little too narrow. He pulls in his elbows and tries not to raise his head as he worms his way back to the little table next to his bed where he keeps his .45. Another blast burns through over his back. "Creep's firing blind," the detective growls. "Only thing saving me." He crawls. The rough wood of the hallway scrapes down his belly, and then finally the floor turns back into that smooth cold tile, slippery now with his sweat.

He fishtails forward somehow to the knit rug, fingers curling to grab and pull him to the rickety table next to the bed. "Must be reloading," he tells himself as he gropes up to the table top to grab his .45 and the phone the landlady let him wire in after he beat up the thug of a husband who tried to whore her out for whiskey money.

Hugging the floor, gripping his .45 in one hand, he uses the other to pull the receiver off the cradle and dial a number. He lifts it to his chin in the weird silence after those big barrel gun blasts and listens as the ring tone gets interrupted by someone yelling something in Chinese. "Chen," he says. "Taggett." And then he just lays the receiver down as the creep on the other side of the door gets another shot through. The bullet holes in the wall behind his bed are connecting to form a deeper darkness in the night-filled room. Taggett stays ducked as he makes sure the .45 is loaded.

It is, so he rises to fire, but he has to hit the rug fast again because the creep outside has another shot. The boom of it seems to shake the building as it blows the crappy mattress Taggett sleeps on into a cloud of feathers. "Time to reload again," the detective mutters and rises again, tightening his finger on the trigger.

And down he goes again. Suddenly there's a flood of lead stitching scars in what's left of the walls and the furniture. "Tommy gun!" curses Taggett, and he stays down, finally getting a shot into the blackness of that little entry hall. Someone out there yelps, and Taggett grins, but then the roar of that Tommy gun wipes the smile off his face as he tries to squirm out of the path of that mob of bullets. As the round shreds the window shade and the window on the other side of the bed from where he's digging himself into the floor, a flicker comes in from the streetlight outside. Taggett glances at what it gives him and crawls on his elbows toward the dark rectangle of the bathroom's open door. The swarm of bullets above him goes away for a second, but before he can do anything about it that shotgun's booming his bed frame into a pile of sticks. Finally he gets the linoleum floor of the bathroom under his belly. He gets himself up on his ass, fishes around behind the tank for a pack of smokes, and lights up. "They'll run out sooner or later," he tells himself. "No one's got that much ammo." He sits there and smokes and watches some creeps use lead scissors to cut his apartment to tatters.

As he settles down to wait for the cops—if his chickenshit neighbors can't peep out of their doors, they can at least call the cops—Taggett starts to think about that hostage situation he and Murphy stumbled into at the end of that climb up the stairway.

Turns out that behind the door they're going up to knock on is some freak who busted out of prison and crossed three states in a couple of days to get to his wife and his daughter and his mother-in-law so he could tie them up with electrical cords and decide what to do with them. Murphy's knock on the door interrupts him. "Get the fuck outta here!" yells the freak. "I'll blow every single one of these bitches to the fucking moon!"

Murphy shoots Taggett a look and makes a calm-down gesture with his open hand. Taggett nods and takes a breath and slips his .38 back into its holster. "Now let's be calm," says the sergeant. "No need to blow anybody anywhere." He's letting that cheesy Irish brogue creep into his voice as he tries to soothe the screaming weirdo on the other side of the door. "Sure, 'tis just a misunderstanding we can clear up easy as pie. We're both reasonable people, aren't we?"

"I got reasons!" belts through the brittle wood of the door into the barely-lit hall. Doors open and heads of neighbors poke out, so Taggett turns around to wave the civilians back to their soft beds. "I got a shotgun too! But I only got two shots, so I gotta decide which of these bitches gets to live! I gotta think! Get the fuck outta here!" The freak's voice is going up in pitch as he hollers; Taggett can almost hear the flecks of spit hitting the inside of the door as the two cops stand there in the shadow between a couple of bare bulbs.

"Sure, sure," murmurs Murphy through the door, "truly a dilemma. We should discuss your options, son. You might find you don't need to kill a single bitch tonight." The sergeant's left hand is still out and level, keeping Taggett steady. "Let's start from the beginning. My name's Murphy. What's yours, son?"

There's a pause that the pulse in Taggett's head fills with sound like an ocean beating on an empty beach, and then the squeaky voice says, "Soames. Bob Soames. Oh, Jesus, what am I doing? My baby, I can't kill my"—the sentence cracks up into a series of sobs and whines, then the sound of a guy clearing his throat. "Uh, Murphy?"

The sergeant's leather mask of a face cracks into a smile. "Yes, son?" Taggett lets out a breath he forgot he was holding.

Soames is back there whimpering. "I don't, I don't wanna, oh fuck, don't wanna, I want, I want, oh my god," that kind of thing, and Murphy is actually winking at Taggett. Taggett rolls his eyes and glances around the hallway. Looks like all the neighbors are back in their rooms behaving or just waiting for the cops to scram and let the night life start up again. From behind that door he can hear something scraping across the floor like someone's dragging away a barricade while Soames just keeps babbling in his high scratch of a whine. "Can't, oh god, I gotta,

I gotta, don't, I can't, I," and along those lines until he starts to sound like a little boy and finally says, "Murphy?"

"I'm here, son." The sergeant's got generations of fatherly Irish in his tone. "I'm right here, everything's fine, no need to do anything you don't want to." He's almost singing the freak a lullaby.

That little-boy voice comes creeping through the door. "I wanna give myself up, Murphy, but I can't—you know, I can't make myself open the door." The freak actually sniffles. "Can you, can you, uh, open the door and come get me?"

"Of course, son," says Murphy and throws Taggett another wink. Taggett grimaces and gives the other man a hurry-up gesture. Murphy puts one hand on his service revolver and the other hand on the doorknob.

Under Soames's sobs and whimpers, under the buzz of the lightbulbs in the hall, under the creaking of the leather in his holster and the wood under his feet, under his own breath, Taggett hears a kind of click. The killing sound.

He opens his mouth to warn Murphy and the door blows into the hall, splinters shredding Murphy's skin around the big burnt hole in his chest. The second shot from Soames's double-barrel blows the sergeant's jaw back through his head to shatter on the far wall of the hall. Murphy's body leans against that wall for a moment then slides down as if the sergeant was just too drunk to stand after a Friday night.

By this time Taggett's grabbed the barrel of Soames's bazooka. The hot metal burns his hand, and he howls as he punches the freak in the face over and over until he feels cheekbones crack and give way. The he drops the punk to the floor as he takes in what's behind, what Soames has been crying about.

Against the wall opposite the door there's a sofa. On the sofa there's an old woman, a younger woman, and a little girl. They're tired up with what looks like the cords from the lamp that's broken on the floor and the radio face-down under it. They're naked, and their skin is scrawled with scars, some maybe a day old, some still dripping the last few drops of blood. The rest of the blood is decorating that sofa and the wall behind it. As Taggett's standing there staring, the freak makes some kind of gurgling moan from down there on the floor. Taggett raises one of his big feet and stomps down hard and hears something crunch under his boot, and then the silence closes in.

It's that silence that pokes Taggett out of his memory as he crouches there in his bathroom. He takes a long look at the wreckage in his room. Those creeps out there have punched such a big hole in his wall with their artillery that the streetlight gets in from outside to throw big shadows of the sharp, splintered sticks of what used to be furniture. The detective can't help snickering to himself. "Knew I could wait 'em out," he mutters. He gets his feet square under himself and checks his gun and takes a breath. Just in case they're a little smarter than he's ready for, he creeps around the counter of his little kitchenette and edges his head so he can see down the entry hall. "Damn," he grunts to himself. "Can't believe there's so much left of that door, just that big jagged hole in the middle."

A noise from the other side of the door freezes him. Some kind of slap, something hitting a hard wood surface, a grunt and another slap and another thud. Then, in that light from the hole in his wall, Taggett can see someone reach through the hole in the door and start to open the three locks he's had installed to keep out the dangerous type. He hears the click of the first lock opening, then after a second the second. He grips his gun and gets ready. The third lock clicks open as Taggett wheels around the corner and brings up the .45. As his finger tightens on the trigger, he hollers, "Get ready, home wrecker! My turn!"

CHAPTER THREE

The arm pulls itself back out of the hole in the door, and a familiar voice comes through. "Easy, boss," Chen says. "Don't shoot a pal before you mean to."

Taggett can't help chuckling. "Yeah, come on in. I guess I'm entertaining this evening."

As Johnny's uncocking the .45, Chen reaches back through the door to twist the deadbolt. The door swings open, and the light bulb in the hall flickers on behind a wiry little Chinese guy with his lips set into a permanent smirk."Geez, Taggett, put some trousers on, will ya?" he says. "You'll give your guests the idea you're a slovenly housekeeper."

Taggett blinks and suddenly notices that he's still naked. He's a little surprised to find out he can blush as he gropes around for something to cover himself with. He finds the pants from his one good suit and a stiff dingy undershirt and shoves himself into the rags while Chen slips down that dark entry hall and around a corner to a countertop and the coffeepot somehow still unbroken on it. "This new coffee?" he says.

Taggett snorts another chuckle. "You're feeling sleepy? Maybe you need more exercise." The detective grabs the .45's holster and a blazer and slips them both on. "By the way, what's out there in the hall?"

"Oh, yeah, sorry about that," says Chen "When I got your phone call, I figured I'd get a little fun, but there were only the three goons outside." The younger man reaches into a drawer and rummages around and pulls out a coffee cup. "I thought we were going to save that phone call gag for real emergencies."

Johnny grabs his hat and shoves it on his head and pokes his thumb back at the jagged hole where there used to be a wall. "What do you call that?" he says.

The younger man pauses for a moment to take it in the way a tourist might take in the Golden Gate. "I just figured you were redecorating. You know, I've always said that you could stand to get some more light into this crappy little suite of yours." He goes back to pouring some kind of brown sludge from the coffeepot into the cup. "I have to say, this coffee don't look too fresh, boss. Maybe you oughta spring for a new—"

"Jesus Christ," Taggett growls. "Enough. Are you gonna tell me who's been trying to mow me down in my bed before the cops get here and you can tell them too?" The detective steps closer to his pal, those hard blue eyes glaring down. "If we need to get our story straight, then spill. We can go get some coffee after we're done here."

Chen blinks and grins back up at Taggett. "Okay, boss, no need to get your feathers all fluffed. Here's the straight story." He takes a sip of that old coffee and makes a grimace and goes on. "After my uncle woke me up out of my dream about me and Rita Hayworth, I ankle it over here and there's these three gorillas set up outside your door. I guess they were too busy trying to roust you to notice me, so I picked up the trash can by the stairwell and bashed the guy with the shotgun over the head, gave the moose with the Tommy a couple of good kicks into the old melon, and ended up smashing the guy with the sledge hammer in the nuts. They're looking a lot more peaceful now." The little man chuckles and takes another sip. "Damn, whatever this stuff you call coffee is, it's growing on me."

Taggett's just shaking his head. "I can't believe you don't carry a roscoe of your own." He walks around Chen and grabs a cup of his own and pours a splatter from the coffeepot. "So did you get any idea who they are?"

Chen smirks and shrugs. "I was a little too distracted to make introductions," he chuckles. "I mean, I sort of announced myself, but we never exactly exchanged calling cards. Guess now they won't invite me to tea for Easter."

"You don't have the personality for it," says Taggett, and the two men take their coffee down the short hall and peer through the doorway at three wadded up heaps of laundry with goons in them in the hall. "You don't leave much for questioning, do you?" the detective says.

Chen takes another sip and snickers and says, "Didn't seem like much time for a conversation considering the firepower these gorillas were swinging. I haven't seen a shotgun kick that hard since back in Shanghai." He prods one of the heaps with his left foot. "Any of these creeps look familiar to you?"

Taggett stands there gazing at the unconscious goons, the scar along his face just now starting to tingle and itch the way it does when a thought's buzzing around in the depth of his brain. "Not at all," he says in a distant tone. "And I know all the thugs in this town. Hell, every single one of 'em has come at me at one time or another. Remember that divorce case?"

"Are you kidding?" says Chen. "That rich freak from up on the hill threw a whole army at us just because you found out his wife was fucking a Chinaman from down here in the pits. I have to say I broke a sweat that week keeping your fat out of the fire. You think this is more of that?"

Taggett shakes his head. "Maybe for a moment, but no go. These chumps look like the same kind of artillery from back then, but they're a little too healthy-looking. You remember what you did to those monkeys when they came after us. They wouldn't have healed from that by now." A dark chuckle pushes out through his smirk. "The ones you left alive, that is."

"What about Callendar?" the younger man says as he takes a big step over the one with the shotgun. He crouches down to swing the gun away from the hand with the little bones sticking out the back. "You think he'd quit so easy?"

The detective takes a moment to let his mind drift from the scene in front of him back to the Callendar mansion that midnight, the rich pervert trapped under those slippery silk sheets as Taggett straddles him smashing big meaty rights and lefts into his soft pale face over and over until he's just tenderizing meat and the freak's begging to give him anything if he'll just ease up. The signed confession's still in a safe deposit box downtown under some square name, just waiting. Snapping out of it, he glances back at Chen and actually winks as he says, "I'm not too worried about Callendar. I know where he lives. And, better, he knows what I know."

From his crouch, Chen says, "Hey, hold on a minute. You see this tattoo?" He's holding the shotgun guy's broken hand up so that the sleeve slides a little down to reveal some of the pink skin of the guy's arm. Thick black lines coil and trace a weird design on the flesh. "This is the mark of the Wangs, isn't it? From Shanghai?"

"But that doesn't make any sense," says Taggett. "We blew up half that town to get them off our backs. They wouldn't cross a whole ocean for more of the same treatment." He takes a sip of the sludge in his cup and goes on, "Besides, I can't imagine such a proud clan recruiting a bunch of potato eaters like these three. Not all the way in, anyway. And look how fresh that tattoo is. You can still see the red around the outlines."

Chen takes a closer look and then drops the hand. It thuds wetly on the wooden floor of the hall. "So who?" he says.

"No idea," says Taggett, "and I don't like it." Right about then the guy who was holding the hammer moans a little and twitches on the hall's bare wooden floor. "You're slipping," says the detective. "Not like you to leave one still sucking air."

"Just turning over a new leaf," says Chen, "in case we end up feeling like we want a conversation." They stay where they are, sipping coffee, and watch the goon squirm on the floor as he fades back into the world. He writhes where Chen broke him and his eyes flutter open and he glances back and forth between the two of them. Through his swelling lips he mutters, "Oh shit."

"Yeah," says Chen as Taggett stands there scowling. "Oh shit. You picked the wrong citizen to bother this morning, friend. Now we're gonna have to teach you how to sing." The younger man and steps over the guy with the Tommy gun to where the goon is still stretched out on the floor. He has to shove the body a little more out of the way with his foot as he passes until he's standing next to the squirming thug. "Do you wanna start telling us who sent you or do I get a little more exercise?"

The creep's jaw works for a moment as he stares up. Then he seems to bite down on something and his eyes roll up and his body starts to spasm, his head and his heels knocking on the wooden floor. Some kind of white foam's pushing out through his lips. "Jesus!" says Chen as he squats down to grab the guy's shoulders. "What the hell? I didn't hit you that hard." His fingers clutch as the fight goes out of the thug, as he tries to shake some life back into the sack of meat he's gripping.

"Forget it," says Taggett and finishes the coffee in his cup. "I guess these creeps are carrying cyanide in their dental work in case someone wants to brace them." He glances back into the apartment as the sun's beginning to shove light in through the big hole they made in his wall. "We'd better get out of here," he says.

Chen's still on his knees holding that last corpse by the lapels. He's shaking a little, but after a few seconds he's back on his feet smirking at his partner. "Damn, boss, you must have really pissed someone off. This seems like a lot of effort to send you a message."

Back in the apartment, looking around for a case to throw some shirts into, Taggett yells back, "Yeah, me and this whole building. You notice that not a single one of the other tenants has even so much as cracked open a front door? And where are the cops? I know I don't have the only phone in the building, so why aren't we hearing sirens?" He finds a couple of shirts wadded up on the floor and some boxers and shoves them in the old cardboard suitcase he's holding. "It's like someone's trying to not just kill me but cut me out of society completely." Tying a piece of twine around the suitcase, he steps back into the hall with his partner and the corpses. "Either way, I better lay low until I figure out what's after me."

Chen looks up and says, "Until we figure it out, boss. You know I'm with you."

The tough detective claps his partner on the shoulder. "Yeah," he says. The light bulb in the hallways, on a timer, turns off automatically as the sunlight filters through the cracks in the walls and starts to turn the dead bodies gold.

CHAPTER FOUR

So there's the two of them a couple of days later in an even worse fleapit: two beds, a telephone, and down the hall a bathroom that they're sharing with a fine class of hop-heads and pimps and runaways. They're at the end of the hall within a quick jump of the rusty fire escape that leads down to the piss-smelling alley between these rickety brick buildings at the bottom of the hill. Chen's in the good bed, the one with only half the bedbugs, ankles crossed as he leafs through the paper. "I don't know how much lower we can lay, boss," he smirks. "Don't see why you don't just find a nice cardboard box on the street and—hey, what the hell, that's this number in the ads!" He stabs the page he's looking at with one of his knife-like fingers. The notice he's poking just says "Taggett: KLondike 5-7039" in a black-lined box. Chen's voice goes up nearly to a whine: "Why should we be living like this if you're gonna tell the whole city where we are?"

"Relax," says Taggett. He's sitting on the edge of the bed nearer the door cleaning his .45, making sure to be ready. "No one knows the address here. Hell, I don't think most of the losers who live here know where it is, really. No, I figure if there's only one way to find us, we can see who comes looking. Then we'll know who to kill. So the phone rings, we tell someone where to meet us, and we see who shows up." He packs bullets into the clip. "We decide who we see and when. No more of these morning visits."

Chen squints back, almost grinning. "In other words, you're setting a trap and we're the bait. You're a cool customer, boss." He turns the page over and refolds the paper. "Did you at least get a pack of cards for while we wait?"

That's when the phone goes off like a bomb on its stool between the two beds. Taggett packs the last bullet into his clip and shoots a glance at Chen as the phone keeps clanging until the younger man rolls off the bed and steps to it. He picks up the receiver and says nothing, his deep black eyes watching Taggett. Taggett looks back, that scar on his face going a little more red. Chen looks like he's holding his breath in the silence until finally a little buzz comes from the earpiece and he lets it out to say, "No, there's no Stumpy here." The two detectives are chuckling a little as the earpiece does a little more humming. "Sure, whatever," says Chen. "I'll make sure and give him that message. Yeah, right, Santino wants the rest of the money, sure thing, writing it down now." He wiggles his index finger around his temple as they grin at each other and then puts the phone back down in its cradle.

"False alarm?" says Taggett.

"I just hope Stumpy pays his debts," says Chen. "This Santino sounds like a tough guy." He stands there over the phone relaxing a little when it goes off again and Taggett almost fumbles the clip as he slides it home. The noise fills the little room like the smell of an unwelcome guest who won't quit puffing his crappy cigar until Chen picks up the receiver again and waits.

The air goes thick with the silence for a moment or two, and then the earpiece makes that buzz. "No," says Chen. "I'm not Taggett. I'm his, uh, associate. You wanna leave a message, maybe tell me what the problem is?" After a moment he says, "Oh, sure, we can tail a guy for you," and glances over at the older man on the bed, who's holding up a five of diamonds with MEET? scribbled on it. Chen nods and says, "But we'd need a picture, of course. No, no, we can't meet in our office, it's, uh, getting fumigated." He shrugs over at Taggett and says into the phone, "Sure, I know that place. No, don't worry about directions, we can get there. Huh? Oh, sure. Taggett's a big guy, tough-looking, got a nasty scar down his face. You'll probably spot him pretty easy. Who, me?"

The kid grins like he can't help himself. "Just look for the handsomest jack in the place and you'll find me. And by the way, what's your name? How will we—hello? Hello?" He actually looks at the earpiece for a moment. "She hung up on me."

"She?" says Taggett.

"Yeah," says Chen. "Some dame with a weird tone to her voice." He hangs the earpiece back in its place, but his eyes are looking into the distance, as if he's studying the gloom that's gathering in the little room as the sun goes down. "So familiar," he says, "like someone I know I've heard before, but I just can't place it. You ever get that, boss?"

Taggett says, "I don't forget," and works the .45, sliding a bullet into the chamber. "So we're meeting this mystery dame somewhere?"

Chen twitches a little, like he's shaking himself awake. "Yeah, she says she wants to meet at Jonesy's."

That pulls a laugh out of Taggett. "Nice lady, to know a place like Jonesy's. I didn't hear you warn her that she was trying to meet a couple of strangers in one of the toughest dives in the city. Did she sound like some kind of street baby?"

"Not at all," Chen says, still standing there over the phone on its rickety wooden stool. "Sounded kind of high class, really. Now that you mention it, I can't figure how she'd know about a place like that. Think she might be connected to some kind of mob?"

"How the hell should I know?" the older man almost snarls. "We do know she's interested enough in my name to dial this number and make up some kind of story about a tail job. You notice she didn't tell you who this pigeon is to her?" Taggett's lips are pulled back from his teeth as the light keeps leaking out of the room. "Whoever this high class broad is, she's barely even trying to trick us. She knows we know what kind of trap we're walking into." He pushes himself up from the bed and takes two strides to the middle of the room where Chen is standing, the phone between them like a coiled snake ready to strike again at any moment. "So when do we meet this mystery lady?"

"Tonight," says Chen. "She was trying to get me to tell her where we are so she could give us directions on the streetcar. I think I gave her the slip on that."

The tough detective reaches over the phone and slips his hand into Chen's jacket and pulls out a beat-up pack of smokes. "So good job," he says as he strikes a match on the stool and lights one up for himself and another for his partner. "I guess we better get over there then. If we get there before she does, maybe we save ourselves a beating we don't need."

So the two men grab their hats off the beds and step out into the hall. A quick turn to the left puts them through the big window at the end of the hall to the landing of the fire escape. They flip up the collars of their coats as they stand for a moment, the wind biting as last bits of the sun push weakly between the buildings and their shadows, and then start climbing down the cold metal ladder to the alley. Chen wrinkles his nose and mutters, "Jesus, Taggett, how do you even live like this when you're on the run? We were a lot better off back at that Hotel Prestige in Shanghai. Remember that?"

Taggett shoots him a look as they trudge down the alley. "That's weird. I was just thinking about that Shanghai deal, that crazy Violet Diamond, wondering if this thing we're trying to break out of has some kind of relation. I guess those Wang tattoos got me thinking." His hand rises to half-consciously scratch the scar on his face. It takes him till they get to the mouth of the alley and turn right for the streetcar station to ask, "So what's got you remembering?"

"I don't know," says Chen. "I was just remembering Jie, wondering if he's still keeping his balance in that gang war over there. He was quite the dictionary, wasn't he?" The younger man lets himself chuckle. "I guess I was just thinking about because of the way that weird dame on the phone was talking. She just reminded me of—" He just stops dead in the middle of the sidewalk, citizens on their way home from jobs stepping around him and cursing. One actually bounces off Taggett as the tough detective stops too. "It can't be," says Chen.

Taggett stands there looking down at him, waiting.

Chen looks up, his eyes going a little wider as the streetlights start to come on and make little futile spots of visibility in the night that's closing in faster and faster. In a voice with not a hint of smirk in it he says, "You remember that night on the boat, right? Toward the end?"

"Yeah," says Taggett. "That crazy ninja assassin with the one eye, and that storm, and the mast snapping and knocking that weird broad with the black dress and the veil off into the ocean. She was a piece of work, wasn't she, never showing her face, and the way she talked, she really—oh shit."

Chen says, "Yeah. Oh shit is right. That dame on the phone sounded just like Mrs. Foulsworth."

CHAPTER FIVE

Chen's realization keeps both of them shut up all the way to the station and onto the streetcar. It's a long ride to Jonesy's, and Taggett spends most of it staring at nothing and remembering the strange person who called herself Mrs. Vivian Foulsworth, that dark figure who kept throwing her shadow across his path a few years back. She and her decrepit husband Edgar threw him and Chen into a weird mess in Shanghai that he still doesn't really understand, something about that crazy Violet Diamond that he can still hear whispering in his mind sometimes and something else about controlling the vice racket in Shanghai. All he knows about Mrs. Foulsworth to this day is that he's never seen her face or really an inch of her skin; she's always wrapped in a black dress and a black veil like every day's a funeral. And she's not often wrong.

"Black widow," the detective mutters in the streetcar that empties of citizens as they step off toward their safe homes. He glares at Chen across the aisle. "Can't believe you didn't recognize her voice, considering what she did to—"

Chen interrupts harshly. "I know what she did to Walt. You think I'd forget that? Think I'd forget how she murdered the closest I ever had to a father?" His voice is breaking a little. "I just didn't put two and two together, that's all. Anyway, why wouldn't she just tell me her name? She knows I know her."

"Yeah," says Taggett. "You're right, that's a weird detail. A bunch of this doesn't add up. Anyway, I'm sorry." He shakes a smoke out of the pack in his fist and reaches across to offer it to Chen. The younger man stares at it for a moment then takes it and lights up and lights Taggett's. "Thanks," says the detective. Right about then the streetcar rolls to a stop and they jump off. The cold wind shoves them on their way as they trudge away from the city lights.

By this time it's good and dark and all the citizens are safe in their holes. The nightlife is starting, but it's starting a little further up the hill where people have enough money to afford it. Down where Taggett and Chen are walking, they can't hear the shouts of laughter as respectable types try to let off steam by pouring gas on it. They can hear families yelling at each other about burned dinner or bad sex through the tenement windows they're passing, and then that sound fades into the sound of wind and moaning winos and bums as the buildings get emptier until they're all the way into the part of town where tough men go to drink and fight instead of going home to stare at blank walls. That's where Jonesy's is.

The two of them are standing across the street from a big square building, looks like some kind of warehouse, that occupies the narrow stretch between a couple of alleys. Most of the building's dark, but lights are flickering rectangularly from the side that faces them. A guy staggers out and past them as they stand there, and another guy comes down the alley, turns the corner, and steps in through the plain wood door with the sign above it about the size of a business card that says JONES.

"Wow," Chen says. "This place really advertises, doesn't it." The wind has died down a little, but now a fine mist of pissing rain is pushing itself in their faces.

Taggett snorts a chuckle. "It's not like this is one of those tourist bars. Look around. Didn't you recognize Killer Dan McGraw stumbling out of there? You think a thug like that can relax in a civilian's bar? Jonesy keeps a place where creeps like that can have a meal or a drink or something without having to get all violent about it." He tosses his butt in the gutter and watches it hiss itself to death in the scummy puddle. "Not the kind of place I'd expect Mrs. Foulsworth to want a meeting in."

The detective opens his coat just enough to check that his forty-five is in its holster. "You ready?"

Chen takes that last drag and throws his butt in the gutter to join Taggett's. "Sure," he says. "Can't wait to show that crazy bitch just how I feel." He cracks his knuckles and stretches his neck.

"Easy," says Taggett and puts a hand on Chen's shoulder. "If this is that crazy bitch, she's counting on that. She knows your temper. If it's someone else, then you don't want to be punching shadows, right?" He squeezes the shoulder and then takes his hand back to pull out a fresh smoke. "Let's get in there and see what we see." He shakes one out for Chen and lights both up, and the two men cross the street.

They can hear the sound of forks scraping on plates and beer glasses hitting counters through the door, along with a low hum of conversation. No, one's yelling or singing or breaking anything. Taggett puts his hand on the doorknob, looks over at Chen to his right, and turns and pulls the door open and all that noise stops. The two of them stand there framed in the doorway staring back at about a dozen of the roughest mugs they've seen in a while until the bartender yells at them to close the fucking door and quit letting in the fucking rain. With that invitation, they step inside and close the door behind them. Most of the tough guys go back to their eating and drinking and muttering to each other about jobs they've done or fights they've won.

Three of the biggest ones are still looking at Taggett and Chen as the detectives stand there craning their necks to try to find a place to sit. Jonesy's turns out to be a big square room with a bar along the wall to the left of the door and three sets of long tables and benches parallel to it all the way to the back wall where the three goons are still glaring and starting to stand up. The place reminds Taggett of a prison cafeteria with a bar and its walls decorated with decades of wanted posters tacked over each other and yellowing in layers. He nudges Chen and says, "Looks like the welcoming committee's here."

Chen says, "Good, I feel like extending personal greetings." He cracks his knuckles again and sets his feet and watches the three toughs make their way down the aisle formed by the backs of the other customers. The bartender's glancing back and forth between the two parties, and he's starting to shake his head and make the speech about how this is a nice quiet place and no one wants any trouble when a look from the biggest of the three guys shuts him up. The place is silent again as the three of them get to the front where Taggett and Chen are standing.

Up close, Taggett can see the way their suits don't quite fit, the fabric stretched tight over the bulge of their muscles, too tight to carry a gun. The one in front's a little shorter than Taggett and a little wider, a face as pink as the inside of a rare steak with a couple of washed-out blue eyes with enough red to show a lifetime of drinking his meals. He's tilting those eyes up at the detective as a deep throated purr with a little bit of Irish in it pushes out his greasy lips. "Pardon me, sir," he says, "but I can't help thinking that this might not be the most appropriate establishment for your business tonight."

Taggett blinks and looks at the guy and says, "Huh? You telling me I can't have a beer in your, uh, quaint little parlor?" He cocks a smirk and keeps his hand from rising to the forty-five waiting in his armpit holster. His scar feels like it must be flashing as red as a railroad signal. He glances at the other two; they're having a stare-down with Chen, who's got his hands loose and open at about waist level. He flicks his gaze back to the guy in front of him.

The light in the place rainbows a little as those lips curve up into a kind of smile. "Indeed, sir. Despite your obvious way with words, this is no place for a law enforcement official such as yourself. The boys and me are concerned that you might get your delicate sensibilities offended." With that the guy actually licks his lips. The two men face each other as everyone else in the place just stares at the explosion getting ready to happen.

And then Taggett starts laughing right into the guy's roast-beef face. "Sorry," he says between gasps of amusement. "Sorry, no disrespect." After a moment he catches his breath and says again, "Sorry. I don't mean—it's just been a while since anyone told me I look like a cop."

The slick smile on the tough guy's face hasn't moved through the detective's laughing jag. "The fact remains that you do," he says. "Sir." The guy's voice has shifted a little back in his throat from purr to growl, and his hand is inching toward something he's got stuffed into the back of the trousers stretched over his thighs like sausage casings. Chen's two guys are making the same kind of move. "Pleasant as our little chat has been, it's time for you to take yourself elsewhere. You understand?"

"Oh, sure, I get it," says the detective. "But before we go, why don't you ask yourself who this guy is," and he jerks a thumb at Chen. "My partner? You ever see a San Francisco cop hang around with a Chinaman voluntarily?" Chen shoots Taggett a hard look and quickly shifts his attention back to the two guys who look like barely leashed attack dogs straining forward. Taggett winks back.

The thug's eyes go a little glassy as the wheels turn in his head. After a second or two he comes up with, "Well, how do we know you didn't just bring him in as a prisoner to finger someone?" The voice is out of growl territory at least; this guy's considering.

"Sure," Taggett says, "I'd bring my guy in here so you could all get a good look at him. If you think I'm a cop, you must think I'm a pretty stupid one." He glances around and finds an ashtray on the end of one of the long tables, reaches over a guy's shoulder to stub out his butt in it. "And when you think about it, take a look at me," he says to the rough guy in front of him. "You think the SFPD would let someone this beat-up looking into plainclothes?"

That gets the short guy chuckling. "To admit it, you do look like a ten pound bag with eleven pounds of shit in it." He makes a gesture at the other two, and they take a step back. At the same time, Chen stands up a little straighter. The rest of the guys in there start in again with their sounds as the goon says, "I guess you're all right for now. But tell me, what brings you here with your, uh, exotic companion?"

Chen flips the detective another hard look and then starts scanning the place again. Taggett goes slowly and carefully into his pocket for a pack of smokes, watching those washed-out blue eyes all the time as they're tracing his every move. He shakes one out and offers one to the guy. He lights them up and they smoke for a moment, and then he says, "I'm, uh, meeting a lady."

The tough guy starts laughing until the laughs turn into coughs and the pink of his face deepens almost purple. "A lady," he chokes out.

"Mister, I don't think this institution has seen a lady in it since…well, since it came to exist. Whoever told you there was a lady here to meet was feeding you some kind of fairytale."

Chen nods. "No sign of her, boss. Don't see any of those tattoos from the other night, either."

"Sure," says the guy. "We've had our share of sailors here, but they find their companionship elsewhere. This is a clean place." That one sets him off for another minute or so of laughing. "Well, clean as it needs to be," he says when he's done. "Anyway, too bad for you that you've wasted your evening." He turns his eyes to the other two and jerks his head, and then the three of them make their way back to where they were sitting. The detectives stand there in the front and watch the customers going about their meals and their conversations.

After a moment Taggett turns to Chen and says, "Well, the hell with this," and yells over at the bartender, "Hey, what does it take to get a couple of beers and some of that corned beef hash?" As the bartender gets busy, the two of them find a place on the bench between a couple of hard looking characters and wait for whatever happens next.

CHAPTER SIX

A few days drag by then, and that night at Jonesy's turns into a pleasant memory of drinking and eating and the waitresses they managed to get back to their little rathole for some exercise. That memory starts to fade, though, and there's Johnny and Chen just staring at each other and playing cards and waiting for the phone to ring in a dingy little room that the sun can't quite reach at any time of day.

"Jesus," says Chen as he slaps down a busted flush on the stool sitting between the beds they're on that holds their game and the phone. "I feel like we've been in this fleapit for a week now. I don't mind doing these little jobs for the locals while we lie low, but the novelty is definitely wearing off." He glances up at Taggett, who's just staring at him through the cloud of smoke floating out of his cigarette. "How long do we wait for that old freak or whoever's playing this little game with us to throw us another bone?"

Taggett just keeps looking at him through the smoke and says, "We'll wait as long as we have to. You got a date or something?" He picks up Chen's cards and his own hand and squares them back into the deck and starts shuffling.

Chen stubs his butt out on the stool and glares. "Maybe I do," he says. "Maybe that waitress at Jonesy's has the hot pants for me, but what the hell can I do about it cooped up in this hole?" He grabs the bottle on the floor by his feet and the glass next to it and pours himself a shot. "We're just making bait out of ourselves for no reason," he tells the older man as he throws the shot down his throat and stretches out on the bed. Looking up at the ceiling, he blows a breath through his lips.

Taggett's been smoking and shuffling through this little speech, watching his partner let off that steam. Slowly and carefully, he says, "I don't have you in cuffs, pal. You want to go out and paint the town, you do what you gotta do." He puts the deck down on the stool next to the phone. "But I gotta stay here and play this out. What else am I gonna do? Should I just sit tight in my office and wait for another army of goons to bust down my front door and shoot—"

A knock at the door shuts his mouth quick. Both men freeze and wait for whatever doped-up loser found the wrong door to get right and move along, but they don't hear footsteps or the creak of that squeaky board a few feet along the hall. Taggett slowly lets out the breath he suddenly realizes he was holding. Then that knock comes again, softly, as if whoever's on the other side doesn't want to bruise delicate knuckles or like the knock might be muffled by black velvet gloves. The drone of the streetcar passing filters through the walls as the two of them stare at the door.

Then Chen's on his feet without the bedsprings making a sound as he leaves the bed. Smooth as a puddle of oil, he drifts toward the door while Taggett eases his forty-five out of its holster. There's a peephole in the door, but somebody's gun might be pressed up against it waiting for a sucker to get too curious at the wrong time. Chen's made himself into a shadow at the side of the door. He looks at Taggett. Taggett nods and stays on the bed with his feet planted on the floor. The forty-five's in his hands and aimed dead-center at the door.

Chen's hand finds the doorknob, the rest of the young man's body coiled and ready as an arrow in a drawn bow. He grips the knob, turns, flings the door open.

Taggett just gets a glimpse of the black shadow framed in the doorway, the black velvet dress, the veil, the small stature so nearly familiar, before Chen lets out a scream like a demon from hell and lashes out with a foot, connecting right in the figure's belly. The figure doubles over with a creaky groan and Chen throws his arms around its neck and flips it into the room where it hits the floor hard. Taggett's still figuring out his move when Chen jumps onto the velvet-dressed figure on the floor and smashes his fist into that opaque veil and does it again and does it again. He's sweating and almost crying and yelling something in Chinese and finally Taggett manages to push himself off the bed and into Chen, wrestling the other man down onto the floor. Chen's lips are pulled back from his teeth as he struggles for a moment and then goes limp. Taggett gets to his feet and looks down at the two figures lying there on the floor. One of them's writhing around babbling something about seeing her and losing control, and the other one, the one with the veil starting to get heavy with blood, isn't moving at all.

The detective has to take half a minute to catch his breath before he can get out, "What the hell?"

"I don't know," says Chen, still lying there, head turned away from the body next to him. "I just saw, saw her standing there and I knew she—knew she was gonna try some kinda—she was gonna—it's Mrs. Foulsworth, Johnny!"

"Not anymore," says Johnny. With the toe of his shoe he nudges the foot of the body lying there. "Wish you'd given her a chance to talk, though. Maybe she could've told us what the hell she wants from us. Wanted from us." He shrugs and lights up a smoke and reaches down offer his partner a hand up.

Chen pulls himself up and lights a smoke of his own, and the two of them look down at the corpse. "Wow," he says. "I really lost it." He blows out a stream of smoke and takes the cigarette out of his mouth to look at the burning ember. "I gotta say, though, I feel…I feel relieved, like I finally got to scratch an itch that's been bothering me for years." He takes another drag. "When you think about something like this, just go over it and over it in your head, you never know how it'll really feel. I've killed my share of mugs, you know, but to finally get my hands on—"

"It's not her," says Taggett.

Chen nearly swallows his smoke as the detective puts the forty-five back in its holster and steps past to swing the door closed. Taggett says again, "Not her. Whoever this is has the wrong shoes on. That Foulsworth freak wore those black clunky shoes with built-up soles, like I guess they wore in the last century. These are almost slippers."

Chen's cigarette drops out of his slack jaw and smolders for a second on the hem of the corpse's dress before Taggett crushes it out with his toe. "No," says the younger man as his face darkens with rage and confusion. "You're wrong. It couldn't. I didn't." He drops to his knees and rips the veil off the corpse and the two of them suck in a breath of shock and stare at the bloodied-up face of a Chinese girl who couldn't have been more than fourteen years old when she died. Chen swallows almost all of a howl and skitters back until he hits the door. His eyes are like black circles as he stares at the blank face gazing up at the ceiling and his jaw's working and thrashing as he mutters something only he can hear.

Taggett glances over at his partner and then kneels down to run his hands over the body, over the folds in the black velvet dress. He makes a sound in the back of his throat as he pulls out a little revolver and then another one. "Well, this is something," he tells himself. "Don't often see little girls with this kind of hardware."

"Jesus Christ, a little girl," Chen sobs from his crouch. "I've done a lot of killing, but never—"

"Cut it out!" Taggett stands and steps to loom over the smaller man. "Come on, kid, look at it for a minute. Someone's trying to get to us with a bunch of faked-up nonsense from that Shanghai deal." He reaches down to help his partner up again. "Those tattoos, that voice you heard on the phone, this." He gestures back at the dead girl. "You know we both saw that Foulsworth broad get bashed into the ocean, right?"

Chen blinks into Taggett's eyes and sniffles and says, "Yeah."

"So even if she survived that, all we really know is that someone's screwing with us, someone who knows a little bit about our history." Taggett shakes out a smoke and lights it and feeds it to Chen. "We just need to get our hands on whoever that is." His eyes blazing down into the younger man's, he says, "And end it."

Chen stares back up into Taggett's eyes for a moment then cuts his gaze back down to the dead girl. "Hey," he says. "Wait a minute, boss. I think you missed something." He kneels down and pulls at a little gold glimmer teasing just at the edge of one of the dress's folds. His narrow fingers prize out a little tube made of some kind of smooth yellow metal and about the size of a single cigarette, and then he stands up and hands the tube to Taggett. "What do you think?"

Taggett holds the tube between a thick thumb and forefinger and it almost gets swallowed up by thick pink skin. He hands it back to Chen and says, "I'm guessing there's something in there, and it's too small for a bomb. Why not see if you can crack it open?"

Chen steps over by the window that lets in a little trickle of light at just this time of evening and starts pressing the surface of the little tube with his fingertips. While he's doing that, Taggett takes the blanket off his bed and wraps it around the dead girl, slipping her little revolvers into the pockets of his jacket. That only takes a few seconds, so Taggett stands there looking at the bundle with blood stains already seeping through until there's a little click and Chen sucks in a breath. "It's a note," he says. Those wiry finger unspool a tight coil of nearly transparent paper with scratchy letters inked on it. Holding it up to the window, he reads out loud.

"Chen. Taggett. You have discovered by now that I have sent a simulacrum to test you; you have, no doubt, failed that test. I wonder how it feels for you to have killed such an innocent, a sweet gamine whose only crime was allowing me to put her in your path. Perhaps she wounded one of you in defense. Perhaps the wound in your minds will fester more amusingly. No matter. You surely have ascertained by this point that you have an enemy whom you cannot see but who can see you clearly and at all times. You must know that you draw breath because I continue to tolerate your miserable lives so long as you amuse me. I will be with you at my convenience."

Chen turns the paper over and says, "Not signed."

That gets a snicker out of Taggett even as the scar flames across his face. "No real surprise there. But we need to scram." He slips the deck of cards into his coat pocket and jams his hat on his head and yanks the phone cord out of the wall. "Don't you have a connection somewhere with the South China Cruise Line?"

Still under the little postage stamp of a window as it darkens with along with the rest of the sky, Chen just says, "Huh?" and then, "Oh, yeah, I was dating a hot little cookie in the secretarial pool. I guess you remember she told me how she could get us a couple of passes if we need 'em."

"Yeah," says Taggett. "We need 'em. Get yourself spruced up and see how fast this chippy can come across. Let's see how far this all-seeing eye can track us."

Chen says, "You got it, boss," and opens the door to let the bigger man through. As Taggett turns toward the window and the fire escape and at least one night sleeping on the sidewalk like any other bum, Chen says, "What about the girl?"

Taggett stops and turns back and says, "What about her?"

Blinking, Chen says, "What do we do with the body?"

"Lock the door," says Taggett. "We'll be long gone by the time she starts to stink."

CHAPTER SEVEN

So the next day Chen's girlfriend comes through, and the day after that they're on the *Flower Song* steaming out of San Francisco Bay, and ten days later or so they're somewhere in the South China Sea, far away from all that murder. Taggett doesn't have to draw his forty-five once in that whole time. He spends the sunny days relaxing in a lounge chair on deck, thinking about nothing, not feeling his scar itch. Nights he spends in his own stateroom, sleeping on a bed with sheets—or sometimes not sleeping, as he's discovered that the girls in the serving staff on the *Flower Song* know a lot about how to serve. As Chen says to him one night in the bar, "Now this is the way to lay low. Like the complete opposite of that last boat trip we took."

"Jesus, don't remind me," says Taggett. "No rudder, broken mast, and that crazy One-Eye pretending to be the captain. I thought we were all gonna die when he went overboard." He polishes off the rest of his drink and winks at the barmaid for another, and that's the way ten days go by.

So naturally at the beginning of the eleventh day that old familiar thump of a cop knocking at the door pounds the detective awake. He opens the door in his shorts and squints at the sudden invasion of light and the little guy who's standing there says "Uh, Mr. McTagg?" in a nasal kind of monotone, the slightly bored voice of the accountant who's sorry to have to tell you about the audit you're about to get hit with.

"Huh?" says Taggett.

The corners of the little guy's nearly lipless mouth curl up into what must be a smile. "Don't recognize the name?" he says. "I suppose that makes sense, first thing in the morning and all. A lot of guys forget their fake names while they're waking up." He reaches into the thin pink blazer he's wearing over a green polo shirt and a blue pants and pulls out a pack of smokes, taps one out for himself, and reaches up to offer one to the detective, who's still standing there blinking. "Should I just call you Taggett?" He lights his smoke and lights Taggett's. "My name's Venz, by the way. I'm the ship's detective."

Taggett stands there half-naked and smoking and staring down at Venz. Finally he comes up with, "Uh, what, what's going on?"

Venz says, "Why don't you let me in, Mr. Taggett. A few things happened last night that we need to talk about." He stands there squinting up at the big detective. "You don't want to talk about this out here on the deck, do you."

Taggett steps back into the room. Venz slips past like a shadow and takes a seat on the couch, crossing his legs and tapping his ash into a cut glass tray on the little teak table at his elbow. Taggett stays on his feet, stepping a little closer to loom over the smaller man. The two of them lock gazes, Venz still smirking, Taggett with the scar drawing a line of fire across his face. Finally he says, "So?"

Venz takes another drag and stubs out his smoke. "I have to admit I'm a little hurt, Mr. Taggett," he says. "I was hoping I'd get to tell you the story of how I saw through your clever disguise. Ah, well." He shrugs and lights up another smoke and offers a new one to Taggett and then slips the pack back into his blazer when the big detective just scowls at him. "All right then. What say you tell me where you were at about ten o'clock last night."

Taggett can't help a smirk of his own. "I was on a small boat in the middle of the South China Sea. Come on, Venz, if you know who I am, you know I'm not here to waste time. What do you want?" He cracks his knuckles and watches the smaller man stifle a flinch.

Venz recovers quickly, his narrow eyes glaring right back into Taggett's. "I want to know where you were last night around ten o'clock. I hear you're popular with the barmaids, so maybe one of them can help establish that you weren't slaughtering the guy in cabin-two. But why don't you give a working girl a break and just answer a simple question." He taps a little grey powder of ash into the tray. "Unless you'd rather keep that important information to yourself for some reason."

Taggett doesn't say a thing as his lips go tight around his cigarette. Venz just sits there, patiently watching, smoking, tapping into the ashtray, letting the silence fill up the space between them. The stateroom's well soundproofed, so nothing comes through to cut that thickening silence open. Finally Taggett spits his butt on the floor and snarls, "Slaughtered? What the hell do you think I am?"

"That's just it," says Venz. "I don't really know, do I. The ticket office put me on to you and your sidekick for promoting a ticket out through some nice young lady's, uh, infatuation with your pal, but I figured you weren't doing any real harm. Now here's this dead guy that I can't explain, and here you are. You see how I might get suspicious." He stubs his butt out in the ashtray and offers Taggett another before he lights a new one for himself. "So I'll ask you again, politely as I can. Pretty please. Won't you tell me where you were while this guy was getting himself opened up."

Taggett puts out his hands and says, "All right, all right. Jesus. This is a hell of a thing to wake up to. Uh, I think her name was something like Sapphire or Turquoise or—"

"Jade?"

"Yeah, Jade." The big detective can't resist a chuckle. "She's real, uh, friendly."

Venz answers with a chuckle of his own. "Yeah, the front office hires 'em that way. You remember what color dress she was wearing?"

"Red," says Taggett. "Tight, too. That's the color for Mondays, isn't it?"

Venz's chuckle turns into a full laugh as his mouth open a little wider than it should be able to. "You're good," he says. "You keep your eyes open. Yeah, that checks out, she was wearing red." He taps his ash again and grins up at the big detective. "She speaks highly of you, by the way. You should be proud."

"Jesus," Taggett growls. "You've got an alibi for me and you still roust me first thing in the morning and grill me? Hell of a way to run your business, little man."

That kills Venz's laugh, and his lips tighten back into a razor-line of a smirk. "My job's getting the truth, bruiser. I do it how I can, and it's been working." He pokes his third butt into the ashtray, which is filling up fast, and starts to reach into his blazer for a new one then stops himself. "Look at me," he says. "I don't usually smoke like this, but—well, listen, I don't usually fly off the handle like that either. I've just never seen—" He swallows dry. "Never seen anything like—anyway, I'm sorry."

He sticks out his hand and Taggett looks at it and finally gives it a shake. "Yeah, I know how it goes," says the older detective. "You never really forget your first."

"Thanks," says Venz. "You think it's too early in the morning for a shot of something?"

Taggett chuckles and says, "Never," and goes to the sideboard and gets rum out of a cut glass bottle that matches the ashtrays and into a couple of glasses. As he's pouring he says back over his shoulder, "So I'm guessing there's some other reason you staged this conversation first thing in the morning. You weren't betting that much on getting me off-balance."

Venz reaches out for the rum as Taggett steps back to the couch. He takes a swallow and sucks his lips for a second and says, "Well, I need help." Those narrow eyes are actually shimmering as he takes another drink. "Like I say, I've never seen anything like this before, and I heard what a tough guy you are, so I figured—" another dry swallow—"I figured you could give me some advice about what to do next."

"Sure," says Taggett. He knocks back his rum and steps into the bedroom to grab a shirt and his hat. "Let's see what you got." By the time he's back in the front room the little detective is up with the door to the deck open and letting in a blast of sunlight. Taggett shrugs into his shoulder holster and walks out into the air.

The scenic moment doesn't last long as Venz leads Taggett down a narrow, dark flight of stairs that lead to a hallway not quite tall enough for Taggett to stand up straight in. They creep along and turn a couple of corners until there's a guy leaning against a door with a sign that says 22. The guy straightens up and hands Venz a note and wanders off back toward the stairway. Venz stands in front of the door and opens the note. "Okay," he says. "George Farrell. Twenty-nine. Looks like he's been plowing a pretty thick furrow through the female passengers. Word is he's got two main ones on the string, and we haven't seen either of them since, uh." He takes a yellowish hankie out of his sport coat and mops his brow. "Since about ten o'clock last night."

Hunched with his head pressing up against the ceiling, the brim of his hat crushed in front of his eyes, Taggett says, "Well, how about that. I guess we've got a couple of suspects right off the bat." He puts a coffin nail between his lips and lights up. "Let's see what you've got."

Venz nods and opens the door with a skeleton key. They step inside to a smell of meat starting to turn, the thick air in the room almost tropical against their faces. The little room contains a bed and a sink and a door to what must be some kind of closet. On the bed is a mattress getting soaked with blood and a body tied by its wrists and ankles to the frame. The body's naked, hacked open in a few places, and missing its penis. Venz is staring at the red wound between its thighs and gagging a little as Taggett bends over it, carefully not touching anything. "You weren't kidding," says the big detective. "This is definitely a rough one."

Venz lights up a smoke and just nods. The two men don't say anything for a lingering moment. Faintly, they can hear the sounds of nearby tourists waking up and coughing and running water, and then that sound goes away too. Then they can hear the flat sound of blood dripping from a sodden mattress to the floor and a kind of a high-pitched murmur that reminds Taggett of a whipped dog. And then that stops.

Taggett looks over at Venz and moves quietly toward that closed door. He takes out his forty-five and holds a finger to his lips as Venz backs toward the room's other door, reaching under that weird pink jacket to pull out a little pistol of his own. Taggett grips the knob of the closet door and throws it open.

The girl inside couldn't have been more than twenty or so when she died, which looks like it was about thirty seconds ago. The foam's still coming from her lips and drying on her chin. Taggett stares down at her corpse and says to Venz, "Looks like there's more." As the smaller man steps closer, Taggett points down at the girl's hands. One's gripping a straight razor, still open and shiny with dripping blood. The other hand is clutching a severed cock. Venz mutters something to himself and bolts for the door, slamming it shut behind him as he gets out of there. Taggett crouches to get a closer look. "Holy hell," he says to himself.

Carved into the girl's shoulder is the same mark he saw in San Francisco on those gorillas that rousted him out of his little office three weeks ago. Taggett stand up and backs off and his calves hit the bed. He turns around and looks down. George Farrell's corpse doesn't say a thing, just keeps staring up at the ceiling with that look of pain and horror freezing into its face as the rigor mortis sets in. Taggett stares back until he sees the same mark on its left shoulder, a tattoo that would be just starting to heal on a living person. "This is gonna be a long day," Taggett says, and then he gets the hell out of there himself, making sure the door's locked behind him.

Venz is standing there in the hall, smoking and shivering. "What do you think?" he says.

Taggett says, "I think I've got more trouble than I expected."

CHAPTER EIGHT

Chen's somewhere else fighting shadows: Mrs. Foulsworth, over and over. They're dancing around some little wooden room like that craphole back in San Francisco, or maybe it's a little cabin on that boat that barely got them back from Shanghai. It doesn't matter. All that matters is the fight. He's giving it everything he's got, but she's amazingly tough for an old broad, like some kind of steel frame lurks under that black veil. He wants to yell, to growl, but there's no sound in that crappy little arena. Just the fight. He can smash his fist into her veil over and over, feel the bones crunching, but not hear any of it as she attacks him with some kind of black steel talons coming out of her gloves. He can feel the heat on his face as she slashes at him and he ducks and weaves until he's backed up against that little room's wall, the rough wood digging splinters into his skin, and that's when he realizes it's not Mrs. Foulsworth at all. It's that girl he killed in San Francisco, the one whose name they never found out, and she's got knives instead of hands, and she's coming at him faster and harder, like a hungry spirit of vengeance. He wants to cry out, but there's still no sound, and he can see eyes through that veil, red as burning coal, as he flinches back into the wall, cringing away from that slashing heat, beyond even trying to fight back.

Then he wakes up, his back against a huge crate in the absolute dark of the *Flower Song*'s cargo hold, surrounded by the creaking of boards and the splash of waves against the hull, which he can barely hear over the harsh whisper of his breath as it slows. He can feel the sweat on his bare chest turning his skin to ice, the floor of the hold scratchy under his bare feet. Sitting there and shivering, he closes his eyes again. Nothing changes. The dark's the same.

He puts his arms around his knees and pulls himself into a tighter ball of tensed muscles and thinks about the last week of restless days and sleepless nights, how he keeps seeing her, Mrs. Foulsworth or the dead girl or some kind of crazy trick his mind's playing with him, casting a shadow around corners or making a black shape through clouded portholes. He's been over every inch of this boat trying to catch a hint of her scent, but she's always not quite within reach, if she's even here, whoever she even is. This black vast hold is the last place he could think of to look, and he can't remember how long he's been down there. "It's the not knowing," he murmurs to himself and clenches his body a little tighter.

It takes him a moment to notice the silence after that. The rats aren't scratching somewhere out in that stretch of darkness he's in. The boards of the hull aren't even creaking. As he's holding his breath he hears just one sound, and he knows it's the killing sound.

So he throws his body over to the left, crashing to the floor to avoid the blow he can still feel the wind from on his face as he goes down, but he's not fast enough to duck the first kick to his gut. The breath explodes out of him as he hunches in pain, the dark of the hold going white for a moment as he grabs out blindly and catches the foot coming back for a second kick. He pulls hard and spins and gets a thickly muscled leg in his arms, ready for breaking, but the other guy throws himself back and flips Chen into the dark to smash against a crate that cracks open a little. Chen grabs and pulls a jagged board away from the crate just before he hears the air parting in front of something that crashes another hole into the crate as Chen ducks back and comes up swinging his plank. He can hear a grunt as someone catches it, yanks it out of his hands, and throws it clattering into the blackness, but by that time he's jumped away to the right and then taken another jump into the darkness. He feels the thump more than hears it as he hits another crate and uses his hand to trace his way around its corner to crouch and breathe for a moment.

The hiss of his breath fills his ears until he stifles himself. He turns his head back and forth, listening: scratching and squealing as the rats wake up and try to find safety, scraping of a crate that someone didn't tie down right against the hold floor, groan of the ship's boards as the ocean pushes them in and pulls them back, whisper of a soft shoe against the floor too close.

The punch catches him on the temple as he tumbles out of the way just quickly enough to keep it from cracking his skull open. He keeps tumbling as the white noise crowding his vision fades to orange and then to red and back to black, and something heavy and keeps chasing him in the dark, massive thuds of footfall tracking him as he skitters on his hands and knees to change direction. As whatever it is gets closer, he turns over to lie on his back and coil his entire body into a kick that smacks the soles of his feet against what feels like someone's face, a nose smashing under his heel. He spins, avoiding grabbing hands, and punches up into someone's crotch and lifts that body enough to scoot under and roll back the way he came, smirking a little at the thud of a body hitting the floor behind him and then groaning out loud as he hears that body get up and start chasing him again in the blackness.

And then his searching hands, groping out in front of him, run into another patch of splintery wood, so he jumps and scrambles and makes it to the top of the crate. He's staying low, crawling on his elbows and knees, trying to glide so the wood under him doesn't make a noise to give him away. He needs a moment to catch his breath. His gut's clenching with soreness and he can feel the side of his face starting to swell. He stops and flattens himself face down on the rough surface and listens. The sound's below him, someone doing a good job of sneaking but not quite good enough to keep Chen from tracking the brush of some kind of slipper over the floor of the hold. As the sound moves away from the crate he's clinging to, he lets out a little breath of relief.

The sound stops, and Chen's lips tighten to hold in the last of his breath. He wills himself to relax the fingertips trying to dig themselves into the wood underneath him. The hold seems gigantic in the absolute darkness, and it's gone silent again. He stays as still as he can, trying to be part of the crate, when he hears a new sound, the slip of metal against leather. He recognizes the sound of a gun coming out of its holster and rolls out of the way just as the explosion fills the space and a bullet whizzes past his forehead, punching a hole of light into the ceiling of the hold. Someone screams on the other side. Chen shifts and squirms to avoid the circle of light on the crate lid, deaf for a moment as he feels the heat of another bullet scraping his shoulder. He keeps rolling and falls off the edge and lies there for a moment face down on the floor and waits for the high buzz in his ears to fade. He can feel himself muttering "Get up, get up," even though he can't quite hear himself saying it. Maybe the creep with the gun is having the same problem. Maybe the creep with the gun is right around the corner, closing in on the young detective. Maybe Chen's out of options.

Three heavy clanks boom out from in front of him, and a door opens in the wall that's much closer than he thought it was. He pushes himself up to his feet and squints and raises an arm to shield his eyes from the rectangle of yellow light that blasts open the dark of the hold. Through the ringing in his ears he can hear Taggett's voice roughly yelling, "Chen! What the hell!" He lowers his arm, still squinting, to see his big partner and some little guy in a salmon-colored blazer framed in the doorway.

From the doorway next to Venz, Taggett watches his partner standing there half-naked and shaking. The whole right side of Chen's face is starting to darken and swell up, and he's bent over to the side with a hand on his ribcage, red stripe of blood on his shoulder. Worse, there's a fear in the younger man's eyes that Taggett hasn't seen there before. "Someone," Chen croaks. "Someone back in there. Took a shot at me. Couldn't. Ah, shit, Johnny, I killed—" and then he's back down on his face on the deck. Taggett rushes over to him, turns him over. Venz takes a couple of steps back and whistles twice, and a couple of goons with drawn guns push into the hold and past Chen and Johnny into the darkness. While the goons are bustling around back there, bumping into crates and swearing, Venz steps back into the hold and looks down at the two detectives. Taggett looks up from his crouch at the little guy and can't think of a thing to say.

"So I guess this is your partner," says Venz, "and I guess we can quit looking for him now." He takes a smoke out of his jacket and lights up and keeps looking down at the two of them.

Taggett's got his jacket off and draped around Chen's shoulders. Chen's just shivering. Taggett glares up at Venz and growls, "You got any more funny things to say?"

Venz blinks. "No, I really don't think anything funny's happening here." The goons come stumbling back out of the darkness shaking their heads and putting their guns away. "Looks like we're alone," he says. "This door's the only way out except for the cargo hatch, and we'd be underwater if someone opened that. I think your friend needs a better story."

"Or maybe you need better men," Taggett tells him. "There's probably a dozen places in here were someone could hide who knows how to." He stands up with Chen's arm slung around the back of his neck, holding the smaller man up. "Now where's the sawbones on this boat? I hope he's sharper than you are."

Venz steps back as Taggett steps forward, and the goons click into place behind him, blocking the door. "Our guy does pretty well with twisted ankles and hangovers, but whatever's ailing your oriental buddy there's gonna be another matter." He tosses his smoke aside and flexes his fingers and looks up at the bigger man. "Honestly, your pal's condition isn't my problem. My problem is that you two eggs get on my boat and all of a sudden guns are going off and paying customers are getting chopped up." His tongue darts over his thin lips. "You'll see our guy as soon as I get some questions answered. Starting with, who'd he kill?" The little detective reaches into his jacket and pulls out a little pistol, just big enough to shoot a man to death. "I think it's time you start talking."

Taggett rolls his eyes. "I guess you've cracked the case of why we didn't just book regular passage under our own names. Yeah, we've got a past. That's not important." He takes another step forward as Venz cocks his little gun. Taggett stops and glares down at him. "Listen," he says. "My friend is hurt. I'm taking him to your ship's doctor. If you know anything about me you'll know that I'll go through you to do it. Just get this. If I have to put him down to kick your ass I'm not gonna stop until you're all the way out of commission. Are you ready to retire?" He flicks his eyes up to the goons, who are glancing back and forth and not pointing their guns anywhere in particular, and then back down at Venz. "We can do all the talking you want once we see your doctor. Lead the way or get out of the way."

The ship creaks as the ocean pushes it around. After a moment Venz uncocks his gun and puts it away, and the goons follow. "Come on," he says and starts through the door and into the corridor. Taggett follows, and the goons fall in behind. Over his shoulder, Venz says, "We're definitely gonna talk, and then you're gonna get off my boat. We'll be docking in Shanghai in a couple of days, and that's the end of your cruise."

Carrying his partner, Taggett says, "That's great. I think we were done anyway."

CHAPTER NINE

So there they are a couple of days and a ferry ride later in a crappy little dockside bar drinking watery beer and watching the dock workers pushing around some of the *Flower Song*'s cargo that followed the evicted passengers. The grey of the sky they're under matches the grey of the harbor water, which matches the grey of the rundown little private dock. Chen squints in the dim and sets his glass down on the rickety table they're sitting at and says, "Gotta say, I never thought we'd see this place again. Especially considering that we killed like half the crooks in town the last time we were here." He picks up his glass for another sip and says, "Small world, I guess."

Taggett grunts and shifts his weight on the flimsy chair he's perched on and takes a long look at his partner. "That's probably the most you've said in the last couple of days. Good to see you snapping out of it."

Chen's eyes flash back from the scene into Johnny's. He lets out a bark that sounds like it could have been a laugh in a better world. "Snapping out of it?" he says. He takes a gulp of that pissy beer and slams his empty glass on the table. His voice cracks a little as he says, "I haven't had a night of sleep in like the last couple of weeks. I keep having these dreams. I keep seeing that Mrs. Foulsworth or that girl I killed or some kind of shadow everywhere I look." He glances back at the dock where some guys are using crowbars on a big crate with a jagged hole in one of its sides. His eyes narrow and his hand drifts up to his chest, feeling through his shirt the bandages over the lingering pain some shadow kicked in his side. "I don't even know how I got down in that hold, I just woke up and there I was in the dark," he says in a small quiet voice Taggett's never heard him use before. "I just don't know what's going on."

Taggett lights a smoke and passes it to Chen and says, "Yeah. But something is. Those bruises aren't in your imagination." He leans over the table, gets up in his partner's face. "That means that someone is screwing with us. Get it? You're not going crazy." He looks around the little corner of the dock they're sitting in, corrugated iron roof held up with wooden poles over the area where a little old Chinese woman's overseeing a bar made out of old crates. He cranes his neck a little to catch her eye and holds up two fingers, so she turns her head and spits on the floor and brings over another couple of glasses of that cloudy yellow stuff they call beer around here. As she's shambling back to her post, he tells Chen, "Listen. If someone's screwing with us, that's something we can do something about." He reaches out and puts his hand on his partner's shoulder. "We're tough, right? No one screws with us for long, right?"

"Yeah," says Chen. "You're right." He shakes his head and takes a sip and looks around again at the same scene they've been staring at for the last hour. "So who do you think's doing it? Couldn't be that Mrs. Foulsworth, could it?"

Taggett says, "I've been thinking about that. Remember that Purple Diamond she suckered us into carrying for her?" Chen nods and Taggett goes on, "Well, I got the impression that she's seen plenty of other weird rocks in her life. That creepy mummy of a husband she travels around with is supposed to be some kind of collector." He takes a drag of his smoke and says, "Even though we saw her go over the edge, she might've somehow used some other little curio like that to save herself."

Chen takes a swallow and says, "Yeah, and there's another thing. I was thinking, we've never seen her out of that crazy old-time funeral costume she wears, right?" It's Taggett's turn to nod, and Chen says, "So she's got a perfect disguise. All she has to do is put on a different dress, and we don't know her from Lana Turner."

"Nice thinking, partner," says Taggett. He tosses his smoke down between a gap between boards under him into the shallow sandy water at the edge of the bay and lights up another. "So there's no reason that crazy old dame couldn't be the one that's after us."

Chen takes another swallow, finishing off the glass. "Okay," he says. "So we take the fight to her, right? It'll be a relief having something real to punch." He takes a moment to crack his knuckles one by one. "And I'll admit I'd like to meet whoever was chasing me around the hold. I owe that guy."

Taggett throws the last of his own glass down his throat and says, "Well, we don't know that yet. I could be saying a lot of this same stuff about One-Eye. Remember him?"

"That ninja?" Chen shudders. "I remember he was out of his freaking mind."

Taggett nods. "Crazy enough to live through just about anything, definitely crazy enough to want to watch us squirm like this. And remember he's some kind of disguise artist, so he could have been tracking our every step all this time without us catching on."

"Damn, boss, you really know how to make enemies, don't you?" The younger man can't help laughing for a second. "I guess if someone's gonna come after us, they may as well be insane and unkillable. Did I ever tell you how glad I am we met?" Taggett snickers as Chen says, "So did you wire ahead to let him know we're coming?"

"Yeah," says Taggett. "That greasy little gumshoe Venz gave me that much before he kicked us off." He shrugs. "No reply, though, so I don't know if our friend got it. Don't even know if he's alive, really. He's got plenty of enemies of his own, no doubt." He raises his empty glass to his lips and scowls as he notices there's no beer in there. "Another?" he says to Chen and glances over at the old woman behind the bar without waiting for an answer. There's no one there. He shoots his gaze all over the little bar and doesn't see her anywhere, as if she's been carried up to crabby old bartender's heaven for her good work.

Right then Chen says Johnny's name in a voice that's gone all quiet and shaky. The tough detective turns his head to see a the empty dock just as he starts to feel the sudden silence. Some crates and trunks clutter up the wooden floor of the dock where the vanished workers must have just left them. The ocean waves lap loudly at the boards, and the seagulls are still yelling at each other, but all the human sounds have stopped. The two men look around the desolate scene and then back at each other. Taggett pulls out his forty-five and puts his glass back down as Chen flexes his fingers and subtly gets his feet under him. "Ready?" says Taggett. Chen nods.

The two of them sit there at the table very still, waiting. After a moment, they notice the low mechanical rumble that's been creeping in to the low end of their hearing. It gets louder, and Taggett sees a cloud of dust or smoke or something coming slowly at them from inland. It's tracing the straight length of the street that cuts south through town to the river. As it gets closer, the grey sky opens up again and some beams of sunlight shoot down to bounce off something shiny at the base of the cloud, which just disappears as the shimmer of light comes on ahead. Whatever it is, it's coming fast and getting louder. Chen's on his feet next to the table as they watch it coming. Taggett cocks his forty-five.

As it approaches the border between street and dock they can see it's a car, and it's driving right on to the wood, right at them. It's almost to them, slowing, when Chen puts his hand on Taggett's shoulder and says, "Hey, I know that car."

As Taggett uncocks his forty-five and lets out his breath, he says, "Yeah. I guess he got my wire."

The Silver Phantom turns and pulls to a stop a few feet from their table with a refind squeak of its brakes. Its back passenger door opens, and a deep voice that sounds like a bowl of maple syrup tastes says, "Gentlemen! Although I must apologize for the perhaps ominous circumstances of my arrival, I must at the same time express the unalloyed elation occasioned in me by the felicitous occurrence of our reunion." As he's speaking, a dark Chinese man dressed in a sharp pinstriped suit gets out of the car, his compact body surprisingly small for the volume of his voice. His thin lips are curved up into a smile that actually cracks the plane of his cheeks and lights his eyes. "Please allow me to extend my most sincere and cordial greetings."

As Taggett's putting his forty-five away, Chen covers the distance from the table to the car and is hugging the older man. "Jie!" he says, grinning. "We were just wondering how you'd been holding up."

"Oh, let me assure you, Mister Chen, my ability to not only survive but, indeed, prosper as well among the least favorable of vicissitudes has long demonstrated itself as one of the central aspects of my being." Stepping back and bowing, he gestures Chen back to the table where the driver of the car has somehow managed to add a white tablecloth and three small clean glasses right in front of Taggett, who at least is quick enough to set them at the table's three chairs. As Chen stumbles back, Jie follows and shakes Taggett's hand warmly. "Allow me to apologize, Mr. Taggett, for not having replied to your communication more expeditiously, but I felt it necessary to take precautions for your appearance that, I'm sorry to say, involved more effort than I had foreseen."

Taggett chuckles as they sit down together. "Yeah," he says. "I suppose you had to spread around a fair amount to get all these guys to clear the dock."

"Indeed," says Jie. He takes a pristine pack of smokes from his jacket pocket and offers one to Chen and one to Taggett. They all light up together, and Jie goes on. "Fortunately, the owner of this dock has a close association with a few of the organizations that I have the honor of representing in one way or another." He snaps a his fingers, and there's that old woman again as if nothing had just happened, back from nowhere and pouring whiskey into the shot glasses in front of each of the men. Jie raises his glass and says, "To friendship, gentlemen, and to the continuing profitability of our combined endeavors."

The other men raise their glasses as Chen says, "Uh, yeah," and the three of them drink. "Damn," says Chen. "That is some exceptional grog." The old woman fills their glasses again.

Jie smiles modestly and says, "Your praise does honor to my humble ability to connect myself with the most prestigious of suppliers. But perhaps we should take this moment to direct our attention to business perhaps less pleasant." Turning to Taggett, he raises his glass and sips and swallows and says, "I gathered from your cable that a series of unfortunate circumstances has led you once again to this particular corner of the world."

"Yeah, we were just talking about that," says Taggett. "Someone's using that crazy mess we waded through a couple of years ago to chase us out of our lives." As the old woman keeps refilling their glasses with Jie's outstanding whiskey, Taggett goes back over the story of that deadly wake-up call, the facedown at Jonesy's, the death of the nameless girl in San Francisco, the sick calling card someone left in blood on the *Flower Song*. Chen takes a few more shots while the older man talks, and he shivers a few times.

Jie listens gravely, nodding his head once or twice, and finally says, "Your analysis seems highly credible based on the events you have endured thus far. Someone is indeed using what you might consider your escapades to exert psychological pressure on you, although to what end we cannot yet accurately speculate." He makes a signal to his driver, who packs up the glasses and the tablecloth and what's left of the whiskey back into the trunk of the Silver Phantom. As the three of them rise and turn toward the car, Jie flips a coin at the old woman and turns around, walking backwards for a few steps to say, "Perhaps I may be permitted to observe that an aspect of your account, based on my consideration of your character, perplexes me."

"What's troubling you?" says Taggett.

Standing by the side of the car, opening the back door, Jie says, "In my limited experience, I have known your first impulse when confronted with a challenge to respond to that challenge directly—indeed, often with a decisive degree of violence. However, the provocations of your unknown assailant in this case seem to have inspired you to a policy of flight, which does not seem, if I may be so bold as to make this assertion, to have resolved the disturbance in which you find yourself."

"Yeah," says Taggett. "I gotta admit I was wondering about that. Guess I developed something to lose." He tosses out his smoke and steps into the car, Chen stepping in after. As Jie gets in the front, Taggett says, "But then I guess I've already lost a lot of it, so what the hell." He reaches into his pocket for a fresh smoke, finds nothing, and reaches into his other pocket and pulls out a note. "Taggett," he reads to the other men, "Even a mind as limited as yours must have ascertained that you can neither run nor hide from my vengeance." He bums a match from Jie and sets the note on fire and tosses it out the window as they go. "Funny," he says. "Seems like everyone's giving me the same advice."

CHAPTER TEN

A little while later he blinks himself awake as the Silver Phantom pulls into the lengthy semi-circular driveway of what looks like an actual castle made of big gray blocks of stone and brimming with turrets and peaked roofs and squatting over the flat Chinese landscape like some kind of medieval troll frozen into place by sunrise. "Crazy dream," he mutters to himself.

Jie turns and says over the back of the seat, "If I may be so bold as to contradict you, sir, this admittedly outlandish manifestation of classical European architecture is, despite its distinction from the context in which it has been placed, no kind of oneiric experience. The superordinate of one of the associations with which I have the honor to be affiliated imported this edifice brick by brick from deep within the forests of Germany to coincide more accurately than the local scenery can with his deep interest in European history and culture." The older man allows himself a dry chuckle. "My esteemed associate believes that true power resides within the same mystical tradition that the National Socialists seem to be exploiting with such rhetorical success."

"I don't know anything about that stuff," says Taggett as the car purrs to a stop. "I stick to the funny pages." He reaches over and gives Chen a nudge in the shoulder.

The younger detective yawns and stretches and rubs his eyes and does a double-take at the scene through the windshield. "Great," he says.

"I finally scored a date with Snow White. Shouldn't there be some little guys around here whistling or something?"

As the driver gets out and walks around the front of the Silver Phantom to open the passenger door, the corners of Jie's mouth turn down a little. "Regrettably, sir, I must advise you in the most emphatic terms to eschew to the utmost extent of your ability the humor which under ordinary circumstances so enlivens your discourse. Our host, a figure of great power, considers his connection to the Teutonic civilization represented by this structure a matter of the highest consequence and thus will tolerate irreverence with disapproval of a potentially lethal degree."

"Huh?" says Chen.

As Jie opens Taggett's door, the tough detective says, "He says don't make fun of the layout, the boss isn't kidding around."

Chen opens his own door and steps out onto the white gravel of the drive and stretches his thin hard body. "Fine with me, I don't care if the guy's Kaiser Wilhelm with a side of sauerkraut. I just need some place where I can get a drink and a meal and a good night's sleep so we can figure out how to start hitting back." He smacks his palm with his fist. "I'm ready to quit running."

"Then I can assure you with absolute certainty, young sir, that the means to attain all that which you desire lie within," says Jie as he leads them over an actual drawbridge that spans an actual moat up to a pair of wooden doors nearly the color of a few centuries of smoke and blood and girded with black strips of wrought iron flaked with rust that smells like painful history. Taggett tips his head back to check the height of these huge doors and nearly loses his hat. They go up at least a couple of storeys. The tough detective lets out a whistle as Jie leads them to a smaller door cut into a corner of this massive gate. He reaches into his coat and pulls out a thick key ring, selecting the right one to open it so that he can guide them down a short dark hallway to another door, flat and featureless. A little rectangular slot slides open to reveal a pair of suspicious eyes that squint a question at the three of them. Jie says something Taggett can't quite catch and the slot slides shut and the door swings inward to admit them.

They step into an enormous room, lit dimly by electric bulbs dotted along its walls, which reach up into a dark distance beyond the reach of the light. The vast sawdust-and-hay floor of this inner courtyard is absorbing the slop from dozens of tables where a bunch of hard-looking characters are weirdly chopping up steaks with forks and knives like a bunch of New York socialites. At the far end from the massive doors they're standing in front of, Taggett can see a kind of low platform with a bigger table on it. Behind the table there's a throne, and on the throne is a huge Chinese man dressed in furs and wearing a horned helmet. Giggling white girls are feeding him morsels from his plate as he surveys his domain. Johnny elbows Chen and points with his chin at the fat guy. Chen nods and makes the sign of the zipper across his lips. At a glance and a hint of a smile from the boss, Jie bows subtly and starts shepherding the detectives toward a place near the boss's platform.

As they edge along the jagged aisle at odd angles between the tables, Taggett notices a lot of creeps with scars worse than his across their faces and missing eyes and ears, and they're sure as hell noticing him. Some guy with an eye patch and a hook where his left hand used to be is staring the tough detective down with one glittering eye and grinding his teeth like a dog about to jump off a leash. Johnny gives Chen another nudge with his elbow and mutters, "What is it with these mugs?" as the low buzz of conversation at each table they pass fades out to a clinking of forks and knives against plates, and then that fades into a little patch of silence around them, fading back into that hum of conversation as they get by.

Chen mutters back, "We weren't here that long ago, boss, and a lot of these creeps probably remember what we did. Hell, we probably did it to some of these guys." The younger man glances around. "I hope our old buddy didn't bring us into something to kill our way out of." His eyes turn back to Taggett's, and they're a little shiny. "I really need a break from that."

"Don't worry," says Taggett. "Jie wouldn't steer us wrong." He takes a seat at the table and puts his gnarly hands palms-down on the smooth white tablecloth. "Anyway, no one's gonna start trouble with the boss right here. Let's just have a meal and some drinks and get some rest and figure out what comes next when we get to it."

Chuckling as he sits down, Chen says, "Or when it gets to us."

Jie says as he pushes Chen's chair back in, "With your kind permission, young sir, I feel I must attempt to dissuade you with all the eloquence at my poor command from the otherwise completely understandable concern you express so cleverly. As Mr. Taggett has elucidated, you find yourself under the protection of Mr. Wing." Having gotten the men seated, he glances around the room and makes a beckoning gesture to someone Taggett can't see somewhere in the depths of the big shadowy room. "The ill will borne you by many of the employees of this organization should, if I may be so bold as to say, present no obstacle to a restful and productive evening's repast." Bowing again as he backs away, he says, "Now with your permission I must endeavor to excuse myself so that I may converse briefly with our host." They watch as he glides to the side of the platform and whispers in the ear of one of the boss's girls, who goes and whispers something to the boss. He nods, and then Taggett and Chen get distracted.

The serving girl coming their way is swaying her hips like a hypnotist swings a pocket watch, her curves rippling irresistibly under the sheer toga that's hugging them. Taggett can feel his jaw going a little slack as he stares. After a moment his stare finds its way to her face to notice her pale blue eyes and hair so blonde it's almost white. The long braids drape over her shoulders and just barely obscure the nipples of her softly swinging breasts. By the time she gets to the table those breasts are just about eye level. He can barely hear her husky German whisper over the thumb of the blood pulsing in his ears. "My name is Helga, Mr. Taggett." she purrs. "Will you say for me how you like your steak?"

Taggett swallows and says into that soft warm breast, "Uh, rare. Bloody. And a bottle of whiskey."

Helga smiles down with a pair of lips that look less like an invitation than like a dare. "Of course. And for you, Mr. Chen?"

Chen just sits there with a dumb grin hanging around his face until Taggett grabs a shoulder and gives him a shake. "Oh! Uh, I guess the same," he says in the rusty squeak of a teenager. Both men just keep staring as she turns and takes her mesmerizing body back to wherever the steaks are coming from.

After a moment Taggett says, "Your own bottle of whiskey. Nice."

"Gimmie a break," says Chen. "That babe had us both buffaloed." The two of them glance back the way she came and chuckle together for a moment.

By the time Jie shows up they've finished both steaks and one of the bottles. Chen burps and actually giggles a little and says, "Damn, uncle, I forgot how you people know how to live! You got more girls like that Helga back there? She can frost my strudel any day of the week!" Red-faced, he burps again and glances around the room he's yelling into. It's emptied out, and a bunch of little Chinese guys are sweeping up the dropped napkins and broken plates and sticky sawdust and hay.

Jie's patting the younger man on the shoulder and saying, "Indeed, young sir. However, the hour grows late, and your activities of the evening past—indeed, of the past week, according to the account I have received from a Mr. Venz of the Oriental Blossom cruise line—lead me inescapably to recommend, subject of course to your agreement, that a course of quiet rest could better improve your state of being than could the strenuous though undeniably pleasurable services offered by girls, as you say, like that Helga."

"Huh?" says Chen.

Taggett chuckles and drains the last swallow from his glass and says, "He says you need to take it easy."

"Oh," says the younger man, and then the bottom half of his face opens up in a yawn. "Yeah, I guess you're right." He grabs the extra bottle of whiskey by the neck and starts to stand up and makes it about an inch off the chair before he thumps his ass back down. Leaning on the bottle a little helps him keep his face from smacking down into the table. Instead, he carefully aims himself at an invisible spot on the tablecloth and starts snoring before his head quite makes it all the way down.

Taggett chuckles and looks at Jie. The older man nods and gives a chuckle of his own. "Allow me to offer my sincerest assurance that our young friend will indeed find his way to a more felicitous place of repose.

I shall myself attend to his secure disposition." He winks at Taggett and hands over a big cast-iron key. "Our host has assigned you quarters one flight up and at the end of the corridor to the right. Shall I employ one of the staff to assist you in locating your chambers?"

The tough detective snuffs out his smoke and shakes his head. "I can remember one flight up and to the right," he says. As the older man's snapping for one of the janitors, Taggett says, "Thanks for coming through for us like this. Not everyone would."

Jie smiles down and says, "Perhaps I have not made sufficiently clear that I am not everyone. Good night, Mr. Taggett. Your path leads you through that door you see to the left of the platform, up a flight of stairs, along a corridor, through a door, and into a bed. I have not a scintilla of doubt that you will find yourself in the morning, having rested and restored yourself, in a far superior condition to confront the circumstances that have led you here."

"Yeah," says Taggett and stumbles a little bit as he makes his way to the door that Jie pointed out. As he's grabbing the knob he looks back over his shoulder and sees a bunch of the janitors bundling up Chen and hauling him toward another door on the other side of the platform while Jie supervises. Taggett steps through his own door and into the deeper darkness of this crazy Shanghai-on-the-Rhine palace. He grabs a candelabra off the wall next to the door closing behind him and lurches his way up a curving set of wide stone steps until he makes a landing, turns right, and doesn't have to walk any longer than the length of a football field plus endzones to get to a smaller version of those giant black wooden doors at the front of the castle. He shoves that heavy key into the kind of keyhole he remembers from working the tenements and pushes that heavy door open. As he does, a blast of wind comes from inside the room and blows out the candles. In absolute darkness his heavy body staggers forward on its own and somehow makes it to the big soft bed that he falls face down into. He's tumbling into the land of Nod before he can even take off his hat.

CHAPTER ELEVEN

A couple of minutes or a couple of hours later his eyes snap back open in the dark. He can feel a little drool on his cheek where it's pressing against the softness of the quilt that's covering the bed, and he can feel that same dark softness inside his skull. The room's full of dense warm air that he feels like he's swimming in as he pushes himself over on his back and searches himself for a fresh smoke. After some groping he finds one and sticks it between his lips and fishes for his lighter.

Across the big room there's a spark and then a little flame, and the tough detective's breath catches as he sees Helga's face behind the fire from his lighter. His jaw goes slack and the smoke falls out of his mouth as he watches her. "You are looking for light, Mr. Taggett?" she says. "Or for heat?" The lighter snaps shut. Taggett listens to the whisper of bare feet drifting along a deep carpet, a sound like breathing that's getting closer to him in the velvet dark of the room. The flame snaps on again and he has to blink and squint a little. She's close enough for him to see the fire dancing in her ice-blue eyes as she breathes. "Mr. Jie tells to me that you are man who needs…what is word…distraction?" Her voice is that same mellow purr he remembers from what must have been this morning. As he's breathing in to say something the flame goes out again, and then she's kissing him.

The soft hot weight of her body is pressing him into the mattress as her tongue slips between his lips, her clever hands loosening his shoulder holster. He makes some kind of noise to get her to stop, but she's a little bit too strong for him and slips the holster right off him, sliding it across the mattress to get swallowed up in the dark. Then her fingers are opening his shirt and the tip of her tongue is flicking over the tip of his. Her hands are soft and smooth as they slide over his skin. His heart's hammering under those hands as his rise to her face as the kiss gets deeper. He can taste a little of tonight's steak and beer on her tongue, in her breath as she whispers over his lips, "This is good distraction, yes?" Before he can even start to grunt a response her tongue's in his mouth again and she's straddling him, grinding herself against him right where he's swelling, right where his hips are bucking up to grind into the wet heat he can feel through his pants. She gives a moan that shoots through him like electricity and takes her mouth from his. He thinks his eyes have drifted shut by this point, but the room's too dark to show a difference.

Then her mouth's on his throat, kissing along the throb in his jugular, teasing it with her little sharp teeth. He lets out a breath that comes out as a deep shuddering groan as she slides back a little onto his thighs. Her hands are caressing down his chest, over his belly, tricky fingers finding and loosening his belt, pulling it through the loops and tossing it somewhere into the vast dark. He groans again, deeper, as she gives his nipple a teasing bite that almost distracts him from the feeling of those fingers opening the button of his slacks, sliding down the zipper, flaps of fabric separating like curtains on opening night, only his boxers between the heat of her touch and the equal heat of his rigid cock. She wraps her fingers around its thickness and squeezes a little. "Oh, Mr. Taggett," she breathes. "So big and hard for me you get."

He's got just enough mind left to kick off his shoes so she can finish pulling his pants off, pulling down his shorts, getting him entirely naked. Her body leaves his for a moment, and he lies there floating in the softness of the mattress somewhere in the infinite space of that dark room, the air forming itself around him into a second skin of wet heat, like he's forming a storm cloud around himself with his lust.

There's a click, and his lighter's lit again. She's holding it a little further away from herself this time so that he can see the shadows tracing her curves like tongues as she sways her naked body for him. "So big and hard," she murmurs again. He can feel his fingers curl tight to clutch the sheets as he stares and she keeps whispering, the soft rattle of that German accent, her tongue against her teeth, driving him somehow crazier. "Such a strong hard man for me, yes?" He can see hints of something glistening at the tops of her thighs in the teasing flicker. The glow from the little flame shimmers along the length of her lips as she licks them. "You have me so hungry, Mr. Taggett," she says, and the lighter flicks out again, and then he can feel her hair on the insides of his thighs as she kneels between them. He barely has time to twitch before she's taking him into her mouth, sucking around his swollen head as her little hand curls around the base of his rigid throb. The tip of her tongue is tracing, flicking, drawing wet lines down and back up his length, forcing breathless encouragements out of him as she takes him deeper, those velvet lips stretching around him, the wetness of her mouth enflaming him.

He can feel his eyes roll up as his body tries to arch deeper into her, but she pulls back, that tongue still swirling around his tip. His whole body's shaking like a worm on a hook. "Not so fast," she tells him. "To those who wait come the good things." Then she takes him again, deeper, that tongue pulling him back into her throat. She's swallowing him as his mind blows up like a balloon to fill the dark space around them. She pulls back a little, squeezing gently with her jaw, just poking his skin with the tips of those sharp little teeth. The pleasure makes him bark.

She pulls back again, all the way off him, and whispers, "You make me want you, Mr. Taggett. Want you inside me." She's still got her fingers wrapped around the base of him as he feels her rise, feels the mattress sink a little as she straddles him, feels her on him. She's grinding along his length, not quite letting him in, as her sly hands find his chest. He's staring up wide-eyed into the darkness at what has to be her face but all he can see is a shadow against a shadow as she takes him into her, as she holds him tight and starts to ride. She pinches his nipples as her hips grind him deeper, as she buries him deep in that tight hot embrace. He reaches out, reaches up to find her breasts with his hands, to clutch and squeeze and thrust into her, yelling words he doesn't recognize as his muscular hands maul her. She's spewing out some weird series of syllables in German or Chinese or something as her thighs grip tighter around his hips and she pushes herself over him.

And then with a deep growl he turns them over on that big mattress so that he's on her, on top of her, driving into her, forcing himself deeper. She starts to wail as he bites her throat, as he fills her with himself over and over, driving deep, taking her, claiming her. He gets up on his hands, his body looming over her invisibly in the darkness, her body invisible under him as he pushes it into the give of that mattress again and again and again and again. Her heels are digging into his ass as she pulls him deeper. Her lips are at his ear. "Fuck me," she pleads. "Fuck me good, Mr. Taggett."

His growls are turning into roars. Bolts of lightning start to streak through the storm cloud around them, the cloud made of their sweat and smell and inarticulate noises, as his vision starts to come in through eyes that have gone as big and wide as searchlights on a battleship. He'd swear he can see her face under him, blue eyes glassy and glittering with tears that stream back along her temples into her luminous hair, lips parted to let out her cries and whimpers and showing those teeth in a feline snarl. He doesn't stop. He can't stop. He bends over her to bite that luscious lower lip, tasting blood as he bites harder and she grips him inside, tighter, wetter, hotter than he can resist. Her voice cracks as she shrieks uncontrollably. He feels himself swelling, feels that pressure at the base of his spine. Her nails open gouges in his back as she screams again. "Johnny! Johnny! O Mein Papa!" He bends to her breast and bites her nipple and thrusts with all his power into her. "Take me!" she screams. "Make me yours!"

And that makes him explode. He rams his full raging length into her and fires round after round of heat into her spasming sex. She keeps saying his name like some kind of magic spell as he slows and starts to catch his breath and shuts her up with a hard deep kiss. He sucks her tongue for a moment and lets it go and feels himself slide out of her, rolling onto his back. "Damn," he mutters.

Lying there next to him she laughs deep in her throat. "You are well distracted, I think, yes?"

"Oh, yes," he says, and reaches up past their bodies to fumble around in the darkness. He finds the jacket she'd stripped off him and uses his fingers to pull out a couple of smokes, and then he somehow finds the lighter on the bed between them. He lights them up and passes her one and spends a minute watching her face in the glow from the cherry end. Her eyelids droop heavily as she smokes. He says, "You can tell Jie I said you were just what I needed."

She smiles and says, "Thank you, Mr. Taggett." She manages to get off the bed to disappear into the darkness, the little red spot of fire vanishing as she snuffs it out. "You sleep now," she tells him. "Such an important man must have a busy day ahead."

"Busy life," mumbles Taggett, but she's gone by then, and he's already asleep and talking into his dreams.

CHAPTER TWELVE

He wakes up again naked under a gigantic brown fur in a room full of light that shafts in from a leaded-glass window high up on the stone wall opposite the bed. He yawns and stretches and looks around for a smoke and finds the fresh pack with a new book of matches on top of it on the little table next to the bed. As he rolls over to light up he notices his forty-five hung up on a hook next to a dark oak door he guesses must be the closet. Coughing and scratching his belly, he smokes for a moment and then steps to the door to open it and see a slick new suit hanging from a wooden hangar. He lets out a low whistle and in a minute or two he's all dressed up, the forty-five in its holster fitting under the jacket with barely a bulge.

As he's slipping on the jacket he notices a piece of paper folded up in an inner pocket. It's a note: "My dear and most esteemed Mr. Taggett, it is with the utmost regret that I may have within my poor power to express that I must reluctantly acknowledge to you an unavoidable obstacle interfering with my ability to join you for the breakfast we had implicitly planned. Please accept my fondest hope that you and our young associate Chen will enjoy the repast provided by our host and that you will then proceed about the business that will have been prepared for you in his name and in your honor. An acceptable confluence of circumstances will find us rejoining each other this evening, at which time I may have the opportunity to apprise you of potentialities for the furtherance of goals which I believe we will find to be mutual."

Taggett's started chuckling even before he gets to the signature. Still grinning, he pulls open the door to the hall, slipping the note back into his pocket and coming face to face with the winking sneer of a little granite gargoyle topping the pillar at the end of the banister. He stops for a minute and winks back and actually starts whistling as he follows the wide steps down to the courtyard.

Chen's already there in what looks like a new black turtleneck to go with his black jeans, digging into a thick slice of ham with a fried egg on top leaking its yolk all over the plate. He looks up at Taggett and grins with his mouth full as one of those Germanic serving wenches sets a cup of coffee at an empty space on the table. Taggett takes a seat in front of the coffee and breathes in the smell with a smile his face doesn't usually make. Chen swallows and says, "This Wing really knows how to treat a guest, eh?"

"You don't know the half of it," Taggett says, taking a sip. While the cup's still in his hand one of the wenches, dressed up for the breakfast shift in blonde braids and a silk dress that clings to her creamy white curves, has slid a plate of ham and egg onto the table in front of him. The heat of her breath over his ear as she brushes it with her lips gives him a little shiver. He turns to her and mutters, "Tell Helga thanks," and starts applying his fork and knife to that ham steak.

The wench gives out a little giggle and glides away as Chen sips his coffee and says, "Where's Jie?" Taggett shrugs and passes over the note from his jacket. He watches the younger man squint at it for a minute or two until Chen says, "What's this business he's got in mind? I thought we were on vacation, boss."

Taggett shrugs again. "I guess nothing's free. I've always had to work for my living." He takes another sip of the coffee and the forks the last of the ham steak into his mouth, a little surprised that he's wolfed it down so fast. "Anyway," he says, "we may as well make ourselves useful. This kind of lifestyle is just gonna get us too soft."

"I wouldn't mind getting a little soft once in a while," says Chen. "All this being hard is just getting me tired." He leans back in his chair and lets out a breath. "You know what I mean? You ever wonder how much more you can take?"

Taggett's eyes narrow as he stares back at his partner. "No," he says. "I never wonder. I just take what I get."

"Yeah, and you pass it around, don't you," says Chen. The metallic clattering of Wing's army of tough guys scraping forks and knives on plates seems to get louder as the two of them just sit there watching each other and wondering what to say next.

After that long moment there's suddenly a guy standing next to the table, a tall Chinese character with his head shaved and his left eye bulged into a monocle and his lanky body dressed in some kind of Kraut general's dress uniform from the War, a uniform that doesn't exactly fit. This crazy figure clears his throat and says, "I am Otto. I will your companion be for today. With breakfast you are finished?"

The two of them goggle up at Otto, and Taggett says, "Uh, yeah." He snaps a glance over at Chen. "You with me?"

Chen looks down and looks back up and says, "Yeah. Yeah, of course, boss." He takes a pack of smokes out of his pocket and lights up a couple and hands one to Taggett and the two of them get up and follow Otto through the little door, down the hallway, and out into the gravel drive. A gleamingly black Cadillac 61 is idling there waiting for them. The driver, whose head comes directly out of his muscular shoulders like a thumb out of a fist, shoves himself out to waddle around and open one of the back doors. Otto opens the other one, and Johnny and Chen slide into the back seat from either side. Then the other two get in and with a rumble of an obviously souped-up engine they're off.

It takes a few minutes down the road for Chen to say, "Otto? Like von Bismarck?"

Without turning his hairless head, Otto says in some kind of tongue-rattling accent Taggett can only imagine he's picked up from movies, "Yes. Otto like von Bismarck." The driver says nothing, maybe doesn't even speak English. The hum of the well-kept engine fills the car as the two detectives watch the scenery go by, sticks of black skeletal trees giving way to little huts giving way to the outskirts of Shanghai.

After a few minutes of this, Chen says, "You're Chinese, right?"

"Yes. Chinese," says Otto to the windshield in front of him. The city's building itself up around them, little houses and shops crammed together and getting taller as the car gets closer to the port. The road that the Caddy's been navigating has started to narrow as the driver turns left and right and right again and left again into a maze of alleys, starting too slow.

Chen can't stop. "And your parents named you Otto like von Bismarck?" he says to the back of the character's head.

"My parents named me Xi," comes the answer with a throatier growl to the accent. "My employer desires me to dress and speak this way and to call myself by this name." The car comes to a stop as a warehouse door rolls up in front of it, a couple of little guys yanking chains hand over hand to open it. One of them sidles up to the driver's window and the driver hands him a few bills as the Caddy drifts forward into the building. Total darkness swallows everything for a moment and then they're idling in the middle of some kind of factory, a bunch of guys turning valves on industrial pressing machines and siphoning off clear liquid into flasks that they take to a bank of ovens that are glowing hot and orange to give off half the light in the enormous room. That glow is coloring half of Otto's face as he's turned around to glare furiously into Chen's eyes. "Will I then be mocked for what I must do to feed my family?" he hisses.

Chen puts up his hands and keeps grinning and says, "Hey, sorry, no harm meant, just making conversation." The driver gets out and opens the back door next to Taggett as the other two men stare at each other for a moment, Chen's grin slowly fading. Then the younger man opens his own door and steps out and opens Otto's and puts out his hand. "Let me put it another way," he says. "I apologize."

From his seat Otto extends a hand and says, "I accept your apology." They shake and Otto gets out and says, "Now let us attend to the purpose of our activities today." He gestures around the room. "You see around you the processing of the poppies we receive from our fields elsewhere into the opium that we ship around the world from our port here in Shanghai. Our men operate these machines to convert the opium to easily transportable powder." A smell of machine oil and burning fills the space along with the hiss and roar of steam and gas, like it's the nineteenth century in here.

Taggett whistles. "Quite an operation. What's it got to do with us?"

Otto makes a little bow and says, "Your directness does you credit, Mr. Taggett. I will explain. My employer is not the only processor of opium in Shanghai, especially since the turmoil generated by your last visit. Many factions struggle with each other for control of this industry. Thus we must have a strategist of the kind that Mr. Jie recommends you as for our defense."

Taggett glances over at Chen in the wavering orange light. The younger man shrugs and gives a little nod and Taggett says, "Okay."

"Excellent," says Otto. "Then return please to the automobile so that we may continue." He and the driver open up the back doors and the detectives step back in and settle as the Caddy backs up through the warehouse door into the buzz and hum of the alley. The car clears the doorway, backing almost all the way to the alley's other wall, when something explodes and the window next to the driver turns into a pile of shards and the driver grips his neck and grunts and slumps over the wheel. Blood's gushing out from between his fingers as Otto yells something and grabs the wheel with one hand and pulls hard as he shoves down on one of the driver's thick thighs. The Caddy slams back into the wall behind it as another shot goes off and Taggett pulls his forty-five and shoots back through the little side window. Gears grind as Otto wrestles with the shift lever and manages to get the car into forward gear, making the tires scream as the car turns and jets down the alley and smashes through three or four carts to get to the main street and stall out again, blocking a lane or two of traffic. Taggett lunges over the back of the front seat and throws open the driver's door so that Otto can shove the body out into the street and slide himself behind the wheel. A third shot blows up the back window over Chen, who's thrown himself into the space between seats, and Taggett throws another couple of shots back as Otto throws the Caddy into gear and stomps on the pedal. The Caddy lunges forward. The driver's door slams shut. Taggett looks back out of the blasted back window to see a purple coupe screaming around the corner they just turned and roaring after them. He sights down the barrel and squeezes off a shot that shatters the coupe's headlight as he kneels on the back seat and then falls over when the Caddy starts swerving back through the maze of this warehouse district.

"Goddammit, Otto!" yells Taggett. "Keep it straight!"

"I take us to a safe place!" Otto yells back. Taggett gets back to his knees and then ducks back down again just as another shot flies through the Caddy. The tough detective gets back up and squeezes off a shot that smashes through the coupe's windshield. The coupe swerves out of the street into a crowd that scatters out of the way screaming, and then it gets back onto the road as the Caddy takes a sudden right into another alley and then another right into another alley. Taggett pops back up to peek through the back and all he sees is traffic. The Caddy slows and takes a left and stops with a soft squeak of brakes. Otto shoves some bills into the fist of the guy who creeps up the driver's door and a bunch of carts full of bulky displays of flowers and fruit close up behind the car to make a wall that looks like the end of an alley.

"Damn," says Taggett. He reaches down and pulls Chen back up to the seat. The younger man's eyes are round and glassy, and his lips are puffing out a little as he pants. "You okay?" Taggett says.

"I don't know," says Chen. "But I think I will be. Let's get those creeps killed."

CHAPTER THIRTEEN

"I've got an idea about that," says Taggett. "Otto, take Chen back to the castle and get together some of those gorillas and meet me in front of the Prestige Hotel in about an hour." He sticks a fresh smoke between his lips and pulls out his forty-five to check the action. Otto's starting the car as Taggett reaches to open the back door.

Chen grabs him by the shoulder and says, "What the hell, boss? Back to the castle?" The younger man's eyes are a little shiny. "What's the plan? Who do we get?" He cracks his knuckles as his voice goes up a little in pitch. "We can catch up with that coupe and just take those guys apart until they cough up some answers, right?"

Taggett puts his hand over Chen's and looks into the younger man's eyes and just shakes his head. "You're not up to taking anyone apart," he says. "You know as well as I do you've still got the yips from whatever happened to you back on the boat." He starts to take Chen's hand off his shoulder but Chen yanks his hand back. "Listen," he says. "I can't watch your back and mine at the same time."

"Yeah," says Chen. "I get it." His hands curl into fists and he's holding them knuckle-down at the tops of his thighs as he turns to stare forward past Otto, who's doing the same kind of staring less emphatically. "You just let me know when you think I'm ready," he says into the car's thick air.

Taggett looks at him for a moment and says, "Yeah." He pulls the handle and opens the door and steps out into the noise of the alley. It's late enough in the day that the sun's got the angle to pop the sweat out under his hat as he watches the carts make a road for the Caddy to back out through. "All right, mouse," he says to himself. "Let's take a look at who's setting the trap." Shoving his hands into his pockets and whistling a random little tune, he starts making his way around the shouting and down the alley and onto the main line.

As he ambles along the wide street, he keeps an eye on the buildings he passes. He's seen a few docking neighborhoods in his life, and this one's another one. He's sauntering up a wooden kind of sidewalk, sharing it with a bunch of tough guys all marked up with bruises and scars going about their business and giving him the hard stare as he smiles politely back, just the goofy American tourist wandering away from the hotel district. Every so often one of the creeps leans into him and shoves him aside as he bumbles along, and the tough detective just smiles and takes it and even tips his hat once or twice. After a few minutes of this he gets to the edge between where work happens and where selling happens and starts to look around with a little more intent and finally turns to pass through a pair of swinging doors under a sign that says YANKEE SAILOR NUMBER ONE FOOD BAR.

It's a little room with floor and walls made of grey wood planks, swirls of dust twinkling in the diagonal rays of light that push in through the dirty windows. To his right, the bar follows most of the wall until it gets to a door with a rusty knob, and seven tables that clearly didn't come from the same shipment clutter up some of the floorspace. The furthest one from the door is holding up some white wetbrain and a bottle with a couple of fingers left in the bottom. Closer to the bar a couple of dockworkers are just glaring at each other across a round table and drinking shot-for-shot. A little to Taggett's left sits an old fellow in a seersucker suit staring back and sipping something thick and green out of a shot glass, holding his big white mustache out of the way of a stain with his thumb and finger. A cracked voice with a hint of Southern drawl creeps out from under the mustache and says, "You seem lost, son."

Taggett clears his throat and says, "Uh, yeah, got separated from my group back at the, uh, I forget what they call it here. Do you know the way to the Prestige Hotel?" He stands there shifting his weight from foot to foot like any other half-drunk stooge as the elderly character regards him.

"Indeed," says the guy. "But perhaps you'll join me first for a sip of the local color. These people make a fantastic liqueur, it'll curl the hair under that sturdy hat of yours." It's almost like he's singing Taggett a little song.

The tough detective shrugs. "I'm ordinarily a whiskey man," he says, "but, uh, sure, I'm here for an exotic experience." He takes a seat across the table from the cute little dude, who raises a hand to get the bartender to bring over another glass. With a twinkle in his washed-out blue eyes, the antique pours a shot for Taggett that oozes from the bottle to the glass like a slug of syrup.

"You know," says the elf, "you're in the right place. This whole town is made for exotic experiences." He takes a sip and smacks his cherry lips and winks. "Experiences of an entirely unexpected kind. And how's your liqueur?"

Taggett looks down at the glass and back up at the old cutie and smiles politely.

With a jolly chuckle the old fellow says, "Yes, quite the nectar, quite the nectar. They say it gives a man visions of paradise, far from this world of woe." He takes another sip and licks a green coating from his lips. "Go ahead, try a taste, forget your cares."

"Well," says Taggett, "I'm really in a hurry to get back to my group at the Prestige, so…" He trails off. "Ah, forget it. You're a recruiter, aren't you?" The old boy blinks back, the picture of innocence. "A recruiter," Taggett repeats. "This nectar's drugged, right? Probably the glass, so I can see you drinking from the bottle, but there's definitely a mickey here. Then once I'm out I wake up under the deck, maybe in irons, working for someone's navy, right?" He raises the glass and pours it out on the floor. Out of the corner of his eye he can see the bartender muttering something into a phone, but the wetbrain and the dock workers don't flinch. The old cutie just blinks across the table at him. "So what the hell good are you to me? You work for the Foulsworths? For One-Eye?"

The guy shrugs. "Yeah, I guess you got me, mac." The gentle Southern lilt is gone, turned into some kind of gutter-Irish brogue.

"No skin off my nose. If you don't wanna drink, I'm not gonna hold your nose for you." That friendly sparkle's left his eyes. His hands have left the table top. "I gotta tell you, though," he says, "I don't know any of those birds you're chattering about." Taggett glances down to see the old boy pushing back his jacket to reveal the buck knife sheathed in his belt. Those blue eyes, dead as a doll's by now, shoot down at what Taggett's looking at and then back up at the tough detective in a wink. "And even a wised-up mark like yourself knows when to move on, right?" says the recruiter. "You believe me now, don't you."

Taggett takes a look over at the bartender, who's off the phone by now, and raises his hands, back to the goofy tourist routine, pasting that dumb smile back on his face. "Oh, yeah," he says, "I don't want any kind of trouble with a professional. I was just hoping for a prettier story, I guess." He carefully stands up from his chair and backs out of the bar and into the street.

As the doors are swinging shut he turns around to hear someone yelling "Prestige Hotel!" He looks around the scurry of the traffic and sees across the street a gawky bucktoothed kid harnessed to a rickshaw. "Prestige Hotel!" the kid yells again, twisting his head around on its stalk of a neck in every direction except right at Taggett.

The detective pulls out a smoke and lights up and lets out a snicker. Then he holds up his hand and hollers across the street at the kid and stands there on the sidewalk watching him tug that rickshaw through the traffic, dodging cars and bouncing that little wooden passenger cart up onto one of its bicycle wheels and then the other. Sweating and panting, the kid says, "You go Prestige Hotel, Mister? Too far for walk, too short for drive. I take you, you see sights, yeah?"

"Yeah," says Taggett. "Why not?" He takes a look around and then back at the kid and says, "You'll get me there one piece, won't you? I've heard these streets are dangerous."

The kid nods and grins and says, "One piece, sure, you have smooth ride, see sights," as he's lifting up the poles he's gripping in each hand so that Taggett can get between them and step up into the cart they're attached to between the bicycle wheels and have a seat on the bench that comes out of the cart's tall back. He leans back as the kid holds the poles at about waist level and darts out into the street and starts running along with the cars and trucks.

As the cart bounces and jostles Taggett can see that the kid's not the beanpole he seemed to be from across the street. Thick ropes of muscle tense and stretch the skin of his shirtless back as he turns a corner and another corner, taking the detective further into the city. Taggett can see the buildings getting bigger as the kid pulls him deeper until with another turn they're in an alley between high brick walls with a dead end Taggett can see past the kid's head. Suddenly the rickshaw pulls to a stop and the kid's somehow got himself turned around to face Taggett. "This you stop," he says, not grinning.

Taggett goes for his forty five but his hand's still in his jacket when he's suddenly on his back staring up at the sky, the breath pushed out of his lungs by the smack of hitting the street with his spine. He's got less than a second to wonder what the hell just happened before the kid has leaped over the bottom of the cart and onto his chest, yelling like a berserker and smashing him in the face with rights and lefts that feel like bowling balls. The detective takes a few punches before he can get his knee up between them and shove the kid up over his head, over the top of the cart and onto the packed dirt of this little alley. Then he throws himself to the side and smacks up against a brick wall, still fumbling for his forty-five, yanking it out, aiming at the kid, but the kid's too fast. He's on his feet and jumping again, back onto the rickshaw, setting it right so that the poles smack on the ground before he jumps at Taggett, who's just swinging his gun around as the kid's bare foot misses his face by half a hair, slamming into the wall beside him. The kid's on the ground but he's got a hand on Taggett's forty-five, gripping it as he uses his other fist to smash the detective in the face again and again. Taggett takes it. He pulls the kid closer with his gun hand so that the blows can't have as much effect and then rears back and butts the kid right across the bridge of his nose with his dome. The kid roars and loses his grip on the gun. Taggett gets off a shot, misses, hears the bullet kick up from the dirt and bounce off one of the walls as the kid gets his grip back and they start wrestling again for the forty-five. Taggett grabs the kid's other wrist. They pull each other back to standing, grunting with effort. Taggett's staring deep into the kid's eyes, watching them bulge and strain and start to get a little bloody. The kid's fingers claw at the inside of his wrist as he plants his knee between the kid's thighs and then does it again and then does it again, feeling something soft squelch against his knee that third time. The kid howls again. He's getting weaker. Taggett forces the gun back and back until the muzzle's under the kid's chin and pointing up, pressing into the soft skin behind the jaw. Those eyes are almost out of their sockets as Taggett squeezes the trigger and sends them the rest of the way, the kid's head just exploding. The new corpse drops to the ground and Taggett slumps against the wall, sliding down to a seat, staring down at the body as it dies, noticing that tattoo on the kid's ankle, the tattoo from San Francisco and from the *Flower Song*. "Guess I got someone's attention" he mutters to himself feeling his breathing slowly get steadier.

A low rumble catches his attention after a moment, so he looks up from the corpse to the mouth of the alley where the Caddy is idling, Otto and Chen in the front and a couple of fireplug-looking goons stuffed in the back and grinning like sharks. The detective pushes himself back up to his feet, feeling that brick wall scrape away at that slick new suit jacket and noticing the rips in his trousers. He looks down at his forty-five and slips it back into its holster and then takes the time to find his hat and screw it back onto his head. Once he's got that done, he reaches into the beat-up jacket and pulls out a crumpled pack of smokes. He pulls out a bent one and pulls it straight and lights up and starts limping toward the car. He can feel his face starting to swell up where those brick-like fists got to it. Finally he gets to the Caddy and leans down into the driver's window and says to Otto, just a little out of breath by this time, "Sorry for the trouble. I thought they would send someone harder."

CHAPTER FOURTEEN

So they leave one of the gorillas behind to pay off the cops and get rid of the corpse, and Taggett slips into the back of the Caddy and says, "Okay, we've got somewhere to start. Turn us around, Otto." The gorilla next to him hands him a handkerchief so that he can smear some of the blood from his face as he guides Otto back through the weird maze of traffic the rickshaw kid had run him through.

From the passenger seat, Chen turns around and says, "You okay, boss? I couldn't see much, but it looked for a second like that kid had your number." There's a smirk on Chen's face that Taggett hasn't seen in a while.

He answers with a smirk of his own as his lip starts to swell. "I guess I needed my back watched more than I thought." He turns and rolls down his window and spits a mouthful of blood out into the street. "Did you see the tattoo?"

"Yeah," says Chen. "Same creeps from back home?" Taggett nods, and the Caddy slows down a little as it gets into that district where the tourists and the working locals overlap and people start wandering into the street with their wagonloads of crap for sale. After a few seconds more it rolls to a stop in front of YANKEE SAILOR NUMBER ONE FOOD BAR. Otto shuts off the engine and gets out and opens Johnny's door. Taggett gets out as Chen and the gorilla open their own doors. As Otto's coming around the front of the car Chen says, "Just gonna leave it out in the middle of the street?"

Otto looks down at him through that crazy monocle and says, "In this part of town this car is known. Everyone knows that anyone foolish enough to attempt mischief soon would be found and"—he takes a moment to sneer—"punished."

Chen chuckles and fakes a shudder. "Tough crew," he says. Otto grins like a wolf and just nods, and then the four of them push through the swinging doors and into the dusk of the bar.

Turns out this is the kind of bar where nothing really changes. The wetbrain's still hunched over his table back by the far wall. The bottle in front of him has lost maybe an eighth of an inch, but he's still got that stupid smile from somewhere far away plastered on his face. The two rough-looking sailors are still over there to the left, between Taggett's group and the unoccupied bar, still staring at each other, still trading shots, the bottle between them still about half full somehow. The sporty old imp in the seersucker suit is there too, staring back at Taggett and smirking. "So," he says, "I see you've managed yourself some reinforcement. Can't imagine what we'd have to fight about, though. I haven't done a thing to you or yours, have I?" He's making an innocent face, but Taggett can see his hand inching toward the knife in his belt. He flashes a glance at Chen. Chen dips his head into a tiny nod, and his body shifts into readiness.

"You can forget about all that," says the tough detective, showing his empty hands. "I just want to ask questions."

The recruiter's eyes flip over to Otto and those thin lips curl up into a sneer. "I know you, don't I," he says. Otto just stares back. "Yeah," says the recruiter. "You're that guy Wing dresses up like a Kraut to drive him around. Don't you ever—"

"Shut up," says Taggett. He steps closer to the table, away from the doors the four of them are standing in front of. Chen unobtrusively takes a step alongside. "We're not here for trouble." He's keeping his voice slow and even and friendly as Chen idly circles around to the recruiter's off side. "I just need to know what happened to the bartender."

The best the old guy can come up with is, "Huh?"

"The bartender," Taggett says. "That little greasy-looking guy that's not behind the bar anymore." The tough detective shifts his arm a little bit so that his jacket falls open to reveal the forty-five in its holster. "Does he often just leave the customers to take care of the place?"

The recruiter snickers. "You really are a wised-up baby," he says and flinches the tiniest bit to get the wetbrain at the back table leaping up from his chair to swing his bottle the way a bouncer swings his billy club at the back of Chen's head. The younger detective drops and kicks and knocks the wetbrain's feet out from under him and punches the guy in the throat to keep him down while the two sailors to the door's left have launched themselves at Otto and the gorilla. The gorilla goes down under one of them as Otto takes a punch to his chest from the other one and grabs the offered arm and snaps it as he throws the sailor into the opposite wall. The sailor on top of the gorilla is throwing lefts and rights like swinging hammers until Otto grabs him by the back of his shirt and yanks. The sailor stumbles back into the table, which tips over onto him as he hits the floor and tries to jump back up but just smashes his face into the sole of Otto's foot and goes back down into the splinters. The guy under Chen's stopped gurgling by this time, and the room goes silent again.

Through all this the recruiter's got his hand on his knife, too smart to draw and get what Taggett's got waiting for him in that shoulder holster. The two of them stare at each other as Chen and the gorilla get up off the floor, the gorilla all red-faced and stepping over to the sailor lying up against the wreckage of the table and giving a hard stomp to the middle of the ribcage. Something cracks and the sailor moans and coughs out a spray of blood and stops moving. Chen and Otto catch a breath and give each other a quick nod of respect and then everybody's looking hard at the recruiter.

Taggett says, "Okay, let's try it again. That bartender was calling someone the last time I was here." The recruiter shrugs and gets a smack across the back of his head from Chen. "Come on," says Taggett as the guy rubs the back of his head and looks all watery-eyed and harmless, "The sooner you tell us what you know, the sooner we can get on with our business and out of your hair."

"How the hell am I supposed to know anything?" says the old guy. "I just drink here." That gets him another smack, this one hard enough to bend him over the table a little. He straightens up and glares into Taggett's face and says, "Listen, I don't mind answering questions like a gentleman, but you need to curb your dog here. This Chink's—"

That gets him a smack across the face from Taggett. "He's not your problem," says the tough detective. "And give up the innocent act. You don't drink here, you work here, and you don't work here without permission." He bends down to put his face half an inch away from the recruiter's and says, "That means you know who the bartender is and who he called and where he went." He pulls the forty-five and tucks it under the cute old guy's chin and pushes just a little into that softness and says, "So tell me."

The recruiter sucks in a breath and holds it and stares into Taggett's eyes. "I'm thinking," he says. "I know you can punch my ticket right here, but you don't know what the big man can do to me." Carefully, delicately, he opens the jacket of his suit with two fingers to show Taggett the pack of smokes in his inner pocket. Taggett gives a little nod and the recruiter shakes out a smoke and lights it up. The four men stand around for a moment and watch the guy smoke.

Then Taggett tightens his finger a little, just enough for the old guy to notice, and says, "Think faster."

"Okay," says the recruiter. "You got me." He leans back in his chair and taps ash off the end of his smoke and says, "You big sides of beef won't get too far anyway, I suppose. Check behind the bar."

While Taggett and Chen keep the cute old guy nailed down with their stares, Otto and the gorilla peer over the bar. Otto's suddenly got his bony fingers wrapped around the grip of an old Mauser pistol from the War. He pokes it down over the bar, his finger tightening, and then turns back to Taggett and says, "Trap door." He goes around behind the bar and bends down and straightens up again to say, "You may want a look at this to have."

"Okay," says Taggett. "Cover this guy." He slips his forty-five back into its holster while Otto turns his Mauser to point at the recruiter so that Taggett can walk away, wooden floor creaking under his solid weight, to take a look at the square hatch in the floor opened to reveal a ridiculously narrow cylindrical tunnel with ladder rungs taking up almost the entire space as it seems to taper down into the darkness. He looks at it for a moment and lets out a snort of a chuckle and says to the recruiter, "Yeah, I see what you mean. We're not going to get down there without some equipment."

Otto says, "Of that I can take care," and snaps his fingers so that the gorilla picks up the bar phone and starts talking Chinese into it. "I am having our man request more heavy armaments, more powerful guns and perhaps some grenades," Otto tells Taggett. "And at the same time he explains to our employer this operation unsanctioned in our territory." He grins fiercely at the recruiter he's got his gun trained on and says, "No doubt I have that he will want conversation with this representative of such an operation. A slow and intense conversation. Perhaps he will allow me to take part in such a conversation." Right then Taggett notices just how sharp Otto's teeth are, like either he's filed them down or he's just mostly shark. "I have a particular fondness to converse with men who choose your profession."

The recruiter takes a gulp of air as Chen moves smoothly over toward the bar, takes a look down that narrow tunnel, and says, "I can get down there."

"Better wait," says Taggett. "You heard Otto, we've got some backup coming. No need to get into something we can't see." He glances over at Otto, who hasn't taken his eyes or his gun off the recruiter. "How long do you see this taking?" Taggett asks him.

Otto says, "Not long. In our own domain we are well supplied." He steps a little closer to the recruiter and grins a little bit more. "And we have many interesting implements with which to stimulate conversation."

"The hell with that," Chen says. "This drip drip drip is killing me." He strips off his turtleneck to reveal a slim and tightly muscled body and shoots Taggett a wild-eyed glare. "If getting to the end of that tunnel makes it stop, you think I'm gonna wait around a damn minute more?" The gorilla makes a move toward Chen but a blast of intensity from the smaller man's eyes freezes him.

Taggett says, "At least take a heater with you." He tosses his forty-five to Chen.

The smaller man catches it and spins and tosses it right back. "I don't need a gun," he says and suddenly tips his partner a wink. "My winning personality's always been the ticket." His lips draw back from his teeth into a kind of a grin and winks again as he flashes a knife out of a secret pocket in the back of his pants and flashes it right back in again the way a magician pulls a cane out of the air and makes it vanish. "I'll be fine," he says and slips down into the hole before anyone can flinch. Taggett can hear the hint the whisper of soft shoes and callused hands brushing over metal bars, but that goes away after a little while.

A few minutes after the last sound of Chen's footsteps has faded a rough grumble of engines tells Taggett that the gorilla's phone call has paid off. The swinging doors part and in comes Jie. He smiles at Johnny and says, "Mr. Taggett, perhaps I may be allowed to observe my absolute delight in your ability, having taken decisive action in your inimitable manner, to apparently wed your specific tribulations of recent times with such apparent fortuity to a difficulty of similarly recent vintage that has caused such concern to my current associate. I applaud you, sir." Stepping forward to shake Taggett's hand, he looks at Otto and says something in Chinese. Otto says something back and Chen steps forward and says to the recruiter, "And you, sir. My colleague informs me that you have yet to confide in us the bagatelle of what your name might be. Do allow me to assure you that we have no need for that detail; however, you will soon provide answers to many question of more practical and relevant import, make no mistake. Before we begin, though, I must insist that you relinquish that blade with which you may be tempted against your better judgment to attempt a futile defense of your miserable life." He holds out his hand as the gorilla steps up on the other side of Otto. The recruiter takes another swallow of nothing and uses the first finger and thumb of his left hand to carefully, delicately, slide the knife out of its holster and place the handle in Jie's upturned palm. Otto puts his gun away and grabs the recruiter under one arm as the gorilla comes around the table and grabs the old guy's other side. The two of them drag him out through the doors and Taggett thinks he hears a yell of desperation just before some car doors slam shut and the Caddy starts up. The sound of the engine slowly fades into the silence of the room with Jie and Taggett and what Taggett suddenly realizes are three corpses with broken necks in it.

The two men look at each other for a long moment. Eventually, Jie says, "I ascertain no sign of Chen."

"Yeah," says Taggett. "He went down the hole." As Jie just keeps staring at him he goes on to say, "I think he's trying to prove something."

Jie says, "Indeed," and the sound of a gunshot comes out of the hole.

CHAPTER FIFTEEN

Taggett yells his partner's name and covers the space between the front door and the hatch in the floor in two strides. He hollers Chen's name again down into the hole. Nothing comes back. He stares down into the darkness and yells again and doesn't even get an echo. He's on his belly, forty-five in his hand, thrusting his face down into the silent darkness.

Behind him he can hear Jie's mellow voice saying something in Chinese into the bar phone. Then there's the click of the earpiece going back onto its hook, and then he hears his name from back there. "Mr. Taggett," Jie says again. "If you'll pardon my saying so, the course of action which you currently appear to be pursuing seems utterly to lack utility. This passage remains inaccessible to those of us who, unlike our youthful associate, have allowed our bodies to thicken with the passage of time." He's crouched down next to Taggett, murmuring suavely, as the tough detective keeps peering down into the blackness. "Further," Jie says, "the silence with which our friend has responded to your entreaties could as easily signify a deliberate stratagem as it could a physical incapacity."

Taggett yells down into the hole again. Again nothing comes back, and the detective's body seems to sag toward the floor. With an effort he pushes himself over onto his back and says, "I told him he wasn't ready."

From his crouch Jie looks down sternly. "Respectfully, I cannot imagine that the opportunity for self-recrimination has as yet arrived," says the older man as Taggett just stares at him. "Indeed, we more effectively pursue our objective of ascertaining and ensuring the safety of our friend by effecting a course of direct action rather than allowing ourselves to be distracted by our emotions, notwithstanding their validity. To that end, I—" The phone on the bar rings to interrupt him. He gracefully rises to his feet, picks up the earpiece, and listens for a minute. Then he says something in Chinese, hangs up, and steps over to Taggett, reaching down a hand. He's smiling as he tells the tough guy, "The brief telephonic sojourn that you have just witnessed has confirmed the soundness of the advice that I was beginning, in my circuitous way, to offer. Your allies in this cause are not without resources, and one of those resources, consisting of a large number of surprisingly observant shadow-dwellers, has located the terminal point of the underground passage that begins under our feet."

Taggett grips Jie's hand and pulls himself up, holstering the forty-five. "Let's get there," he says.

"Indeed," says Jie, and the two of them walk out through the swinging doors, leaving the empty bar to the dead thugs already starting to stink the place up. The two men step into the Silver Phantom and Jie starts up and starts driving. By this time the dusk is closing in on Shanghai. The city buildings are turning on their lights, making that evening glow that welcomes commuters the commuters on their home and the tourists on their way to the entertainment. Jie and Taggett are driving the other way, into the dark.

The sky's turned from purple to black by the time the Silver Phantom gets them to a little dirt road that trails off from the highway into the flatland. They're both leaning forward a little, peering ahead into the yellow ovals of road that the headlights reveal, until the road narrows even more, turning into a pair of ruts dug into the soft earth, and then what looks like some kind of two-storey farmhouse, almost like a barn, looms up into view and Jie stops the car. The headlights go out and the two of them sit there staring into the darkness.

After a while Taggett says, "Well, I guess there's no one guarding the place."

"Perhaps," says Jie. "Alternately, a sniper rifle could be trained as we speak on the source of the headlights a presumed security team must have seen as we approached, awaiting, perhaps, the glint of light from a car door opening to reveal the location of a target." Taggett pulls his hand back from the door handle and takes out his forty-five and slumps down a little in his seat, sighting down the barrel through the windshield up to where he saw a second story window in the headlights a minute ago. Glancing down at him, Jie fakes a smile and says, "You appear to be developing a stratagem."

Taggett glances up and shows Jie his teeth in sort of a grin. "Yeah," he says. "I'm thinking if you go out the door and someone takes a shot I'll see his muzzle flash and take him out. That should give you time to get around the back of the car and start taking your own shots." He pulls back the hammer with his thumb and says, "Ready?"

Jie doesn't quite start laughing, but Taggett can see his chest pull in a little as if he's stifling something. After a discreet motion of his Adam's apple, the older man says, "At the risk of overstepping the limits of propriety by way of an excess of candor, I must observe that your proposal greatly overestimates my agility." Taggett snorts out a chuckle. "However," Jie goes on, "we could, in my opinion, tempt the fire of this presumed sniper through a less hazardous course of action." He puts his hand on the door handle and nods at Taggett. "At my signal, throw your door open, violently, while remaining inside the car yourself." He throws a sharp look at the tough guy and says, "Understand?"

Taggett nods and grips the handle with one hand and the forty-five with the other and watches Jie's face. The older man nods and they both pull the handles and push the doors and nothing happens.

So they sit there so still they're not even breathing for another minute or so. Nothing keeps happening. Finally Taggett just mutters, "Ah, hell," and rolls out of his side belly down on the dirt sighting on the house from under the car door. After a moment Jie does the same. The night stays silent. As if they'd planned it, they roll away at the same time from the sides of the car and start crawling on elbows and knees to where the house makes a darker outline against the sky. Taggett's trying not to hold his breath as he drags himself through the sucking soil and waits for the bullet with his name on it to find him.

After too long they find the front of the house. Taggett presses his palm against the splintery wood and follows the front wall to a doorknob. He hears Jie breathing about three feet away, the width of a door, and makes a little kissy sound. Jie responds with two little kissy sounds and Taggett yanks on the doorknob, flinging himself around the door as Jie dives through and rolls and comes up with a Tommy gun swinging around the big room as he pivots. Taggett does the same and fetches himself up against a wall. By this time the moon's up and throwing a tease of light through a window a little to the left of Taggett's head. He can see Jie creeping into a shadowed corner and a door in the opposite wall and a spiral staircase going up and down through holes almost centered in the floor and ceiling. As he's looking around, the door opens and closes and he cocks the forty-five and points it, but it's just Jie slipping through. Taggett shrugs and approaches the staircase twisting down into more darkness.

He grabs a tubular steel rail with one hand and tests the steps with his foot as he's pointing the forty-five down along the staircase's curve. The step holds. Carefully, he takes the next and then the next, pale moonlight fading out behind him as yellow lamp light seems to be expanding in front of him as he gets closer to the bottom. Finally he can hear the sound of his shoes on solid ground. Glancing around, he can see that he's in some kind of hallway with a door at the end leaking out a rectangle of yellow light around its edges. He puts out his hand to find a cool surface that feels like some kind of ceramic and use that to guide him along toward the end of the corridor.

He gets to the door and freezes and listens. There's a floor creaking above him, probably Jie poking around up there. Taggett carefully places his hand on the doorknob and curls his fingers around it and slowly bends his wrist. The knob turns. Taggett yanks the door open.

He dives and rolls into some kind of office, his forty-five leveled at the kind of desk a receptionist would be sitting behind in a normal world. There's no one there, but Taggett hears clattering and rustling from behind the door to his right, opposite the door he just busted in through. He sidesteps to it and checks the hinge to see that it opens in, so he steps in front of the door and turns the knob and slams it open.

There's an executive office in front of him, with a big desk taking up the space in front of the opposite wall, a leather sofa over to his left, and a plush blue rug over the wooden floor. At the desk a Chinese guy in a sharkskin suit lounges with his feet up, unlit smoke dangling from his lips, big six-shooter pointing right at Taggett. The detective gets just that fraction of a flash to see all this before the guy at the desk has tightened his grip on the trigger and blasted a hole in the door behind him. He feels a sting across the outside of his thigh and goes down shooting and gets the Chinese guy in the shoulder. The guy howls and drops the gun as a door opens behind him and Chen comes through and grabs the guy in a full nelson and shakes until Taggett hears a click and the guy goes limp.

Chen gets across the room about the same time that Jie comes charging through the hole where the door used to be. Chen gets to Taggett first and says, "Stay down, boss, you're bleeding." Jie takes his pocket square out and fashions a tourniquet and ties it around the top of Taggett's thigh as the tough detective watches Chen. The younger detective's got a red line tracing back along his right temple and his left eye has swelled shut. "Jesus," says Chen. "We've got to get you to a hospital."

"Forget it," says Taggett and leans on the other men to pull himself up. The room goes out of focus for a second as his leg seems to swell up with pain. "I'm no worse off than you are," he says.

Chen glances back at the guy he just killed and says, "Maybe. Anyway, we need to get you out of here before you bleed all over this pretty rug. Jie, did you see anyone?"

Jie shakes his head, Tommy gun in one hand as he helps hold Taggett up. The three of them hassle through the outer office and down the hall and up the spiral staircase and through the front door into the darkness when Jie says, "Wait!" The three of them stop and a deep moan forces its way through Taggett's lips. "I had no opportunity to ascertain the vacancy of the edifice's upper area," says Jie, "and thus cannot in full confidence assume the absence of snipers to track us as we attempt our return to our conveyance." Taggett groans again, more in irritation than in pain.

"I'm with him," says Chen. "Either there's someone up there or there isn't. Anyway, you got in somehow." He takes a tighter hold of Taggett's shoulder and says, "If it makes you feel better, why don't you walk backwards behind us. You can keep a bead on the upstairs with that chopper until we get to the car. You brought a car, right?"

Jie chuckles, "Indeed." He turns himself around and tilts up the Tommy gun so that the three of them can drag back through the soft sucking of the ground to the Silver Phantom. By the time they get there Taggett's moaning a little with every step and breathing hard, eyes shiny and skin clammy. They lay him down in the back and Chen takes the shotgun seat as Jie gets the car started up and into reverse. After a minute they get themselves back onto the highway.

As the Silver Phantom makes the bump from dirt road to asphalt Taggett lets out a groan and says, "All right, you talked me into it," and passes out.

CHAPTER SIXTEEN

The black velvet of unconsciousness wrapped around Taggett doesn't keep him from letting out a weak moan every time the Phantom hits a bump in the road, and it's a bumpy road. As he fades in and out he can see Chen turned around in the front seat to keep a worried eye on him, Jie hunched over the wheel and peering deep into the wall of night they're driving toward.

And then he's flat on his back, lying on what feels like a couple of hay bales in what smells like a cow barn. He turns his head and pukes onto the dirt floor. His leg has turned into a throb of agony, like a bag filling up with hot blood every time his heart thumps. He turns his head the other way, and there's Jie and Chen and some little chinless guy wearing a filth-caked version of a chef's outfit, the coat that used to be white and the big baggy pants. Chen's looking puzzled while the other two are hollering at each other in Chinese. Jie reaches into his jacket and pulls out a big wad of cash and hands it to the little guy, who tucks it away somewhere and keeps on hollering.

"What the hell?" says Chen, almost squawking from his worry. "Is he gonna get to work or not? Get the X-ray, get that bullet out of him!"

"No X-ray!" yells the little guy. "Animal doctor only! Must cut!" Taggett feels the sweat squeeze itself out through his pores as he lies there and listens to this. The hay's poking into his back through his shirt. He can feel his body squirming, his jaw clenched as he tries to make himself quit and keeps failing. The little animal doctor takes a step toward him. Chen lunges after him but Jie grabs the younger man and somehow holds him back, murmuring something in his ear as the animal doctor gets closer and glances past Taggett.

Taggett whips his head around to see a door open and let in a blast of clear light and then close again. He feels a mutter of "How the hell long" pushed through his pressed lips and swallows the rest as he watches the luscious redhead dressed up as a nurse and swaying toward him out of the murk that's crowding in around the edges of his field of vision. He blinks, but she's still there, raising a finger to her lips to softly shush him as he feels something bite him in the back of the neck, and then his veins fill up with ice, and then the dark swallows him up again.

Someone's screaming and crying at the top of an endless stairway that Taggett's trying to climb, but his leg keeps buckling, so he has to crawl. The shrieking just gets louder. He knows that someone up there is getting carved up alive. He's clutching his forty-five as he keeps forcing his body up those stairs, slipping on blood, bruising himself on the hard sharp corners of steps that get steeper as he pulls himself toward the animal howls of terror and misery. "Didn't hear it," he's growling to himself. "Didn't hear the sound, won't get killed." But still he's got no traction. The door at the top of the stairs is just getting smaller and further away. Hard to believe that whoever's screaming behind that door is still alive. "Didn't die," he keeps mumbling. He keeps crawling, his body working without him. "Didn't hear the sound, not my time," even as he starts to recognize the voice of the screaming victim up there. It's his own, of course.

And then he's in that fluffy cloud of a bed in his room in Wing's weird Bavarian palace. Big sconces of candle-shaped bulbs have the room lit up in yellow circles with dark borders as Taggett lies there for a moment blinking and breathing hard and then pulls himself up to sit against the big wooden headboard so that he can see the shape of his body under the furry blanket. It's too thick for him to tell, though, so he raises a hand and brings it down on where his right thigh should be, just to make sure. Through the thickness of the blanket he feels the slap of his hand on his thigh's hard muscle just as he feels the thrill of pain that happens when you smack a fresh bullet wound. The pain and relief force a complicated yelp out of the tough detective.

In a chair next to the bed Chen twitches awake and says, "Huh?" The crust of black bristles around the younger man's lips tells Taggett that he's been in that chair for at least a couple of days. The bandage on his head tells Taggett that he's been through a scrape of his own. Chen's eyes take a moment to focus before he can see Taggett sitting up, and then a grin spreads itself over his face. "Hey," he says, and swallows the lump in his throat. "You feeling nice and rested?"

Taggett blinks at his partner and works his jaw for a long moment, trying to lick some moisture into his cracked lips. Finally he manages to rasp out a "What the hell happened?" Chen pours a glass of water from a pitcher on a bedside table and hands it to Taggett, who manages to get some of it into his mouth as he's spilling the rest down his chest. He swallows and repeats the question in a voice that comes a little bit closer to one he'd recognize from himself.

"You got shot," Chen says. "Jie's doc says you took one high in the thigh without getting your bone smashed to pieces or your vein ripped apart." He takes the glass from Taggett, pours again, passes it back. "The guy says that doesn't happen to anyone, and he's stitched up more than a few of these gangsters. You're lucky, is what this guy says."

That makes Taggett chuckle and wince. "I'd be luckier without a bullet in me," he says.

"Jie's guy took care of that," Chen says and hands Taggett a little box that rattles when the tough detective shakes it. Taggett glances from the box back to Chen and the younger man laughs. "There's your souvenir from Shanghai, boss," he says as Taggett reaches to drop the thing on the table on the bed's other side. The tough detective lets out a little moan as he twists but waves Chen back into the chair.

"I'm okay," says the tough detective. "But what the hell happened to you?"

Chen raises a hand to the bandage on his forehead and flinches a little as his fingers brush the bandage. "Well," he says, "I went down into that tunnel without even thinking. Once I got to the bottom, there was plenty of room to stand up, but it was dark, so I just put out my hands and started walking forward." He lights up a smoke and hands it to Johnny and lights up one for himself. "Some creep, must have been that scrawny bartender you were talking about, had some equipment down there with him, a flashlight and some kind of artillery he wanted to ventilate my skull with. Good thing for me he needed the light. I heard him click it on before it quite caught me, so I ducked out of the way of his pellet and threw my knife back down the beam of light." He chuckles for a moment and then catches himself and shudders. "That little gurgle of his that told me I got him in the throat—I have to say I forgot how good it can feel to kill the right creep."

"You ducked almost out of the way," says Taggett. "You could have been killed."

Chen takes a long drag and says, "Yeah." He sits back and the chair and looks Taggett right in the eyes. "I guess after a while it doesn't matter."

"I guess you're right," says Taggett. The two of them sit they're in silence for a moment and then he says, "Okay, so first thing in the morning we head back to that country house. I want to see what it looks like in the daylight. Then we—"

Chen says, "Nix. The sawbones says you're damaged goods for a while, boss. He says to Jie you need to be on your back for at least a week. Anyway, that house got burned down the night after our little visit." He leans forward to put his hand on Taggett's shoulder for a moment and says, "You rest up. We'll shake some trees around here and see what falls out. I think Otto's still working on that recruiter. Don't worry, you'll be in on it when we figure this thing out."

Taggett scowls but says, "Yeah, okay." He slides back down into the bed. "I guess all this conversation is tiring me out anyway." A big yawn surprises him and opens up his whole face for a moment.

Chen gets up and says with a wink, "Hope you're not too tired yet." As he hikes across the huge room to the door he throws another wink and says, "You might need some of that energy." He tugs open the door and Helga slips in past him wearing not much more than a sheer nightie and a grin.

Taggett takes her in with his eyes and says, "Don't wait up" as Chen steps out and shuts the door behind him.

So the next few days go by like that, Helga bringing the patient his breakfast and sticking around to make sure he gets his snack. After a few days on that plan, though, the tough detective has to get himself out of bed, so Helga shows up the next morning with a cane for him. And that starts another few days of this big white guy limping around the castle and crashing into walls and generally getting in the way. The other guys in the castle start sneering at him even more openly as he stumbles down the big stone staircase for breakfast in the courtyard. Sometimes he sneers back as he's struggling back up to his room.

This goes on until the morning a week and a half or so later when he and Chen and Jie are just finishing up their plates of steak and eggs as Otto steps up to the table and clicks his heels and clears his throat. They all look up at him, friendly smirks curving their lips as he pulls a little white envelope from his sleeve and then places it on the table so that they can all read the pencil scrawl on its front: GIVE TOO JOHNY TAGIT. "This has been found," he says, "by a worker in one of our establishments."

Chen chuckles and says, "That's sweet, Johnny. The downtown whores are thinking of you." He takes another sip of his coffee and snickers some more, and even Jie's got his hand in front of his mouth to hide his grin.

Otto's face hardly moves at all as he says, "Perhaps not. The envelope has been found in the hand of a corpse." That shuts everyone up. The men at the table glance around the courtyard, but all the thugs who are still there are still dedicating themselves to their breakfasts. "It seemed an important message to deliver," Otto says.

Taggett looks a little more closely at the dingy envelope. "Yeah," he says. "I'd say this gets my attention." He picks it up and presses it all over with his fingertips. "Doesn't feel like anything but paper, so we've got that going for us," he says. "Do we know who got killed to deliver this?"

"No one of importance," Otto says.

As Taggett's grabbing the steak knife off his plate Jie crooks his finger at Otto, who bends at the waist to get his ear next to the older man's mouth. "At a later time," Jie murmurs, "you and I shall discuss the propriety of your manner and timing of delivery as well as your ability to gather information. Perhaps you could pass the time between this moment and that conversation by devoting yourself to a more pertinent task." Otto goes a little pale and nods and straightens up and gets out of there.

While all this is going on Taggett's using the steak knife to rip the envelope open. He dumps the folded paper inside it onto the table and spends a moment or two looking at it before he touches it. "Looks dry," he says. "I guess it won't poison me." He picks up the flimsy, tissue-thin note and reads:

Deer Mister Johny Tagit

Yu have bin lookin fur that gang from that bar down town. I no were that gang is. Bring 500 dolars to that bar and ile tell yu. Cum aloan at midnite on wensday.

Sined, a frend.

Taggett looks back up at Chen and Jie. "What do you think?" he says.

Chen cracks his knuckles and says, "Today's Wednesday." Jie nods.

Taggett grabs his cane and stands up and says, "Well, I guess we've got a lead."

CHAPTER SEVENTEEN

The three of them spend the rest of the day making plans. Taggett cleans his forty-five thoroughly and practices a few moves with his cane, shadowboxing with Chen. Jie disappears for a couple of hours and comes back with five hundred American dollars in small bills creased with black lines of grime and limp with sweat. As he's packing them into a woven wicker case he turns to Taggett and smirks a little. "As you have no doubt ascertained," he says, "our host is not without access to significant amounts of capital, much of which he understandably refuses to employ for the storage of its physical manifestation what we might consider aboveground institutions."

"You mean he has to keep the cash somewhere and he doesn't want a banker's eyes on it?" says Taggett as he keeps clicking bullets into the magazine.

Jie chuckles like someone's favorite uncle. "Quite perspicaciously interpreted," he tells the tough guy. He gets the money stuffed in the case and the lid shut over it with a brass clasp to keep it from popping back open.

Taggett slides the magazine into the forty-five and says, "So you think this mess has something to do with where you keep your money?"

"Perhaps," says Jie. "The success of the operations with which I have associated myself has necessitated a degree of vigilance that mortals such as myself cannot hope to maintain." He sighs and pinches the bridge of his nose for a moment. "Your arrival here may have been providential or fortuitous," he says. "However, I cannot deny the possibility of a relation between your arrival and the difficulties faced by this organization, as evidenced perhaps by the message delivered to you by Otto, which reflects the common knowledge that you and we have become associated."

Taggett shrugs and holsters his forty-five and says, "Well, maybe we'll find out more about that tonight. We should all take a nap until it's time to go." He grabs his cane and pushes himself up the wide stone steps and into that dream of a bed.

And then Helga's kissing him awake and he's limping back down the stairs to the courtyard where Chen and Jie are waiting for him. The three of them walk past the workers mopping up the dinner mess to the little door and down the hall and out to the driveway where Otto's waiting behind the wheel of the Silver Phantom. No one says a thing as he drives and soon enough they're through the glitter of the hotels and back down into the darkness of the working district by the wharfs. He parks the car across and a little up the street from YANKEE SECRET NUMBER ONE FOOD BAR and kills the lights. Taggett takes a glance at his watch. Eleven-thirty.

Chen murmurs from next to him, "You know this is a trap, right?" The younger man cracks his knuckles.

Taggett just snickers. "I've told you before," he says, "the best way to find out who's trying to trap you is to walk into the trap. I think we're ready for some answers, don't you?" The way his scar is itching makes his eye twitch in what must look like a wink.

"Yeah," says Chen. He twists himself around to kneel on the seat so he can keep an eye on the dark through the Phantom's back window. Taggett's watching the bar. Jie in the front passenger seat is observing the occasional bum stumbling along the sidewalk next to the Phantom. Otto seems to be looking straight out through the windshield. And there they sit for half an hour and then another fifteen minutes while no one enters or leaves the place or moves on the car they're sitting in. Chen says, "Stood up again. I'm starting to feel unpopular."

Taggett says, "Well, let's go in and see what's waiting." He opens his door and steps out into the street. Jie puts a hand on Otto's shoulder to keep him in the car as Chen gets out, and then the older man's on the sidewalk with his Tommy gun in full view. Otto keeps staring forward. Taggett's already crossing the street as the other two double-time it to catch up with him.

Like the rest of the neighborhood, the bar's dark and quiet. Chen says, "You wouldn't think a few bodies would throw off the business like this. Guess they figured we'd be back." Taggett shushes him and leans a little forward on his cane to take a good look at the swinging door.

"Not locked," he says and takes a step to the side and pushes one of the sides of the door open with his cane. The three of them stand there for a moment listening to the surf noise of the faraway traffic while nothing seems to happen in the bar. At a glance from Taggett, Chen drops to the ground and rolls into the bar. Jie pulls the lever on his Tommy gun and follows, and then Taggett steps in, letting the door fall shut behind him.

The bar smells a little like a boxer's room after a losing fight. Hints of blood and spit linger like a poisonous mist in the still air in there. The tables and chairs are scattered around in pieces except for one shadowed in the back just beyond the reach of the streetlight's halo. Jie's got his Tommy gun trained on it as Taggett's eyes adjust and he sees the guy sitting there. None of them can make out the guy's face, but they can all see the way the light bounces greasily off the gun on the table in front of him. No one says anything for a lingering minute.

Then Taggett says "What the hell" and strides to the table and slides the gun away from the guy's hand. The tough detective turns back to his partners and says, "This guy's dead."

"What the hell," says Chen as Jie glides to join Taggett at the corpse's table. The older man pulls out a flashlight and flicks it on to reveal a pudgy Chinese guy with a face the color of fresh snow, eyes bugging out. The hands on the table in front of the corpse look like puffy gloves with a couple of missing fingers. Between them there's a pretty good sketch of Taggett on a tattered square of paper. Chen snorts and says, "I guess the trap rusted shut."

Taggett glances back at his partner and then gets back to going through the dead guy's pockets and pulls out a needle and a bent spoon with its bowl burned black and a little stack of cards with Chinese writing on them. He drops the junkie's works on the table and hands the cards to Jie. "This mean anything to you?" he says.

Jie hands the flashlight to Taggett and squints down as the detective points it at the ragged little cards. The edges of them flutter a little in Jie's breath. "These miniscule placards appear to bear an address, or more accurately they describe the location of a particular edifice," he says. "However, it appears to be an address native to a section of this fair metropolis with which I am, regrettably, unfamiliar."

Taggett grins in the shadow behind the torch he's holding and says, "That's good news. If you don't know this place it's because someone's kept it from you." He puts the light back down onto the corpse's puffed-out face. "This guy must be some kind of junkie block captain carrying around his boss's address in case he needs to sign up soldiers, looking to get himself ahead by rubbing me out. Maybe someone's trying to muscle in on your opium trade, Jie."

"So I guess we've got another visit to make," says Chen, cracking his knuckles. He turns back toward the door as Jie pockets the cards and Taggett gives the corpse another once-over with the flashlight. After a second or two the detective shrugs and cuts the light and the three of them step back out of the thick air of the bar into the street with its cool breeze smelling a little of rotten fish from where they lie dead in piles on the docks. Taggett's got his neck on a swivel as they cross toward the Silver Phantom but no one's around at this time of the night.

"Cops must be asleep," he mutters, "or we're up against an operation that can't pay 'em off to arrest us for that dead guy in there."

As they approach the Phantom, Jie says, "Alternately, the circumstances in which we have recently found ourselves could serve as a preliminary component of a more sophisticated stratagem to lure us to unfamiliar territory and employ the necessary disadvantage that this unfamiliarity would create to attack us more successfully." By the time he's done with all that they're opening the doors and slipping into their seats.

Taggett just shrugs and says, "You know how I feel about traps."

Jie answers the shrug with one of his own and hands the card to Otto and says something in Chinese. Otto looks at the card and then back up at Jie and doesn't say anything at all, just holding the older man's gaze. Jie's face hardens and he says something else in Chinese, finishing his point with a slap to the driver's face that knocks the monocle out of his eye. It dangles on its chain as Otto starts the engine and pulls into the deserted street. As he drives he screws the monocle back into place, only the paleness of his face showing any sign of emotion.

He makes a turn so that they seem to be driving along a rough parallel to the waterline along a paved road that narrows to a track after a while and starts bending and curving to swerve around the dips in the swampy ground. Little shabby buildings loom up in stretches of shadow and fly past as Taggett watches. He glances at Chen and lights up a couple of smokes and hands one to his partner and waits for whatever's about to happen.

Finally the Phantom slows and pulls to a stop alongside a dark building sagging with neglect. Otto pulls the brake and says, "We have arrived." Without a word Jie and Chen and Taggett get out, leaving the doors open. Taggett takes a breath and coughs, gagging a little from the smell of decay that's hanging around this surprisingly large shed in the middle of nowhere. Jie leans back into the car to give Otto another hard look and then the three of them pull their feet through the stretch of muck between the Phantom and the solid-looking wooden door centered in a wall of peeling planks. Taggett plays light from the torch over the door. A rectangle of darker slightly darker paint shows where a sign used to be. The three of them stand there in the mud and stench and look at it.

Chen breaks the silence to say, "So do we knock or ring the bell?"

"We go in," says Taggett and steps forward to grab the door's knob. It turns and Taggett lets out a soft low grunt of surprise and then pulls the door open. The smell gets worse, flowing at them and over them like a putrid river through the open door. They go in anyway.

The cheap wood floor creaks under them as they step through the door into a big room dimly lit by little candles flickering along the baseboards of the filthy walls. In that creepy flicker Taggett can see rows of bunk beds with what look like wadded-up loads of laundry in them. And then he notices the buzz of the stuttering, watery snores coming from the wrecked bodies in there. Taggett's scar is burning across his face as the three of them stand there and stare at the scene the way a wino might look for a message in his own puddle of puke, weirdly hypnotized by their own revulsion.

Then a figure in a lower bunk a little to their left shifts and turns a face toward them, a face with a ragged red hole where its nose used to be and blind white eyes that shoot daggers into Taggett's. It noiselessly moves its lips for a moment until a rusty voice pushes through, mumbling something in Chinese, slowly getting louder and shriller until it collapses into a spasm of wet coughing and then a slow rattle and then nothing but a pile of meat. The rest of the sleepers keep snoring.

Taggett can feel himself shaking as he whispers to Jie, "What the hell was that?"

Jie's shaking too. "I, I have difficulty translating precisely," he says. "I believe that most of that poor specimen's mouth and tongue must have rotted away." He blinks a few times and swallows and goes on, "He seems to have been repeating something about the answer that you seek, that it is near, that it—" He interrupts himself. "My god," he whispers. He turns to Taggett and Chen and says, "I know the cause of your erstwhile assassin's demise and the reason for those placards he carried. This is a leprosy hospital."

"God," Chen gasps and turns for the door that must have swung shut behind them. He grapples with the knob for a moment that lingers until he manages to shove the door open so that the three of them can push out into the night. As they're stumbling out Taggett's hand brushes something tacked to the door jamb and grabs it reflexively. The three of them stand there gulping air for a moment, trying not to throw up. The door slams shut again behind them.

After another stretching moment Taggett pulls out his flashlight to see what he's grabbed off the wall of the leper hospital. Chen says, "God" again as the three of them gape at a small and dainty pair of black velvet gloves.

CHAPTER EIGHTEEN

The ride back to the castle takes a while, and the lying awake in his bed staring up at the ceiling and wondering what the hell those gloves are supposed to mean takes a while longer and the nightmares about gnarls of flesh that scream like little girls take forever, so Taggett doesn't wake up the next morning until it's too late for breakfast. He pries himself up out of that fluffy bed with his cane and creaks downstairs into the courtyard where most of the tables are empty except for two or three little groups of thugs playing mahjong or something. As Taggett leans on his cane looking around Chen comes in through the other door blinking and sucking his lips. Taggett lights a couple of smokes and hands one to his partner and says, "You okay?"

Chen takes a drag and coughs. "I don't know," he says. "I had to take like three showers last night just to get the stink of that place off me."

"Yeah," says Taggett. "We're definitely getting pulled into something weird here." He looks around the big empty room. "I'm still trying to figure out why we'd find Mrs. Foulsworth's gloves in a leper hospital. Hard to imagine her taking them off, especially in a place like that." He takes a drag. "So I figure someone left them there for us to find, but how could anyone know we'd be there? And what was that freak yelling about?"

Chen claps him on the shoulder and says, "Let's just forget about that part. That old weirdo was dying, probably thought he was giving out his last words to his girlfriend or his god or some crazy ghost." The younger man chuckles. "We've got bigger fish to fry anyway," he says. "And speaking of, I'm starving. You think it's about lunchtime?"

"I don't think lunch is part of the service here," Taggett says.

"You are correct," says Otto, who's somehow suddenly standing about half a foot away from the tough detective as if he'd just popped up out of the floor. As Taggett stifles a flinch Otto goes on, "Our employer has expectations for his workers. Daytime is for working or for sleeping, not for lunch."

Chen laughs. "So what are you doing hanging around here?" he says. "You're not just waiting for dinner, are you?"

Otto looks flatly back and says, "No, I work. I have been awaiting the two of you. Now I drive you." He fiddles with his white gloves while the muscles in his face twitch the tiniest bit. "I am," he tells them, "the driver."

The three of them stand there in awkward silence that the clicking of tiles doesn't do much to break. Finally Taggett says, "Okay. So where are you driving us to?"

"I have not been informed," says Otto. "However, I may suggest a destination. You spoke of a desire for lunch."

Chen says, "You know it. These crazy hours are gonna make me into a shadow of myself if I miss too many more meals. I'll turn into one of those dancing skeletons." He chuckles and pretends to weave around on rubber legs for a minute until Taggett tells him to snap out of it.

Otto stands there and stares the way a substitute teacher waits for a class to settle down and finally says, "Then I will drive you. I know of a place in town that will serve you the good Western food you need." So they follow him through the door and down the hall and through the door and into the Silver Phantom and a few minutes later they're passing the Prestige Hotel and making a couple of turns and parking in front of a quaint brick building with a sign on it that says DELICATESSEN.

Chen's doing some more laughing. "I can't believe you're taking us to a deli in Shanghai," he says. "What's next, a pizzeria?" As Otto opens the door for Taggett on the passenger side, Chen steps out from the back and just stands there in the street and stares. The building they're in front of could come from the village in the shadow of the castle they just left, white beams framing the brick and an actual German flag hanging over the door. "I thought this Kaiser act was just some kind your boss is making you play along with," he says. "But a whole restaurant?"

Otto tightens his lips and says, "Apparently my employer has tastes shared by others." Once they get to the sidewalk in front of the white wooden door to the joint he takes his monocle out and polishes it and pushes it back into his eye socket. "I bring my employer here twice a month or so," he says. Then he steps forward and opens the door to usher them in.

A cloud of solid fragrance grabs them as soon as they enter and floats them over to a square table covered with a red-and-white striped cloth. A Chinese woman about the size and shape of a fire hydrant stomps over and says something in German. Otto says something German right back, going on for a while and pointing at Taggett and Chen. She looks at him and looks at them and stomps away and comes back a moment later with three thick steins full of dark brown beer. "Now we're talking," says Chen and takes himself a big swig.

Taggett says, "This place got a can?" When Otto just stares at him he says. "I gotta take a whiz."

"Oh," says Otto. "Yes. Uh, follow that hallway and use the first door on your left." He's pointing back at a single swinging door to the side of the glass counter showing off stretches of sausage and bowls of glistening sauerkraut. "Go through there," Otto's saying.

So Taggett pushes through the door into a dim hallway with a couple of guys just standing there in it wearing black suits with white shirts and skinny black ties and smoking. Taggett says, "Anyone in there?"

The tall one with a nose that looks like someone shoved an apple into his face when he was a kid and left it there to get all brown and gnarled says, "No, we're just waiting for an order. Go on in."

Taggett squints and lights up a smoke of his own and goes on in. As he lets the door shut behind him he finds himself in a surprisingly modern bathroom, big enough for two stalls and a urinal along with a sink. Someone even laid out for white tile to cover the walls. "Guess the upper class around here likes to shit in style," Taggett mutters to himself as he steps to the urinal and pulls himself out so he can do his business. He hears the door open and glances over to see the little fat one of the guys from the hall stepping in and turning the faucet on the sink to start washing his puffy little hands. The fat guy looks over and Taggett drops his gaze back down to the target practice he's doing in the urinal when something drops down over his head, some kind of plastic bag with hands around its neck at the bottom, around his neck, trying to choke him as the bag suffocates him, getting tighter around his nose and around the cherry of the cigarette in his mouth which melts the plastic which sticks to his face burning and melting into his skin as he smashes his heel back into the foot of the guy behind him and wheels around with his elbow and hits the creep's ribcage hard enough to crack something. He uses his elbow to shove the guy around against the wall next to the pisser and whirls and puts his fist into that ugly tumor of a nose and feels it squish and does it again and then again until the tall guy stops squirming. Taggett glances over to the sink. It's still running but the little fat guy's not there. "You should've had a third guy to do lookout so you two could gang up on me," Taggett tells the tall guy and then shoves him into the stall, tying his ankles to his wrists with the tie from his ill-fitting suit and propping him on the toilet so no one'll find him for a minute or two. Then he reaches down and maneuvers himself back into his pants and flushes the urinal. That must have been the fat guy's cue as the door swings back open and he saunters in.

"I told you that American wouldn't be so tough," he's saying as Taggett just lunges forward and clocks him across the forehead with his forty-five. The tough detective grunts as he catches the fat guy's weight and stores him in the other stall tied up just like his partner. Pushing the door closed and locking it with a quarter, he steps over to the running faucet and rinses the blood off his knuckles and combs wet fingers through his hair as he catches his breath. A smear of pain at the top of his thigh reminds him that he's left his cane at the table. He grabs the sink for a moment until it fades a little and then turns off the water and pushes through the door.

As he's turning toward the deli a pale-skinned Asian fellow steps into the hallway wearing what looks like a white silk suit with a pearl-colored tie and a fedora to match. This fancy character stops a few steps in and seems to goggle for a moment at Taggett. "Apologies," he says in a clear tenor voice straight out of the radio. "I had expected to meet some, uh, associates. Have you seen them?"

Taggett shrugs and says, "I don't know, I haven't seen anyone around, Mister, uh…"

"Sing," says the guy. He grins, thin lips revealing little sharp teeth. "I am Mr. Sing."

Taggett nods to him."Johnny Taggett," he says and puts out a hand. In return Sing reaches out a hand in a light tan kid glove to shake. "Uh, good luck finding your friends," says Johnny.

Sing says, "Many thanks, Mr. Taggett. And perhaps I can suggest that you seek some care for the burns on your face." This close, Taggett notices that Sing has eyes almost the color of a lion's. "Left to linger," Sing says softly, "such injuries can prove quite unpleasant, even deadly." The leather-covered grip on Taggett's hand tightens and Sing says, "Perhaps we understand one another, Mr. Taggett."

Taggett tightens his own grip and says into those weird orange eyes, "I think we do, Mr. Sing. Nice to have met you." He loosens that grip, but Sing doesn't quite let go for a beat, and then they're not shaking hands any more. Sing goes into the bathroom and Taggett limps down the hall in a hustle.

When he gets back to the table Chen and Otto are tucking into a huge plate of sausages and kraut. Chen's laughing about something and Otto's watching him do it as Taggett stands next to the table and grabs his cane and says, "We need to get out of here."

Still laughing, Chen says, "What the hell, boss, we just got here. Listen, Otto was just telling me about this guy that ate so much Kochwurst that he—" The younger man stops himself. "Damn, Taggett, what the hell happened to your face?"

"I'll tell you about it later," says Taggett, "after you finish your story. In the car." He glances around the room, sees that the door to the hallway hasn't burst open just yet, so he turns back to his partner and says, "In a minute or two all hell's gonna break loose and I don't want to be here when it does." As the other two men get up and Otto peels off some bills and drops them on the table, Taggett says, "I just met a guy."

CHAPTER NINETEEN

A few days later Taggett's standing in the mouth of an alley in the pissing rain of a big-city dusk and staring up at a second floor window. Otto went in there a few minutes ago. Taggett cups his hands around a match to light up a smoke and thinks about last night's conversation with Chen.

"You ever notice that guy's always around when some weird trouble's happening?" the tough detective said as he sawed off a hunk of Wing's steak and washed it down with a slug of Wing's beer.

Chen pushed his fork into a clump of spinach and lifted into his mouth and said, "Yeah, I see what you mean." He looked around the courtyard at all the other tough guys shoveling dinner into their faces and said, "So what are we gonna do about it? Do you wanna brace this Otto guy and see what spills out?"

"No," said Taggett. "I don't wanna queer our thing with Jie before we find out what the hell's been going on." He took a minute to chew and swallow another hunk of that buttery steak and said, "I've been thinking I need to see what this guy does when he's off duty." He leaned a little closer to Chen. "You think you can find a way to keep Jie busy for a few minutes?"

Chen snorted a laugh. "Child's play," he said. "I'll just ask him directions to somewhere and give him a chance to practice his vocabulary on me. He can't pass that up." Smirking, the younger man got up out of his chair and lit up a smoke and said, "Better be careful, though. That fancy talk'll rub off on me. You'll come back from wherever Otto takes you and you won't understand a thing I say. Give me a few minutes." He wandered off into the big room and a while later Taggett saw that strange German figure slip out the front door.

Shivering in the rain, Taggett mutters to himself, "A whole damn night and day of following this creep around and here I am none the wiser." He takes another drag off his smoke and coughs a little and glances around this crappy little Shanghai residential neighborhood Otto has led him to. There's a guy walking around in circles and yelling something, probably about the fish shining in slimy rows in that wood cart he's pushing. There's a squad of kids running around and shrieking. There's a smell of something getting fried in peanut oil and someone's singing what sounds like Al Jolson tunes in one of these buildings. This kind of thing goes on for hours as Taggett stands there and watches that second-story window reflect the darkening sky.

Finally Otto comes out without his field-marshal costume on. He's just wearing a shirt and trousers like all the other Chinese guys milling around as he stands on the sidewalk in front of his building and gives the whole scene a suspicious glare. Taggett shrinks back into the shadow of his alley and lets Otto start moving along and then follows as cagily as he can, considering he's about a foot taller than everyone. Otto leads him for what seems like a random series of rights and lefts as the night thickens around the dark buildings until he finally takes a turn into another alley several blocks away. Taggett hangs back for a moment and then steps around the corner to see an empty space between two brick buildings with a brick wall at its far end. None of the walls has a door in it and Otto's nowhere. Taggett curses and lights up another smoke and looks around. He's pretty nearly downtown. "Hell with it," he mutters to himself. "I'll just have to pick him up another day." He turns away from the alley and sees that he's just a few yards away from a streetcar station. "Perfect," he tells himself. "I'll take a streetcar to the Hotel Prestige, spend the night, see if I can find out where this weirdo's slipping away to." He pats his pockets, finds fare, and yawns hard as he drags his feet to the curb to wait for the last car of the night.

Soon enough it shows up and Taggett pulls himself aboard and says "Ni hao" to the driver. He clinks a couple of coins into a metal box and grips the poles that connect the car's floor to its ceiling until he can swing himself into a seat and let his eyes drift nearly shut for a second or two. The car rocks gently as it hums down its track in the middle of the street. The rain's getting serious, hitting the car's tin roof hard enough to start making a sound like machine-gun fire and jarring the tough detective out of a sleep he hadn't caught himself falling into. He looks around the car, notices the little puddle under him where his fedora and coat have dripped their rainwater onto the floor. As he stares, water from his puddle reaches out into the center aisle where it joins the puddles under the three or four other people nodding along to the bumps in the road. He squints a little to see a middle-aged woman, a couple of sleepy teenagers in school uniforms, a guy nodding over the briefcase he's holding in his lap.

As the car slows his scar seems to suddenly tear a line of fire across his face. A couple of guys get on, their brown fedoras tilted down over their eyes, thin rivulets trickling straight down from their brown dusters, coats just big enough to conceal pistols. Taggett straightens up in his seat and twists his neck to look behind him to see there's too much room between him and the end of the car for his comfort. He slides into the aisle, keeping his eyes on the sharp-featured guys who are walking up from the front of the car, and backs his way into a seat in the last row. The guys in the long coats take seats in the row in front of him, one directly, one on the other side of the aisle. The light in the car flickers as it passes through a breaker and makes a CRACK that makes everyone jump in their seats and then sink back into the buzz and sway. Taggett keeps his eyes peeled, his hand lingering up around his lapel within grabbing distance of his forty-five. The guys sit there staring straight ahead.

And then Taggett's got his forty-five in his grip and the hammer pulled back and his finger tightening on the trigger until he recognizes the driver cringing back and yelping, "Mister! Mister! Wake up! End of line, mister!" over and over until the tough detective eases up and uncocks and slips the forty-five back in its holster. He blinks groggy eyes and takes a look around the car for those guys in brown. They're gone. The car's empty. The driver's still standing they're in the aisle with his hands up shuddering and babbling as Taggett pushes himself out of the seat and shoulders past him into the night.

The cold gives him a slap in the face that drags fingernails down along his scar. Nothing's left of the rain but a bunch of puddles and a fog that shrinks the scene to the few feet around him as he sways a little, his body as heavy as a boxer's in the thirteenth round. The streetcar hits the world with a CLANG and slides itself into invisibility, leaving Taggett alone in the darkest part of the night. He could be on a sidewalk with a brick wall inches away. He could just as easily be standing in the middle of a street waiting to get mowed down by some drunk. He shivers a little, eyes wide, head on a swivel, reaching into his pocket for that last smoke in the pack, pulling it out and pulling it back to straight and sticking it in his mouth. He's got his hand on the book of matches in his other pocket when he sees a faint red dot somewhere in front of him. That freezes him. As he stands there, mist collecting around his hat and dripping onto the pavement, he can almost see the shape of a guy standing there smoking and watching him, cherry glowing at the end of his cigarette just enough to give him away. Taggett bites back a snicker and shoves the smoke back in his pocket and waits to see what happens next.

After a minute the cherry flickers out, but he can hear the guy's shoes hitting pavement back along the streetcar line, leading Taggett the way he came. He and the shadow he's following trace back through a district of closed-up shops lurking unlit along the sidewalk and after a few minutes he starts to recognize the silhouettes of the tenements near where he picked up Otto back around the sundown that seems like it happened a week ago. Another snicker almost gets out of him as he realizes that he'd gotten on the wrong streetcar and never would have made it to the Prestige anyway and then the sound of footsteps in front of him stops. He holds his breath, head swimming a little as he slips his hand into his coat, over his holster. The scrape of a match a little ahead on the wall he's next to, closer than he thought he was, reveals a glimpse of jawline and then the end of a cigarette and then sputters out into the street. The footsteps start again. Taggett waits a couple of lingering seconds and then starts following again.

Another minute and a couple of turns later they stop again. Taggett puts out his hands to find out whether he's still near any walls. He's not. He may as well be floating in midair, the fog is so thick. The tough detective blinks the water out of his face and keeps waiting, quivering just a little from the tension of trying to make a statue of himself. After a few too many seconds a breeze starts to ruffle through his clothes and over his skin like an icy-fingered pickpocket. The blackness behind the fog is starting to take on a little more yellow as the sun must be starting to come up somewhere. The fog's thinning. Taggett blinks and gets himself ready to find out who he's been trailing. His hand's on his forty-five. The air clears as the night fades into dawn.

He's standing alone in a narrow dead-end alley made of brick walls. No one's in front of him, and he knows that no one brushed past him to get back to the street. The detective grunts and raises a hand to scratch at the scar flaming on his face. Then he gets to work.

He starts with the wall to his left. He's got his pocket knife out, and he's tapping it on bricks in the wall, listening for a difference. He takes a few minutes to work his way down to the wall at the end of the alley, and then he slows down even further. He presses his ear to each brick at shoulder level and taps and presses with his fingertips. Then he goes back and examines each brick one row down. About a third of the way through, almost to the middle of the wall, he feels a brick just a little bit smoother then it should be. He stops. He taps the brick and then the brick above it and then taps that first brick again. He pushes on it, tries to slide it one way or another. It doesn't give. He steps back and takes a look at it, then steps to it again and shoves the side of his face into the wall. A faint clanking of chains and gears seeps through the wall into his ear. "This has to be it," he tells himself and leans back and opens his knife. He pokes around the edges of the brick until he feels something catch. His lips draw back into a grin that's almost a snarl as he pushes his knife a little harder.

And then the ground's not under him anymore. His heavy body drops and he lets go of the knife so that he can grab the little lip of surface between the wall and the pit he's falling down into. Feet dangling, he grips with his fingers and pulls himself inch by inch to the left. He has to turn two corners to get to where he can pull himself out. His body's shaking like a prisoner getting electrocuted as he hauls it up through force of will to lie flat on his belly in that blind alley. Over his moaning gasps of breath he can hear the city waking up around him, cars humming along the street behind him, the CLANG of the first streetcar of the day as it carries the maids and janitors uptown. He drags himself an inch or two to the lip of the big square pit that he just pulled himself out of, the pit that just replaced the last five feet of the alley, and peers into the shadows at the rusty metal spikes pushing out of the bottom fifteen or twenty feet down. "Holy hell," he mutters. "What am I stumbling into here?" Slowly he gets his feet under him and fishes that last wreck of a cigarette out of his pocket and twists it back into some kind of shape and lights up. He takes a deep drag as his mind whirls and he staggers across the street to catch the right car to a bed at the Prestige and then a lot of thinking.

CHAPTER TWENTY

A few hours later he's slamming the back door of a taxi in front of Wing's Bavarian nightmare and shoving some bills in the driver's face as he stomps through the gravel driveway and hammers his fist on the little door. The slot slides open and a pair of Chinese eyes stares out at him. He glares back. After a minute the door opens and he shoves past the guard on his way to throwing open the door to the courtyard.

Breakfast is just finishing. The thugs are standing around in loose groups, smoking and belching and half-listening to the orders each group is getting from a guy in a uniform like Otto's. Taggett stands with his back to a corner looking around until he spots Chen and Jie sitting at a table near the platform the boss eats on. A couple of the waitresses are clearing out their dishes and flirting with Chen. Taggett watches until the girls are gone and then strides over there.

Before he can pull back a chair to sit in Jie's already saying, "My dear Mr. Taggett, may I extend my greetings after too great a span of absence." The older man's black eyes are sparkling up into Johnny's. "May I also permit myself the observance that your name has found itself the subject of a great deal of conversation within the highest ranks of this concern with which I have associated myself, a predominance occasioned by that very absence to which I have alluded previously." The mouth that all this is coming out of seems to be smiling, but the sparkle in those eyes reminds Taggett of a gila monster he saw once in a newsreel. He stays on his feet.

"Yeah, sorry about that," he says. "I've been trying to figure out what's going on in your house. There's something you're not seeing."

The look on Jie's face doesn't change as Chen glances back and forth between the two of them. "If I may be so bold," says the older man, "as to allow myself an expression that may be perceived as harboring the slightest degree of reprimand, I must observe and, indeed, remark upon your regrettable ignorance of what I do or do not comprehend within my experience."

Taggett puts his hands up and says, "No offense meant." He takes a moment and a couple of breaths. "It's been a weird couple of days," he says. "And you're right, I don't know what you know, but I can tell you that whatever you're tangling with is probably bigger than you think it is, big enough to be running every square foot of this city, big enough to be setting god-damn booby traps under the streets." His voice cracks a little as he remembers last night and how those metal spikes gleamed wet from the bottom of the pit he nearly died in.

"And perhaps," says Jie, obviously continuing his thought without noticing what Taggett is saying, "your experience has led you to consider the possibility that the source of this, as you say, tangle resides in an element of unsuspected betrayal within this organization." Taggett nods while Chen's jaw goes a little tight. The younger man starts throwing glances around the courtyard as it empties. Jie's eyes stay on Taggett. He says, "One could then further presume to suppose, if one may, that you have in your absence begun to investigate more specific possibilities as to the precise identity of this source of entanglement." Taggett nods again. The courtyard's vacant now except for the three of them. After another moment Jie says, "Thus, considering the indubitable depth of the investigation I allude to, I must confess a belief—indeed, I must go so far as to declare it a hope—that you have in the course of your mentation developed a theory as to that identity." Taggett takes a moment to light up a smoke and look around the room and then he shakes his head just as Otto is gliding up to the table.

He clicks his heels and dips his head in a little bow. "Gentlemen," he says. "I am pleased to find you all together here. Mr. Wing desires your presence. I will lead you to him." He clicks his heels again and lets his hand rise to the chain on his monocle as he makes a little show of waiting for them. Chen spurts out of his chair and stands next to Johnny. Jie takes his time, that blank gaze of his moving from Taggett's face to Otto's as the older man straightens up. Otto gives him that look right back and then leads the three of them to a door in a farther corner of the courtyard and through it to another one of those wide stairways made out of some kind of grey stone. The temperature goes down as they climb those shallow steps that seem to be curving around some big central pillar, no one saying anything. There's just enough light for Taggett to see Chen giving him a quick questioning glance. The tough detective glances back and gives his head a little swivel of cool it for now.

After a while the stairway ends in a hall that branches left and right from it. Otto turns right and leads the little group down a corridor that suddenly isn't from the Black Forest of the nineteenth century at all. The linoleum floor sparkles under bulbs in the ceiling overhead as the four men walk past regularly set office doors, each with a name Taggett doesn't recognize on it. Over the flat clicking of shoes on tile he can hear a faint hum of typewriters chattering, telephones buzzing, murmurs of deals getting made and business being done. The hall ends in a plain set of double doors with stainless steel handles. Otto pulls open the left side and straightens up even stiffer and clicks his heels and says, "You may proceed." Jie gives him another long look to let Taggett and Chen step through before he follows. Otto pushes the door shut from the other side.

They're standing in a waiting room with sofas along the walls either side of the doors and an expanse of soft purple carpet between them and a desk with a pale redhead behind it. Behind the desk and to its left a rectangular panel the size and shape of a door blends in to the tasteful green wallpaper. The redhead looks up from her reading, notices the three of them, presses a button on a box in front of her, murmurs into it. The box says something in return and she gives the group a professional smile. "Mr. Wing is ready for you," she says. Her red-tipped finger moves to another button on the box and the panel in the wall slides open. The men walk in. The panel closes behind them. They're in a little room with no windows and no furniture and nothing on the walls. Chen coils into a fighting stance as he's shooting glances around the little cell. Jie's standing in the center of the floor and seems to be examining the way the walls fit the ceiling. Taggett's hand is on the butt of his forty-five. Above them some kind of machinery kicks on and whirs for a bit while Taggett gets a weird kind of roller coaster sensation in his gut and then the machinery above them kicks off again and the panel in front of them slides back open.

A voice with an accent like a radio announcer's says, "Gentlemen, please come in." The three of them exchange glances and step out carefully into a big room with a gleaming wooden floor that reflects the light coming in from a window that seems to take the place of one of the room's walls and commands an imperial view of Shanghai. In front of that window a little man with a brush mustache sits at a desk. He blinks at them through round glasses with silver wire frames and says again in that weirdly artificial tone, "Please come in, gentlemen. I've been expecting you."

Taggett takes his hand off his forty-five and says, "Mr. Wing?"

"One and the same," says the little guy. "Please, come have a seat." He gestures to three sturdy-looking chairs that line up in front of the desk. "We have much to discuss, Mr. Taggett, Mr. Chen," he pauses for a moment, "and Mr. Jie. How pleasant to meet you at last."

Taggett looks over at Jie and sees the older man just standing there with his mouth hanging open. "You," says Jie, but he can't seem to find the rest of the sentence. He tries again. "I seem to have become the victim of some sort of misunderstanding," he manages.

On Taggett's other side, Chen chimes in with, "Yeah, I've seen this Wing, and he looked like about three of you, mister." He cracks his knuckles. "What kind of game—"

But the little guy's just laughing in a mellow way as he stays standing behind his desk, his hands flat on the surface. "You've met an actor, Mr. Chen," he says. "I see no reason for my employees to know who I am."

"Sure," says Taggett as he steps toward the desk. "The heat comes down and everyone's pointing fingers at the big guy with the Kraut fetish while you just slip away." The tough detective cracks a smirk and settles in the center chair in front of the desk. "Or you just stay up here in your tower and keep an eye on your elevator."

Wing keeps chuckling. "You're as perceptive as I've been told, Mr. Taggett," he says and reaches over the desk to light Johnny's smoke. He goes on, "I certainly hope the other two of your party will be joining us soon. I am, after all, a man with much business to do." The laugh continues in his tone of voice, but his eyes have gotten serious as they train themselves on Jie. Taggett twists around in his seat to see the older man standing there tight-lipped. Wing says, "I'm starting to worry about you, Jie. You seem a little disturbed. You don't want to worry me, do you?"

Jie swallows and just says, "No," and quietly seats himself in the chair to Taggett's left. The tough detective blinks at him as Chen slips into the remaining chair.

"Well, then," says Wing. "Let's consider the situation we're in, shall we?" He sits back down behind his desk and lights himself a black cigarette that lets out some kind of floral-scented smoke. "You, Mr. Taggett, and you, Mr. Chen, arrive at my doorstep at just the same time that my operation comes under attack by an enemy who seems to have intimate knowledge of just where and when to strike. Would you say that's accurate?" From behind the thick lenses of those spectacles Wing's eyes blaze blackly into Taggett's.

Johnny takes a drag off his smoke and shrugs. "I wouldn't know about that, Mr. Wing," he says. "We showed up when we showed up, you got attacked when you got attacked. Not everything's connected to everything else."

"Then why don't I put it another way," says Wing with some more of that chuckle in his smooth tone. He turns to Jie and says, "These foreigners you vouch for appear, I think you'd say fortuitously, and then suddenly my supply buildings start to blow up and my soldiers start to die." The chuckle's entirely gone from his voice as he takes a breath and another drag from his cigarette. "Does that paint the picture clearly enough?"

Jie says, "Although, of course, your interpretation of the meaning borne by the contiguity of these two particular events must bear a certain degree of plausibility based on your as always perspicacious understanding of our particular milieu, I must concur with Mr. Taggett that the relationship between his arrival and the attacks to which you allude has only the coincidence of timing to support your, again, utterly reasonable if in this instance mistaken suspicion." His tone has become as suave as Wing's as the two of them lock eyes and let the silence in the room solidify for a moment that lingers like a bad smell.

"Or maybe something else," says Taggett. He's sitting up in his chair as if the light going on in his brain just woke him up. "What if we got steered here."

Chen snaps his fingers and says, "Damn, boss, that does add up. That army of thugs coming after us back in the States, that weird crap on the boat just as we're coming into Shanghai…." He trails off as his body lunges out of its chair and starts pacing around the room. "We're damn pawns!" he yells.

And now Wing's laughing for real. "Of course," he says. "And now you're about to say we should band together against our common enemy." He takes another drag, still addressing Jie while Taggett glares Chen back to sitting down. "Do you suppose whatever pushed Taggett here makes us partners?"

"Whatever pushed us here makes us all partners," says Taggett. Wing turns his gaze back on the tough detective. "Obviously Chen and me are part of some kind of assault on your business," Taggett says. "But I don't think we're the part you think we are. I think we're a distraction."

Wing glances back at Jie and seems to study his face the way a cop looks over a crime scene for clues. Then he turns back to Taggett and says, "Go on."

Taggett takes another drag off his smoke and says, "You've definitely got a leak in your pipes, but it sure as hell isn't me. How could it be? What the hell do I know about your business or even care?" He pulls another smoke out of his pocket and starts to light it with the butt of his last one, but Wing's already leaning over the desk with a lit match. Taggett nods thanks and says, "Whoever's doing you dirty's been inside for a while."

"Just what I was thinking," says Wing as he glares back at Jie, who's got his usual neutral expression back on and blandly gazes back.

Taggett says, "It's not Jie. Think about it. There's no way he'd use us if he knows you know about his history. I'm assuming you check up on your people." The room's entirely still again by this time as Chen's quit fidgeting and started just staring at the showdown going on across that shiny black desk. "So you'll know what he's been through," says Taggett, "and you'll know he doesn't turn."

"Everyone turns," Wing says, "but I see your point. I've been good to you, haven't I, Jie?"

Jie blinks a few times and says, "Your kindness to me, at least insofar as expressed by your representative, has indeed brought me fortune of the kind which any employee would envy. And in this context, I must permit myself the luxury of continuing by way of the observation that as I consider myself an astute businessman, of course neither of your caliber nor of your ambition or indeed any ambition above my current entirely satisfactory status, my small degree of accumulated wisdom must clearly show me the foolishness of attempting to betray or, indeed, even inconvenience you in your goals, for which my instinct for self-preservation has brought me to desire success as if they were my own."

"Think about it," says Taggett. "He's got no reason."

Wing finishes his cigarette and stubs it out in an ashtray the same shade of shiny black as the rest of the desk. He keeps looking at them through those little round lenses that make his eyes look big enough to fall into the way you'd fall into a pit of quicksand. The three of them watch him thinking until he finally says, "You make a persuasive case, Mr. Taggett. All right." He leans back in his chair and steeples his fingers under his chin. "Let's assume that your problems and my problems have the same source. We'll have to decide what to do about it. Jie, why don't you put some drinks together for us. You'll find the bar over against the wall." He points to it with his chin and Jie gets up to start getting busy with the bottles while Chen keeps pacing around and socking his fist into his open palm. Wing says, "Now then, Mr. Taggett. Wait, did you hear—"

The three chairs in front of the desk fall straight down through the broken boards as the crack of a small explosion of some kind fills the room. Taggett goes down with his seat as Chen throws himself to the floor and yells down into the jagged hole, "Boss! Boss!" He starts to cough from the cloud of smoke and dust that flies up into his face. If Taggett's still alive down there he's not answering.

CHAPTER TWENTY ONE

Chen's on his belly shouting down into the new hole in the floor and then a couple of gunshots from below ramp his shouts up into screams. Jie turns on Wing with a look on his face that makes the little boss do something behind his desk that makes a door spring open next to the elevator. Jie grabs Chen by the back of the collar and pulls him to his feet and the two of them run through the door and clatter down a metal spiral staircase and smash through a panel at the bottom into the waiting room. Taggett's on his back on the floor in the middle of the room, bleeding through his nose and looking dazed and holding on to his forty-five. Some goon's rag-dolled up against the wall opposite Taggett's feet with a brain splatter about where his head would have been dripping down onto the corpse. Next to where Jie and Chen are standing and breathing like wild horses the receptionist's slumped over her desk, a cute little twenty-two unfired in her fist as she bleeds from the big hole in her skull down the front of the desk onto the lush carpet. Taggett pulls himself to his feet, blinks dully at the other two men, says "Missed me," and falls right down again, passed out.

The two men look at each other for a split second and then grab the big detective by his armpits and haul him to the double doors. Chen lets out a yell and kicks them open and then the two of them start dragging Johnny down the linoleum hall followed by the muffled jangle of phones through office doors. Luckily for the two smaller men Taggett slides smoothly along the tiles. He's starting to squirm by the time they get to the turn for the stairs and the office doors are starting to burst open. By the time they're on those wide shallow stone stairs he's got his feet under him and the three of them can run full tilt.

They get to the door at the bottom of the stairs about the time the siren starts going off and the clatter of shoes on stone from above tells Taggett to keep moving. They get into the courtyard and slam the door behind them. Jie finds a chair and jams it up under the doorknob just as the door on the other side of the fake Wing's platform opens and a crowd of three or four thugs in black pajamas, plus the fake Wing himself in some kind of half-assed Viking armor big metal plates over his chest and thighs and a crazy helmet on his head with actual antlers sticking out, comes through. Breathing hard, Taggett pulls his forty-five. Chen just yells and leaps and a thug goes down when that first kick connects with his face, snapping his head back with that familiar crack that means your spine's been severed. The next thug goes down screaming from a quick punch in the nuts that smashes them so hard that some kind of fluid turns the creep's pants dark and stiff as he bleeds out. By that time the other two thugs have rolled forward and started advancing on Taggett. He drops the one on his right with a single shot to the gut and smirks a little while the thug writhes and bleeds and squeals on the floor. The other guy's frozen for a second as Taggett shifts his aim and pulls his trigger but the click of the hammer as it falls on an empty chamber takes the smirk off Taggett's face and puts it on the other guy's. Taggett curses and gets the forty-five back in its holster just in time to get his hands between his face and the thug's fists. He grabs and holds and the two of them dance for a moment before the tough detective rears his head back and butts the creep dead between the eyes. The guy blinks at him with eyes already starting to swell up and then kicks his legs out from under him. Taggett hits the floor hard but doesn't let go. Locked at wrists and ankles, the two of them roll around almost silently, just grunting and growling with effort, until Taggett ends up on top. He drops the guy's hands to grab him around the neck and start squeezing. The thug's throwing lefts and rights that smack against the sides of Taggett's head the way a gang of prisoners might swing hammers to break up a boulder but the tough detective gets his knee up between the punk's legs and smashes hard and keeps gripping that throat with his big hands until the punches turn into weak slaps and then the guy quits punching and starts just grabbing at Taggett's wrists and then he doesn't even do that anymore. Another half a minute and Taggett gets up off the corpse and stands on shaky legs looking up at the fake Wing on his little dining stage.

The big guy in the Viking armor looks down at Taggett and takes a moment to laugh before he turns and blocks Chen's flying kick with a beefy forearm. Chen's wiry form flies back and crumples onto the floor and the fake Wing laughs again. Then the laugh cuts off as if someone's flipped a switch as he turns back to Taggett and growls, "You disrespect your host. You hide your knowledge of enemy activity. You bring saboteurs to the home of your host." He seems to get even larger as he talks, voice getting deeper and louder as he raises his fists. "This disrespect cannot—"

"Disrespect!" Taggett turns to see Jie standing rigidly and staring at the fake Wing. "You dare speak of disrespect who would represent yourself as the host to whom you allude with such pretension!" Taggett has never heard the older man shout so loud. "You cannot, foul cur, aspire to the right to have let such a word form itself in the execrable pit of vipers that composes your wickedly deceptive mind! You earn no less than oblivion for the crime you attempt to commit against the very concept of respect!" Under Jie's words Taggett hears a sound that makes him step a little to the side to get off the line between the other two men.

The fake Wing rumbles a laugh that sounds like a rusty chainsaw starting. "Little man," he says."So proud of his intelligence, so easily fooled. Pawn who thinks himself king." The boards of the platform creak under the big fur boots he's wearing. "Soon I shut your mouth." The boards creak louder as he gathers his weight to leap but instead he paws at his throat, thick fingers slipping off of a blade that shines a little in the courtyard's light. Taggett looks back at Jie again just as the older man's tossing his second blade into the fake Wing's eye socket. The fat man staggers forward, falls off the platform, plants his face on the stone floor as he turns into a corpse. Taggett goes and pulls Chen up off the floor.

The three of them glance around the room at the bodies they've left on the floor. Chen says, "Well, I guess we're off the payroll." A sound like a shot from the other door gets them snapping their heads around to see the chair Jie jammed up against it starting to crack. Chen snickers and says, "Looks like we're getting an escort out."

"Let's avoid that," says Taggett and the three of them run to the entrance door. Taggett smashes a fist into the guard's face at the end of the hall as they burst into the daylight and over the gravel of the drive to where the cars are and tumble into the Silver Phantom. Jie starts the engine with a roar with Chen next to him and Taggett reloading in the back seat and the wheels spit that gravel as they spin the car onto the main road.

After a while the sound evens out to the smooth hum of tires over pavement. Taggett looks over at Jie to see the older man's knuckles almost shining out from his hand because they're as white as the bones beneath as he grips the wheel. The tough detective takes a glance back through the window to make sure they're not wearing a tail and says, "You had a good thing going there, Jie. Sorry to lose it for you."

Without turning Jie says through his clenched jaw, "Please do unburden your spirit of such self-recrimination. Wing's duplicity would have necessitated my departure in any eventuality, albeit in a manner decidedly less abrupt and peremptory." He takes a long breath and lets it out and says, "An association constructed upon a foundation of such literally unspeakable mendacity can offer only an illusory profit to its participants."

"Yeah," says Taggett. "But I'm sorry anyway." He checks the back window again as Jie slows down for the beginning of the city traffic, regular jobholders filling up the narrowing streets as they file from offices to diners for lunch or drag themselves home from the dog end of the third shift. Still with his head on a swivel, trying to get a view on every angle around the car as the buildings close in, Taggett says, "So what's next?"

Jie's taking the breath for his answer when Chen says "Hold on. I know that car coming in from the right." Taggett throws a hard look that way and here comes a beat-up purple coupe roaring up an alley and on to the street behind them. And then another couple of coupes come screeching out of that same alley only to slow to the crawl of city traffic inching toward downtown. Taggett grinds his teeth as he cocks his forty-five. The coupes are three or four cars back and the tough detective can almost hear the way their engines are growling like frustrated wolves. Jie gives the wheel a hard twist and throws the Silver Phantom right into an alley and speeds through it to swerve left into the traffic of the next street over, the Rolls's brakes complaining as he pulls it back to the sluggish pace the citizens use and Chen lets out a long breath. "Damn," he says. "You really know how to work this thing!"

"So do they," says Taggett from the back seat as the coupes pull back in behind them, now only a couple of cars back. He rolls down the window on Chen's side and takes off his hat to stick his head out for a second to gauge the distance. An arm reaches out through the passenger side of the purple coupe and Taggett pulls his head back in before the creep back there can squeeze off a shot. Then he tumbles down onto the seat as Jie pulls the Phantom into a sudden U-turn and right through that same alley and right again so that they're back where they started headed the same way. Taggett pushes himself upright and peers through the back window and the coupes show up behind the Phantom as it passes the next alley. The purple one is only one car back and that car between them could turn at any moment and give some creep a clear shot straight to the back of Jie's head. "We need to get this parade out of town," Taggett says. "I've got an idea. Remember that leper shack we got to visit?"

Jie's eyes go wide for a moment and then narrow again. "Indubitably," he says and takes the next turn toward the wharfs and the road that follows the river upstream. As the traffic thins out he starts the car into an irregular kind of sway across the width of the road to keep the goons behind them from getting a good aim. The road degenerates and starts to make its own swerves around the mud slicks and quicksand pits of the developing swamp. Soon enough the big square mass of the leper hospital rises up as they approach it to loom as a shadow against the nearly white sky behind it. Jie pulls up close to the hulking wreck of a building and whips the back end of the Phantom around to shoot gouts of wet muck into the thick air. The coupes stop in a row but no one gets out. Taggett does.

"Go ahead!" the tough detective yells. "Start shooting! See what you unleash onto yourselves!" Nothing moves in the landscape. "Shoot some holes in the building, see what comes out at you!" While Taggett's bellowing Jie give Chen a nudge and the younger man edges the passenger door open and slips out and creeps around to the back. Still no response from the goons in the coupes. Taggett points a thumb over his shoulder back at the stinking building and yells, "You know this place, right? Steered us here trying to get us sick? Scare us?" His voice is going hoarse as it gets louder. Behind him, Chen's got the trunk open and Jie seems to have shrunk down into the passenger-side footwell. Taggett hollers at the unmoving goons, "You want to see how scared we are?" as Jie hands him a grenade and he pulls the pin and throws. It lands in front of the purple coupe and sends a spray of thick putrid mud up into the air and that gets the goons opening their car doors and trying to scatter. By that time Taggett and Chen have tommy guns aimed and ready to spray death at the scrambling punks. A second later and Jie's on the other side of the Phantom with a roscoe of his own. A second after that they all stop firing because everyone else in the foul swamp is dead.

After a minute the acrid smell fades as the metal of the killing machines cools down. Taggett's ears are still ringing a little as he turns to Chen and says, "Hold on a minute. I need to check something." He hands his partner the machine gun and pulls himself across the field as the mud tries to suck his shoes off until he gets to the edge of the road where the coupes and the corpses are parked. The bodies of the goons lie face down and face up and faceless around the useless hunks of metal the cars have become. Taggett kneels down and looks closely at the corpse lying next to the driver's door of the purple coupe. He grabs the ankle and pushes up the leg of what used to be a sharp set of slacks to reveal the tattoo he was looking for. "Yeah," he says to himself. "Sure, why not." He drops the ankle and slogs his way back across the field to the two men shivering just a little in the cold of that dense building's shadow. Chen gives him a look and he nods back and the younger man rolls his eyes. Then the three of them get back in the Silver Phantom so that Jie can start driving them back to the city.

CHAPTER TWENTY TWO

The three of them ride in silence until the Phantom rolls over a set of streetcar tracks downtown. Something in that thumping interruption of the engine's drone makes Taggett snap his fingers and say, "Jie, take this next left and swing back around. Follow the tracks. I just had a thought."

Jie regards him for a second through the mirror and says, "Sir, I must humbly and with great reluctance express misgivings. You must agree that our circumstances require the most expeditious route away from the hazards of a city whose entire underground seems at this point arrayed against us." He guns the engine a little to get through an intersection. "In anticipation of such a downturn of fortune as this," he says, "I have, with the help of an acquaintance whose identity—indeed, whose very existence—I studiously and with some effort have concealed from my erstwhile allies in the Wing organization, established for myself a sanctuary that we may temporarily occupy as I arrange transportation to environs more convivial not only to the business that suits me most particularly but also to your continued safety in the face of the mass apparently arrayed against you." The tires give a little shriek as Jie takes a right and then a left through an alley just wide enough for the Phantom and explodes into a busy downtown artery, speeding up to match the city traffic. Jie says, "It is to that location that we proceed currently."

"I get that," says Taggett. "And thanks. But I'm sick of running. I want to find out who these creeps are so I can finish this crap." He glances over at Chen and the younger man nods back. Taggett says, "I think I saw something last night I can use." He tells them about losing Otto in the alley, that weird streetcar ride, the indistinct figure luring him back to where he started, the floor of that alley opening under him, those bloody spikes he could smell as he pulled himself up by his fingertips. Jie has the car turned around and headed for the streetcar line about halfway through Taggett's story.

The buildings are casting shadows all the way across the street by the time they get to the alley Taggett remembers. The Phantom pulls over to the other side of the street and the three men sit inside and look at that little stub of a street, so short they can see the blank dead end of it from where they are. Chen snorts and says, "You're telling me Otto lost you in there?"

"It was foggy," says Taggett. "And he knew something I didn't."

Chen chuckles again. "I guess so," he says. "So you figure he was working for this Sing character that had you roughed up in the can?"

Jie's turns to give Chen a puzzled look and say, "Sing?"

"Yeah," says Taggett. "Pale guy, real sharp dresser, looks like he might be from Indo-China. I thought he was the guy Wing thought we were working for." He pulls out a pack of smokes and passes one to Chen and lights up. "Christ, this case is making me dizzy."

Blinking, Jie says, "I assure you, I have in no capacity encountered anyone of that description named Sing, much less a personage of the importance you seem to have assigned to the individual to whom you allude."

"I believe that," Taggett says. "I'm pretty sure Wing was never at war with anyone, at least not the war he was trying to hang on us." He takes a drag and keeps watching the alley. "Think about how nervous this guy is, the way he hides himself. A guy like that with that big an organization has got to get rid of his crew every so often just to keep himself nice and safe in the shadows. Hell, Jie, you were probably next on his list." In the driver's seat the older man colors a little as he sucks in his lips. "I figure he just took advantage of the two of us stumbling into his game to start wrecking it so he could keep his hands clean."

Chen says, "So Otto's been driving us around just to get our faces in public?"

"I think it's more than that," says Taggett. "That deal with Sing was probably a set-up to get me associated with a fake enemy. I'm guessing he figured that my dead body would be good evidence that I was mixed up in his little war." He takes another drag. Citizens walk along past the opening of the alley on their way to their own important lives. No one goes into or comes out of it."On the other hand," Taggett says, "that trip out to the leper hospital was something else. Think about how we got out there. This guy shows up with a note and a bunch of doubletalk about where he got it from and we just pile in the car and go on the tour."

Jie's face goes even darker and his jaw clenches. "You think he's working for Mrs. Foulsworth?" says Chen.

"Or One-Eye," Taggett says. "Or both. All I know is that someone with a lot of resources and a weird sense of humor is pushing me around the damn world. I barely even care who's doing it any more. I just want to know why." He takes the last drag off his smoke and throws the butt out into the street and says, "So I want to find out what's in this alley. Last night before it opened under me I heard some kind of mechanical noise in the back wall." He lights up another. "Plus, I know Otto went in there and didn't come out."

Chen says, "Maybe he fell in the pit."

"No," says Taggett. "I'd've seen his body on one of those spikes." That gets a snort of laughter out of Chen. Taggett takes a drag and says, "So there's something in there and a way to get to it. We just need to see someone do it."

Jie coughs politely from the front seat. "If I may say so," he says, "without implying disrespect for either your experience or your methods, I must strongly suggest serious consideration of the constraints under which we find ourselves, specifically our current status as fugitives from the Wing organization, which, although perhaps debilitated to a certain extent by our having eliminated in our escape from its headquarters many of its soldiers and its ostensible leader, must even as we speak be finely scouring the various boulevards and alleys under its control for the particularly recognizable conveyance in which we apparently insist on prolonging this conversation." The older man takes a handkerchief from his coat and pats it over his brow. "Please allow me to extend my apologies for the unbecoming sarcasm with which I have expressed my perhaps inessential opinion." He folds the cloth over and puts it back in his coat. "Our experiences today have presented a formidable challenge to my powers of diplomacy."

"No, you're right," says Chen. "I can almost feel these goons creeping up on us while we sit here chatting about this blank alley." He tosses his spent smoke onto the sidewalk. "Boss, we don't have time for a stakeout," he says. "Let's get over there and find out what's going on."

Taggett frowns a little and scratches at his tingling scar and says, "Yeah." The three of them step out into the street and stand for a second as the streetcar clangs past full of tired workers on their way back to whatever civilians do when they're not doing jobs. The men step over the tracks and stand at the lip of the alley looking into it. Taggett says, "Careful. I don't really know what sets off the mechanism. I thought my knife caught something when I was poking around but my mind might have been playing tricks on me by then." He takes a drag on his smoke and a glance both ways along the sidewalk. "It was a weird night," he says.

Chen twists and looks over his shoulder at the buildings on the other side of the street and says, "Maybe someone up there has some kind of electric signal that opens the trap and there's nothing behind these walls."

"I don't think so," says Taggett. "It was too foggy last night. No one across that street could have seen me walk in." He tosses his spent smoke into the alley and watches the cherry flicker out in the shadows. "And I don't think it was a pressure switch, or it'd've tripped long before I got to the back of the alley."

Chen snaps his fingers. "That's what it is," he says. The other two men blink at him as he grins. "You told us you got to the middle of this left wall, right?" Taggett nods. "So you didn't make it to the back," Chen says. Taggett grunts and nods again and Chen says, "So how do you know that's really the back?"

"Damn," says Taggett and starts down the alley with the other two flanking behind him. His shoes click on the surface with a weird hollow echo. He notices he's trying not to step down too hard and lets a harsh chuckle out between his lips. In a moment the three of them are facing a brick wall that looks just like its mates to the left and right. Taggett takes a breath and lets it out and says, "Now what?" Chen and Jie glance at him and shrug. "Thanks," says Taggett and raises his hands and pushes against the bricks and grunts with surprise as his fingertips encounter the rough canvas of a painted tarp. The other two actually gasp. Taggett presses a little harder and lets his fingertips glide over the surface until they reach a seam and push to find an empty space behind the fake wall. He leaves one hand on the canvas as the other reaches into his jacket for his forty-five. Another glance to his left and his right at his partners and he yanks the curtain aside and dives through into the dark.

His knees and shoulders thump on a splintery wood floor as he comes back up aiming forward. The other two slip in behind him and there they stand just this side of the heavy canvas false wall that muffles the clang of the passing streetcar. Jie snaps a lighter to life long enough to find a switch that activates a dim yellow light in a cage that hangs from a flat ceiling. The light reveals rows of stiff-looking chairs that face a podium with a desk behind it and to the left beside a plain door in the back wall. Taggett holsters his forty-five and creeps around behind the desk to break open one of the drawers. The other two step behind him as he pulls out a pair of black gloves. Chen sucks in a breath. "Jesus," says Taggett. He breaks open another drawer and pulls out a pamphlet with a bunch of Chinese writing on it and hands it to Jie.

The older man's eyes shift over a couple of lines and he goes pale. He says, "This publication represents itself as promotional material to aid in the recruitment of mercenaries for the purposes of reinforcing the temporal power of what seems to be a religious organization." He glances down at the paper and looks back up into Taggett's eyes and says, "The organization is named the Clan of the Violet Diamond."

"Oh shit," says Taggett. He can hear his own voice as if he's standing at the other end of a long tunnel from himself. His head's filled up with a dull roar like the sound of waves smashing into a shore. As he feels his face go warm and his scar begin to burn the sound fades into the clicking of shoes on pavement beyond the curtain and coming closer. He pulls out his forty-five and cocks it.

Jie puts a hand on Taggett's shoulder and whispers, "I must caution reticence. To reveal our presence here too hastily may bring us the penalty of opposing two forces, each of which by itself possibly strong enough to overwhelm us, simultaneously." Taggett nods and puts his weapon away and stands ready with the other two. The footsteps come to a sudden stop. The streetcar gives a clang as it buzzes past. The beige expanse of the back of the curtain billow in a little at about chest height on a short man and then the seam parts and a platoon of thugs comes bursting in. Two of the six fall where they stand with Jie's razors projecting from their throats. While they're lying there gurgling Taggett vaults over the desk and grabs a chair and smashes it over some goon's head hard enough to knock the guy into one of his partners. They go down and Taggett starts kicking and stomping until the punks quit twitching. He glances over to see Jie and Chen behind the last two choking them out. It doesn't take too long for two faces to turn purple and two sets of eyes to roll back and two limp bodies to drop the last inch to the floor, thumping a little as Jie and Chen lower them. The three men stand there for a moment breathing hard and listening. Nothing seems to be happening on the other side of that door behind the desk. Taggett wipes a little sweat off his forehead and replaces his hat and steps over there to grab the gloves and the paper. Then the three of them step to that huge curtain. Taggett takes out his forty-five and uses it to push aside one of the pieces and peek out into the alley. Nothing out there but the darkening night. The workers are in their homes having their dinners and there's hardly anyone on the streetcar going by the mouth of the little alley.

"Let's go," says Taggett and the three of them shove through the canvas and run down the alley to the street and freeze at what they see. The Phantom's wrecked. Thick scars along its side make ugly stripes in its shiny finish. The sledgehammer those creeps used is leaning up against the front of the car at the end of a ragged line of big dents and holes in the hood. Shards of glass are trying to glisten in the street from the smashed up windshield. "Jesus," says Taggett as the three men stand there stunned and staring at the car's corpse.

Jie lets out a growl and takes a breath and says very evenly, "This development most definitely adds a complication to the sequence of events that I had hoped to facilitate this evening." He turns to Taggett. "With your permission, I must attend to the reconstitution of this vehicle without delay, and sadly, the circumstances of my effort compel me to request with utmost urgency that you refrain from accompanying me as I pursue this objective," he says.

"Sure," says Taggett. He pulls out a couple of smokes and hands one to Chen and lights them up. A cold wind pushes down the street as the detectives look at each other and then around at a city full of hostile strangers and then back at Jie.

The older man smiles and says, "Gentlemen, please allow me to assure you that I have no desire to leave you without resources." He hands Taggett a calling card that he's pulled from his jacket. "A streetcar journey of, I must admit, a perhaps inconvenient duration will convey you almost directly to this address," he says. "At the conclusion of this odyssey of sorts, you will find yourself in a district the nature of which should bring about in you both a pleasant sensation of nostalgia for the disreputable conditions of the existence to which you have become accustomed in your native land."

Chen snorts a little laugh. "So we're back off of Easy Street?"

"Perhaps momentarily" says Jie as he laughs along politely. "When you have presented yourself, you may use my name as introduction. Ask for Stuart."

Taggett takes a drag and says, "Thanks. See you soon." Jie smiles and turns and walks away into the fog that's beginning to thicken. Taggett and Chen start going the other way to the streetcar station and whatever's next.

CHAPTER TWENTY THREE

The streetcar's warm and empty as Taggett and Chen stagger onto it and fall into a couple of seats. Chen lights up a couple of smokes and offers one to Taggett and says, "Hell of a day."

"Yeah," says Taggett, and they ride in silence for a little while. The darkness around the car makes the windows into flickering mirrors that catch their faces as they stare at the buildings slipping past the track pulling them deeper into the filthy heart of the city. The two men squint a little as the car pushes through the tourist area and past the Prestige Hotel. The bell shoves aimless gawkers out of the middle of the road but the car doesn't stop to let anyone on.

Finally Chen says, "So this is all about that crazy ring she gave you?"

"Yeah," says Taggett. "I guess. I can't remember the last time I thought about that thing." The windows have turned black as the streetcar passes out of the business district and turns a corner to skirt a residential neighborhood. "Must've slept through this last night," Taggett mumbles to himself. Chen shoots a look at him and Taggett blinks back and says, "This is like the third time I've been down this line. I think." He holds up a hand. "Just need a moment to figure this out," he mutters to either Chen or himself. The younger man keeps looking at him.

The streetcar makes another turn and city lights show up again. By this time the fog's made itself into a wall that spreads the lights out into smears of red and yellow that cling to the car's windows like a skin of oil that shows ghosts of the two men's faces in reflection. Taggett's thinking about that Violet Diamond, the way it makes weird dark whispers creep in around the back of his mind, how that bizarre Mrs. Foulsworth talked about it as some kind of ultimate prize. "What if she's alive," he says to himself or Chen or the thick air in the streetcar. "She wants it back? Why go through all this?"

Chen laughs and says, "Well, hell, boss, we know she's out of her tree, right?" He pulls out a smoke and lights up. "Maybe she's trying to teach you some kind of crazy lesson," he says."Like she wants us to know what she can do."

"Maybe," says Taggett as the car's bell clangs and it pulls to a stop. A couple of sharp-looking dudes step on and stand there swaying as the car starts up again. Condensation drips off the brown fedoras the dudes are wearing and off of their long brown trench coats. Taggett mutters, "What the hell. I remember these guys." They make their way up the center aisle and take seats in front of Taggett and Chen. No one says anything. The streetcar hums and then cracks like lightning as it hits a breaker. Taggett glances at Chen. The younger man's starting to coil up, getting ready to strike at the sharp dudes who seem to be getting Taggett so edgy. The dudes are staring straight ahead at the yellow circle of the streetcar's headlight pushing against the wall of fog that just keeps sliding backwards. The clown colors keep smearing over the side windows. The dude in front of Taggett yawns and a trickle of water spills out of the brim of his hat as he tilts his head back. Taggett watches him. The dude glances across the aisle at the other dude. The two of them could almost be twins: the same razor-straight cheekbones, the same almost triangular jaw, the same pointed beak of a nose, the same black eyes that Taggett can't see anything in the depths of as he stares. He takes another look across the aisle at Chen and the younger man shoots back a look like a dog yanking at a leash. Taggett puts up a hand to keep him holding. The dude across the aisle yawns while the dude in front of Taggett turns back to stare ahead into the nothing. The streetcar hums and rattles and clangs its bell and slows to a stop and then starts up again. Taggett feels his lips moving and hears himself growling under his breath, "This is too crazy. Too much. Am I dreaming?" The dude in front of him says something in Chinese that makes both dudes raise thin fingers to thin lips to politely stifle a matching pair of high-pitched snickers. Taggett sees Chen's eyes go wide and knuckles go white in fists ready to knock those smirks to the floor of the car. The lights in the ceiling flicker and dim and flare up as the car slows to get ready to stop. The dudes get their feet under them and stand and sway up to the front and one of them says something to the driver that gets another of those hidden chuckles and then the car stops and the dudes get off and Taggett and Chen start breathing again.

Chen pulls out a couple of smokes and reaches across the aisle to offer Taggett one. The flame of the match does a little jitterbug as he lights them up. Taggett takes a drag and smiles at his partner. Chen blows out a big puff of smoke as he laughs and says, "Did that just really happen? Come to think of it, what the hell did just happen?" He glances around the car. "Those guys had me ticking like a bomb, they were so weird. Totally the kind of freaks that've been after us all this time." He takes another drag and lets out another trembling breath of smoke. "You think that Violet Diamond is bringing them out of the woodwork?"

"It's starting to look that way," says Taggett and shrugs and takes a deep pull on his smoke. "Or maybe these crazies have always been around and we're just starting to notice." He reaches into his coat and pulls out the card Jie gave him and squints at it in the car's flicker. "Anyway," he says, "we need to find Jie's guy." He hands the card over to Chen. "This make any sense to you?"

Chen does some squinting of his own and then some shrugging. "Beats me, boss," he says. "Maybe it's some kind of map?" He turns the card over and turns it over again and says, "These Oriental addresses work like riddles. Think I should look at it in a mirror? Hold it over a candle?" The young detective peers at the card with a face like a monkey might have as it tries to do a crossword puzzle. "Hell," he says, "we don't even know when to get off the streetcar."

Taggett chuckles and takes the card back as the car's lights flicker and it slows and the driver yells, "End of line! Last stop! Got to go!"

Chen says, "Well, that's an answer, I guess" and unfolds himself from the bench to pad down the aisle toward the front of the car with his eyes open and his head on a swivel. The car's door makes a rectangle of darkness with tendrils of fog swirling around it for Chen to step into. He stops for a moment and peers into and takes that step and the night takes him in.

Taggett glances after him and then turns back to the driver, a bronze-colored little guy shifting and fuming in his seat. "You need something?" the guy says with a hint of the growl a Chihuahua guards its territory with in his tone. "I gotta get back to base, gotta check in, why you hold me up?"

The tough detective tries not to chuckle as he considers that tone. He shows the driver Jie's card and says, "I'm sorry to take your time. Can you tell me how to find this address?"

The driver doesn't take his hard little hands off the wheel and keeps his eyes on Taggett's for a moment that stretches almost to the point where Taggett has to do something about it. Just as the detective's fingers are starting to curl into a fist the driver drops his gaze to the card and starts to laugh. "No place for you, white man," he says. "You go there, you get murdered."

"But that's where I need to go," says Taggett. He's still holding the card in one hand and flexing the fingers of the other until he wills himself to relax them. His voice drops into a growl of its own as he says, "Will you tell me how to get there?"

Those angry eyes flick to Taggett's big hand and then to the bulge in his jacket where the forty-five pushes against the fabric and then up to Taggett's eyes burning darkly back down. "Okay, okay," the driver says. "No need get crazy, you crazy enough. Go straight down this street." He points at the black rectangle of the open door. "Go down until you hit river. You find what you look for." As Taggett glances away into that darkness the driver says, "You get what you deserve, crazy white man." Taggett shoots a glance back at him to see the rage gone in those eyes, replaced by simple blankness. "Time to go," says the driver.

"Yeah," Taggett says and steps out into the night. He can just barely see Chen smirking in the light from inside the car as it clangs hard and rumbles away until the dark and the fog swallow it all the way up. The two of them stand there for a moment in the silence and then Taggett turns the way the driver pointed and starts walking. His shoes click on the pavement as he strides down the middle of the street and he can just barely hear Chen beside him as the younger man's rubber soles squelch in the little puddles the fog leaves.

Little night sounds creep into that silence. Somewhere on the other side of the big blank buildings that line the street the detectives are groping their way along a couple of cats are yelling at each other, getting ready to mate or fight. Through a high window the two men can hear the kind of tuneless whistle that every night watchman uses to keep himself awake. Every so often a car's drone swells and fades somewhere behind them, getting fainter as the two of them get closer to the halo of greenish-yellow light that's starting to blossom like an oversized flower in the thick fog at the end of the street.

A different kind of noise starts to reach toward them from that direction the way a smell reaches toward you from a corpse. Five or six different bands are playing as loud as they can, shrieks of brass driven into the air by thundering bass drums throbbing with crazy jungle rhythms. Women and men are shouting each other to be heard over that racket in English and Chinese. The women are yelling prices and the men are yelling counteroffers. Soon enough Taggett and Chen have gotten to the source of all this.

The street's narrowed into an alley that spawns a network of alleys from it at all sorts of weird angles formed by little shacks and huts and sheds pumping out that sick electric light and that crazy piercing noise and smells of booze and puke and fried meat. Women in grimy underthings are leaning against various walls puckering their lips and hollering filth at the men staggering by from shed to hut to shack. Sometimes one of the men grabs one of the women and hauls her a little further down into the darkness of the maze of stinking alleys. As the detectives stand there staring the door of one of the larger shacks explodes open and a couple of guys spill out into the slimy mud of the street and roll around punching each other until the one on top pulls a knife and stabs the one on the bottom and drags him down another one of those alleys. Taggett mutters to himself, "Five Points."

"Huh?" says Chen.

Taggett grins at the younger man and says, "Jie was right. This place is just like what I remember from New York." He takes a deep breath as the jazz blares around them. "I even remember these smells," he says. "Bar food and puke and sweat and blood." The two of them jump back from a tiny flood of filthy water that leaves a residue of yellow scum on the pavement as it slides along downhill. "This is home," says Taggett. "Let's find Stuart." He pulls Jie's card out and takes another look at it and a look around at how the building are huddling against each other. "Huh," he says and shows Chen the card. The younger man blinks and takes the same look around and actually gasps as he gets it.

"Are you trying to tell me this really is a map?" Chen says. "These shapes, these lines—it's this crazy nest of alleys from above, isn't it?" Taggett nods and Chen starts laughing. "Jesus, these Orientals," he says and then he stick out a finger and starts turning around as he compares what he sees on the card to what he can make out in the neon of the shapes of the buildings. Finally he stops and points at one of the larger ones. "That's the one with the circle around it," he says. "Ready?"

"Yeah," says Taggett. The two men walk up to a long low shed with a blur of trumpets shooting out through a front door hanging off its top hinge. They push through into a big room the size of the building it's in, bar along the short end to the left and the long wall opposite the door covered with photos of the whores outside and their mothers and their mothers before them. Some kind of grill is hissing and spewing out the smell of the sausages sizzling on it over to the right next to the record player turned all the way up for dancing.

There's no dancing. The floor's too littered with the jagged sticks of what used to be tables and chairs for anyone to dance on even if anyone was there. The bartender's ducked behind his bar with just the top of his head peaking up so he can keep an eye on what's happening over by the grill. What's happening is a big white guy with hair down over his shoulders pounding a fist the size of a canned ham into the face of some poor local slug who's just leaning back against the wall and taking it. The big guy's yelling with each blow, "THIS is WHAT HAPPENS when you STEAL from yer BETTERS, boy!" The slug just spits out teeth and blood and nods as if he can make the beating stop through sheer politeness. The big guy doubles his target over with a punch to the belly and says, "All right, ye've learned yer lesson." He shoves the slug over toward the bar. "Go get a drink afore ye die on me, ye foul embezzler. I know where to find ye." The deep voice comes from somewhere way back in the big guy's throat, almost as if a guard dog had learned to talk. "Consider ye how ye'll pay me back, miscreant," he says. He watches the little guy limp over toward the bar and then notices the two detectives standing in front of the door. His whole massive body turns toward them as he says, "This ain't no show for slummers, gents. Any fight ye see's a fight ye're in, get my drift." He cracks his knuckles and starts moving toward them over the smashed glass on the scratched-up gloss of the dance floor.

Taggett's eyes go wide as he gets a good look at the guy's face. It's like looking in a weird mirror. The guy's got Taggett's broken nose and Taggett's square jaw and a scar like Taggett's. Chen's standing there looking between them and shifting his feet apart, coiling to leap. Taggett squares up as the guy comes at him and says, "Stuart?"

The guy stops in his tracks and looks at Taggett. "Strangers don't say my name in public, son," he says. "Now ye're getting promoted from a beating to a killing." He reaches into his pocket and pulls out a switchblade and flicks it open. His bleached-out blue eyes get a little brighter as his lips pull up into a grin that looks like a wolf's snarl. "Ready to die?"

Taggett puts up his hands and says, "Hold on. I'm not exactly a stranger. Jie sent me. I'm Taggett."

Stuart stands there and takes another long look at Taggett and then folds the blade back into the knife and puts it away. A jagged-toothed smile opens up under those ice-blue eyes. "Aye," Stuart says, "he's spoken of ye. In need of shelter, I hear." He sticks out a hand and Taggett takes it and winces a little from the pressure of the handshake and the roughness of the hand that's dishing it out. "I'll help ye," says Stuart. "Meet me down to the docks in half an hour's time and I'll ferry ye to safe harbor." He glances down at Chen and sneers a little but doesn't say anything to the smaller man. To Taggett he says, "Pass the time with a drink or two. Ye look in need of it. Tell Chang back there that it's on me." With that he drops Taggett's hand and pushes back through the door into the festering night. Taggett lets out a breath and turns with Chen toward the bar.

CHAPTER TWENTY FOUR

A couple of drinks later they're back out in the night and the fog. Taggett's carrying an antique lantern that the bartender gave him and Chen's padding carefully alongside with his hands out and ready to strike as they inch along the alley the bartender pointed them down. The guy said that this was the only way down to the river that wouldn't get the two detectives killed or kidnapped. Even so, Chen's flinching at the sounds of glass breaking and the inhabitants hollering at each other. Taggett's got his free hand on his forty-five. The alley's barely wide enough for the two of them to walk side by side. It keeps shifting right and left at weird angles that have the detectives almost running into walls before they make it through to a wharf that's not more than three or four planks nailed together and edging out into the river almost invisibly. The beach is just a little less dark than that stinking alley, walled off by the backs of buildings from that neon throb back there. The water slaps against the shore as the two of them stand and wait.

"This look a little like a graveyard to you?" Chen says and lights up a smoke and hands it to Taggett. The fire at the tip of the match dances a little in the still air as he lights up one for himself and tosses the burnt-out stick into the river.

Taggett holds the cigarette between his lips so he can keep one hand on his forty-five while he waves around that lantern. He chuckles out of the corner of his mouth and says, "Yeah, there's probably more than a few bodies around here. Seems like a good place to leave them." They stand there for a little while longer and watch the lantern's reflections get sucked into the dark depth of the river.

Soon enough a kind of creaking slips over the noise of the waves. A shadow moves toward the center of the light's dim reach and then resolves itself into a rowboat with Stuart pulling at its oars. The big man twists the boat parallel with the planks coming off the shore so that he's facing the detectives and lets out a brief shrill whistle. "Come aboard if yer comin'," he snarls. "And douse that light. I knows these currents like me own skin, and I wouldn't be leadin' the local bobbies to my little asylum." The two men clamber onto the boat, stumbling as it shifts under them and thumping onto a hard bench. Taggett blows out the lantern. The boat sways and shoves his body back and forth as Stuart tugs and twists at the oars some more to get them all out into the river.

After a few minutes of this he pulls the oars up and slides them into the locks along the boat's sides. "May's well let the river do the work for a while," he says. Taggett blinks at the little pale spark of Stuart's match as it flares and then sucks down into the bowl of a pipe that glows faintly in the thickness of the night. The ember in the pipe gives off just enough light to make a shadow-face for Stuart that Taggett sees grinning at him. The detective looks down to pull out a couple of smokes and offer Chen one and light them up. "So," says Stuart, "me man Jie tells me yer swamped in some kind of mystery."

Taggett sits as still as he can and watches the shadows squirm over Stuart's big face to make weird new expressions that grin and leer at him. Finally, he says, "Yeah."

Stuart's chuckle makes the glow of his pipe swell for a second. "A man of few words, I see," he says. "Good on you, lad." He sucks his pipe for a moment and says, "Never could keep me own counsel too well, sad to say. Too be-smitten by the sound of me own voice, I reckon." The big man's black eyes seem to twinkle as they reflect the cherry in the pipe. He says, "However and on the other hand, I have to admit that me gift of gab has made itself useful to me more than once or twice. Keeps everything straight and aboveboard, ye catch me drift?"

Chen snorts a chuckle of his own and says, "Yeah, the guy that's taking us to his secret island in the dead of night's no man of mystery."

Taggett gives him a quick elbow to the ribs. Chen shoots a glare at his partner and then looks back at Stuart to say, "I mean, thanks for the shelter but you've got to admit you're pretty mysterious as people go."

"I suppose," says Stuart. The hulking shadow outlined against the slightly less dark of the lingering mist shrugs. "Same time, ye gets what ye sees when we deal. No false-front with me." He reaches out and actually gives Taggett a pat on the shoulder and says, "It's the false-fronts that trouble ye most, eh?"

Taggett tenses and almost takes a swipe at that heavy paw. Instead, he lets out his breath and says, "I guess you know as well as I do most fronts are false." He takes a second to take a drag and let the little slurps of the water against the side of the creaking boat put a little more space between the two of them. Then he says, "I try not to let it bother me."

Stuart actually goes *har har* as he says, "A fine policy for yer peace of mind, sure." A long whistle comes out of the fog from somewhere behind Taggett and Stuart taps his pipe out into the ocean and whistles back. As the two detectives toss out their own smokes the big guy grabs the oars and starts wrestling the boat around again until it's nestled against an invisible deck. "Go ahead," says Stuart and the two of them stumble from the boat to a floor of wood so smooth it's gone slick in the fog. As Taggett makes the steep step up he slips and bangs his shin on the edge. He reaches back and grabs Chen and the two of them help each other off the boat, clinging to each other for a moment to stay on their feet. Stuart stays in the boat, still chortling. "Be seein' ya," says the big guy as he pulls at the oars and merges with the rest of the darkness.

And there they stand again. The river waves splash against each other a little in front of them as they stay as still as they can. Whatever they're standing on might not be more than a step or two wide and a flinch in the wrong direction could drop them into that black water. Taggett shoves his hands into his pockets and listens to Chen's breath shudder next to him. Time stretches.

A stealthy footstep off to his right makes Taggett whirl and almost fall to his knees. He catches himself as a puny yellow glow swells out from a lantern hanging from the fist of an African guy about Johnny's size. The guy's skin reflects the light slickly. Taggett and Chen just stand there gawking. The guy twists a knob at the lantern's base and the glow enlarges to reveal some dark kind of wooden hut they all seem to be standing next to. He tilts his head toward it and reaches out to rap the other dense fist on the wood and make the hollow thud of knuckles on a door. "You go in," he says. "I stay here. Keep watch." He opens his hand to push the door open into the hut. As the two of them duck under his arm to step inside he hands the lantern to Taggett. Then he pulls the door closed behind them and pads away on bare feet over the glossy wood.

Taggett turns the lantern up a little more to show them the room they're standing in. There's a flat ceiling about a foot above his head paralleling the flat wood deck they're standing on. A couple of coffin-sized mats for sleeping on line each of the walls and a piled-up coil of rope sits weirdly in the middle. Chen moves closer to it and says, "Hey, I've read about these." He gives the rope a nudge with his foot. "The rope's fake. There's a trapdoor under it for getaways."

Taggett's walked over to the far wall by this time and he's looking down at one of the mats. "Where's the trapdoor lead to?" he says.

Chen shrugs and snickers and says, "Watery grave, I guess." He steps over to a bedroll along the wall opposite Taggett and near where the door should be. The ring of shadow around the lantern's glow has turned the door of this windowless room into just another part of the wall as if this weird cell grew out of the deck around the two of them. Chen kicks the mat the same way he nudged the fake rope. "Can you believe it," he says, "I was in a damn castle last night."

"Yeah," says Taggett. He lies down on his mat and lets his hat tilt over his brow and paint a shadow over his eyes. "I was at the Prestige Hotel," he says. "Everyone's gotta sleep somewhere." A yawn takes over his face for a second and he closes his eyes and then he's in some kind of weird purple void. He might be standing on a floor he can't see but he also might be floating. At this point he might not even be inside a body. The whole world is that pulsing purple light even as darkness starts to creep into it like a slow cloud of smoke curling itself into a bottle and filling it while he's looking at or inhabiting or becoming part of nothing but darkness.

Then he's climbing up that endless staircase next to old Sergeant Murphy. The wood's complaining under their weight and someone in one of those apartments must be filling a tub. Taggett can hear the water splashing somewhere. Murphy's talking in a scratchy whisper. "Destiny," he's saying. "We know what's at the end of this climb, don't we. All that blood, that pain. That killing." The two men keep trudging up those steps in that tenement darkness. "And you can see what it's doing to your little friend, can't you," says Murphy in that creepy creaking rasp that Taggett can feel in the back of his brain. "Do you think he's ready for this life your bent partner sucked him into, the life you're dragging him through? Do you mind the way you've made him into a killer like you?" It's like the two of them are standing still and the staircase is just sinking under them step by step. Taggett's trying to get his hand on his nightstick and knock the false face off of whatever's climbing next to him and talking through Murphy. He can't do it. He can only keep pushing himself forward. The demon beside him just snickers and winks and says, "We know what you are, don't we. Remember how you'll feel in a minute when you see me go down, when you have to step on my body to blow that freak out of his misery. Remember how it'll look in there and how you'll just keep staring into it." The scar across Taggett's face itches deep as he remembers. "Looked like a slaughterhouse, didn't it," the thing says. "It'll look like a mirror." Taggett manages to push a low moan of protest out of his chest at about the same time a door slams hard somewhere in the building. The thing with Murphy's face hisses, "Unfinished business, Taggett. You're holding something that was never yours to keep. Listen!" That door slams again and someone screams and something splashes into that tub they've been filling and then his eyes open into the dark little hut.

No way to tell how long the lantern's been out and no sound in the cabin but Chen shifting in his sleep as if he's fighting something. Taggett blinks and waves his hand in front of his face to make sure of the absolute darkness. Another shot goes off with a clap like a slamming door. Taggett sucks in a breath and rolls away from the wall as Chen grunts himself awake. Another shot goes off and a bullet punches a hole high in the wall above Taggett and then in the hut's roof. Taggett can hear Chen ducking and rolling until the two of them manage to collide around the middle of the floor somewhere as another shot makes a slightly lower hole. A half second later a shot smashes in from the other side. "They're gonna shoot this place to ruins around us," Chen says.

Taggett says, "No, they're saving their bullets, zeroing in on us. We gotta get out of here." He swings his leg and makes contact with the fake pile of rope as another couple of shots come in from either side of the hut, coming lower, letting in drafts of the cold river air and the smell of hot metal. More shots from a third side. "They've almost got us boxed," Taggett says and lashes out with his foot to kick that coil. The sole of his shoe smacks against something hard as he drives his leg into that iron weight of fake rope. The fourth wall of the little hut grows new holes from a fresh set of bullets. The thing that Taggett's kicking scrapes an inch or two along the floor and makes a noise almost loud enough to compete with the ironic round of applause that's going on outside as the walls start to turn into lace. Both men are kicking now. The pile moves to reveal a square of much thinner wood that Chen can smash with a single stomp. The track of a bullet stings along Taggett's side as he rolls over to throw himself into the weird slick shimmer of blackness. He goes in.

The water blinds him and grabs him and throws him around and snatches off his hat and pushes him what must be downstream. He flails his arms in it and starts to shove himself along through its thickness. His chest is already throbbing and pulsing like something's flying around in there and trying to get out. The shots overhead are getting faster, but they're muffled by the water he can feel plugging his ears like cold fingers. Now his chest muscles are starting to stretch and ache and burn. He swims. Some pale light is breaking through the surface above him to show him the shape of the boats the thugs are paddling around up there as they shoot Stuart's little hideaway to splinters. They're too close. If he comes up now they'll just fill him with lead and let him sink again. He has to keep swimming. The water's pulling him in some direction he can't even figure out. His lungs are keeping time with the beat of his heart as they push against his chest. A red haze is fading in around the brightening glow filtering down from above. The red's taking over. His arms and legs are turning into clay and then into concrete. A bubble bursts out from between his clenched lips. Everything goes black and then purple and then black again.

And then he's laid out on the deck of a motorboat with Chen crouching over him and Jie working the rudder as bullets fired from just out of range drop into the water behind them. He can feel his body shake as the boat vibrates under it. A couple of drops fall off of Chen and hit Taggett square in the face and he flinches. The younger man keeps looking down at him. "You all right, boss?" he says.

Taggett turns his head and pukes up some water and coughs. He reaches up to Chen and pulls himself up on the younger man's hand to a sitting position, leaning the back of his head against the side of the boat as it bucks and jumps along the choppy river. The sky's gone grey above him. He reaches into his coat and pulls out a soaked-through pack of smokes and snorts and throws it in the river. "Yeah," he says and spits after it. "Fine."

CHAPTER TWENTY FIVE

They end up in a shack in the middle of a swamp growing out of a narrow bend in the river that Jie's hustled the boat into. Chen's got a fire going in the little black Franklin stove in the shack's corner and the two detectives have their clothing hung up on a line Taggett strung in front of the stove. Now they're both sitting up against a bristly wall in their long johns and watching the steam come off the wet duds while Jie sits in a flimsy in the middle of the floor with his back to the stove. No one's had a thing to say all this time.

Finally Chen breaks the silence with a "What the hell, Jie? Was that supposed to be the safe place you were sending us to?" He spits on the planks that keep the shack from sinking back into the swamp. "And what the hell's with that Stuart guy? Did he sell us out?"

Jie takes a deep breath and lets it out and says, "My ignorance of Stuart's actions this past eventful night and morning does not prevent my continued reliance on the depth of trust inherent in our previous associations. If I may be so bold, however, as to allow my individual emotions to add to the stress caused by the dangers of our current circumstances, my major regret is situated in my apparent abandonment of the two of you to the attack which you so recently endured at the hands of those mysterious forces." He's looking down at his feet as he says this. "To the extent that I may be allowed to defend myself," he says, "I may assert my intention, to the extent of my sadly limited ability, preemptively to thwart exactly such an attack when we parted ways last night."

"Huh?" says Chen.

Taggett lets out a chuckle as he's thumbing the wet bullets out of his forty-five's clip and setting them carefully down on the floor next to him. "He's saying he was trying to save us by winning the war," says the detective.

"Indeed," says Jie. "The extent of the damage to the Silver Phantom and the brutality of such an attack by members of Wing's organization upon property belonging to that very organization revealed undeniably to me the almost feverish incessancy of the organization's pursuit of the two of you. Perhaps, admittedly, under the influence of the undeniable emotion aroused by my discovery of Wing's continuous betrayal and deception, betokening an intolerable lack of respect, I determined in the words of the venerable adage that I could most effectively dispatch the serpent threatening you and thus terminate its ominous motions through an act of decapitation."

Taggett lays his gun down on the wood next to the row of bullets and says, "Well, I like that story better than the one where you had to get the car fixed." That gets a snort of a laugh out of Chen and then a yell from out in the river makes all three men snap their heads around the way rats freeze when they hear a cat growl. After a moment of just the crackle of the fire in the stove and the dripping of their clothes onto the shack's fuzzy wood nothing happens. They relax and Taggett says, "So did you get to Wing?"

Now it's Jie's turn to let out a rueful chuckle. "In a manner of speaking," he says. "I did indeed accomplish the voyage from the cult's hidden meeting room to the castle which so recently has served as our dwelling and base of operations. My knowledge of the organization—indeed, my integral role in it—enabled me to circumvent the castle's security with minimal effort." He reaches into his coat for a pack of smokes and offers it to Taggett and Chen and then lights them up. "Ultimately, however," he says, "I gained access merely to a courtyard emptied of all its inhabitants down to the remains of the men we had dispatched that very morning. Upon further examination, the entire edifice proved to be occupied only by eerie silence." He glances at the door of the shack sagging in its frame and says, "With the notable exception of Wing, whom I found in his office, splayed limp over his desk, bled as white as an ancient Greek statue with a pool of his miserable ichor spreading viscously over the floor."

"You got robbed," says Chen.

The older man's jaw tightens as he says, "Indeed. Fortunately, the villain's assailant evinced sufficient charity to have abandoned in his murderous haste an intimation of, if not specific identity, then perhaps allegiance to a significantly appropriate organization." He reaches back into his coat and pulls out a piece of paper thick and heavy with blood and lays it on the floor. Then as he levels an unreadable gaze right into Taggett's eyes he pulls out the flyer that they found in the weird hidden lecture hall at the end of the alley and lays that on the floor next to the blood-soaked paper so that the detective can see that the two are identical.

"Jesus," says Taggett. "The Clan of the Violet Diamond."

A corner of Jie's mouth twitches up as he inclines his head slightly. "Further, I must append an item of information that seems particularly apropos," he says. "Having despaired of my opportunity to have given Wing the justice demanded by honor, I determined next to locate Stuart and thus rejoin him and you at his bastion. However, he proved elusive. In prosecution of my resolve to discover his whereabouts, I investigated the lobby of the Prestige Hotel, where he occasionally plies one or another of his trades." He looks at Taggett, who's still staring at the documents on the floor, and then he looks at Chen, and then he says. "I saw there a woman attired completely in a black velvet dress which concealed most details of her small frame but could not dispel the effect of the thoroughly opaque veil concealing her facial features."

The younger man leaps to his feet and smashes his fist into his open hand. "I knew it!" he says. "That bitch Foulsworth!"

"Perhaps," says Jie. "I merely observed her, or, to employ a more accurate term, the figure, seem to glide across the lobby floor and enter one of the elevators." He calmly looks up at Chen and says, "One might surmise from this observation that your Mrs. Foulsworth, if indeed the eldritch character detected by me last night can be identified as that personage, makes her residence in the Prestige Hotel, a supposition that could eventuate progress in our quest to discover the nature of the forces pursuing you with such relentless persistence."

Chen's still pacing back and forth across the shack's rough floor. Taggett's still staring at the papers. Chen whirls and faces him and says, "Come on, Johnny, let's go get her! I can't wait to tear that veil off and spit in her face." He's still punching one hand with the other one.

Taggett says, "It might not be that simple." He looks up at Jie. "You never found Stuart, did you?"

"Sadly," says Jie, "My investigation of his whereabouts proved unsuccessful."

"But you found us," says Taggett. He starts to pick up the bullets and jack them back into the magazine. They click as he pushes them down into place. "So I guess you knew where Stuart was going to stash us," he says and pushes the last of the bullets into its slot. Then he jacks the full magazine into his forty-five and says, "But you just got done telling us you spent the whole night looking for Stuart." He works the forty-five's action to get a round into the chamber. "So maybe you knew where those thugs were headed with their guns," he says. His gaze shifts from the steel of the forty-five to Jie's impassive face. He says, "Anything you wanna add to the story?"

Jie looks flatly back at Taggett and says, "I had not in fact concluded my account." The water drips off the clothing in front of the stove onto the floor to make a sound like a clock counting off seconds. "However," says Jie, "I must confess a degree of difficulty has ineluctably associated itself with the task of articulating a comprehensible account of the events leading me to the circumstances of what I can only consider an extraordinarily fortunate opportunity to serve as your rescuer."

"I never thought of you as speechless," says Taggett.

Jie says, "That condition's lack of precedent in your experience should, in my opinion, serve to demonstrate the equally unprecedented nature of the events I must in some fashion describe without creating in my auditors the impression that I have taken leave of my earthly sensibilities." He takes a breath and readjusts his tie. "As I was departing the premises of the Prestige Hotel, unsatisfied in my pursuit of Stuart, I began to take the precaution of purloining a vehicle from the hotel's garage, intending to thus evade as I continued my investigation the many eyes of those thugs who had so wantonly destroyed the Silver Phantom. I had begun to manipulate the ignition wires of a conveyance when an aural experience that I could not at first identify interrupted my actions. Thinking myself in jeopardy of capture, I scanned with great alacrity the parking enclosure but could discern no source for the noise and so continued my activity, chiding myself gently for the extent of my apprehensive imagination's temporary overtaking of my senses." The older man chuckles a little as he goes on. "I had barely managed to begin again when the interruption recurred, but this iteration accompanied itself with more detail in the way of a photograph slowly developing itself into legible existence." His gaze leaves the floor and stabs right into Taggett's eyes. "It was your voice."

Taggett actually sucks in a breath as Chen says, "What the hell?"

Jie nods and says, "I must admit that I expressed a similar sentiment as I burst from the vehicle into the utter emptiness of the garage. I could not, however, deny the veracity of my senses; I had heard your whisper in my mind with a clarity that bespoke undeniable reality. I distinctly perceived your whisper saying, 'In the river. Diamond in the river.'"

"Diamond?" Taggett says and stands up and steps toward the jacket hanging in front of the little stove. He stops and turns and looks at the older man and the papers curling up on themselves on the floor.

Jie nods again. "The coincidence of my inexplicable perception of a voice indubitably yours," he says, "and the revelation of this apparent cult operating without my knowledge within a city I had thought myself intimately familiar with brought me to immediate action. I completed the process of acquiring transportation and sped directly to the quarter to which I had directed you earlier that evening. The narrow construction of those alleys, of course, necessitated an abandonment of my conveyance for the purposes of continuing on foot, and as I entered that darkness, I apprehended a vague purple glow strengthening in its intensity as I made progress toward the area most likely in my opinion to divulge your location. Initially, I attributed the glow to the neon of the low district wherein Stuart so often finds his recreation, but the steady and continuing growth of its power dissuaded me of that hypothesis, especially as it seemed to guide me past the distasteful cacophony of that area and to a motorboat loosely tied to a small dock nearby and nearly hidden by the Stygian shadows of night. Just as I apprehended that novel method of transportation, your whisper returned to fill my cranial cavity with echoes of, 'In the river. Diamond in the river.' This unsettling set of unfathomable sensory data impelled me into the motorboat, which I found myself able to start with almost suspicious ease, and my determination to follow that purple glow, along with the characteristic aural evidence of a gun battle as I approached, led me to you and Chen as you made your aquatic escape."

Through this whole speech Taggett's been running his hands over the stiffening pants and shirt and coat on the line, patting down his empty suit the way he'd pat down some creep back at the precinct. At the bottom of his jacket he stops and says, "Yeah" and curls his fingers around something hard and sharp. "I should have known," he says. As the other men watch he reaches into the jacket and seems to get his arm in up to the elbow before he pulls it back holding a silver ring with a glittering gem set into it. The air in the shack thickens and gets darker and seems to start pulsing with a purple glow that gets slowly stronger as it fades in and out. The little sounds of wood snapping in the stove and water dripping on the floor turn into indistinct whispers that seem to make cracks in the light.

"Holy hell," says Chen. "You keep it with you?"

Taggett's staring at the Violet Diamond in his palm. His lips move without speech for a second and then he looks back up at Chen and says, "I don't know. I keep trying to put it in some hotel safe and leave it for the next sucker but I always seem to keep sliding it back into my pocket." He gazes back down into his hand and narrows his eyes and curls his fingers into a fist around the ring. "And then I keep forgetting," he says as he clenches tighter. "I should probably throw the damn thing in the ocean."

The darkness starts to fade as Taggett clutches the ring harder. Chen's actually got himself backed up against the wall as far from the diamond as he can be. Jie hasn't moved. He sits there like the Lincoln Memorial in that rickety little chair and calmly says, "May I inspect this fascinating artifact?"

Taggett feels his lips pull back from his teeth for a snarl but instead he just says, "Yeah," and steps toward the older man away from the heat of the stove. "But be careful," he says once he's standing over Jie and still clutching that diamond the way a legbreaker might clutch some guy's lapel. "This thing gets in your head."

Jie nods and holds out his hand. "With respect, I must admit that I have experienced some education in the field of the occult; indeed, I may with all due humility consider myself an expert in defending myself against those who would employ dark arts," he says. "Thus, you may with a high degree of certainty rely on my caution in examination of this clearly puissant object." He's still got his hand held out with a look on his face like an accountant waiting for change at a news stand. Taggett lets out a breath and shrugs and lets the diamond drop into that steady hand.

The shack goes dark again so fast that Taggett falls over. The floor scrapes up his bare skin as he scoots back into the stiff fabric of his dried-up suit. Slowly that throbbing purple glow starts up again to show the outline of Jie clinging to his chair and shaking and writhing. "No," he keeps saying. His voice is coming from somewhere beyond his body and vibrating deep in the shack's thick air. "Must protect," Jie says. "Owner. Holder. Never abandon." Taggett can see Chen through that sick purple glow. The younger man's got his knees drawn up to his chin as he stares. Jie's mouth is stretching open as he keeps yelling. "Death! All pretenders die! Unfinished business!" The voice coming out of him sounds like it's made out of howls and barks and growls and then he's just screaming. Purple light is starting to shoot out of his eyes and mouth.

Taggett gets his feet under him and grabs blindly backwards and pulls his shirt off the line and lurches over the floor to where Jie's starting to sweat blood. He puts one hand on the older man's chest and uses the shirt to grab the diamond with the other hand. Jie falls off the chair. Taggett hurls the shirt with the diamond in it even as those whispers are creeping around his head again. The bundle bounces off the stove and falls with a soft thud to the floor. The light swells back into the shack through its little window and the sound of three men breathing hard fills the empty space where all that darkness used to be.

Taggett kneels down over Jie and runs rough hands over the older man's body. "No broken bones," he says, "but he's out." He looks over at Chen. "How are you holding up?"

Chen opens and closes his mouth once or twice and finally manages to say, "Like the Rock of Gibraltar, boss, if the Rock of Gibraltar was made out of jelly." He uses the wall to help him get to his feet and says, "What the hell?"

"I don't know," says Taggett. "First thing is we make sure Jie's all right." He glances over to the wadded-up shirt in front of the stove. "And then we can start figuring out what that crazy old broad has stumbling around in." He loosens Jie's tie and looks up at his partner. "Ready for some answers?" he says.

Chen cracks his knuckles and nods.

CHAPTER TWENTY SIX

So Taggett manages to slip the diamond back into his suit jacket as he and Chen get dressed and then Jie lets them help him back into the motorboat. Chen pulls on the motor's cord the way a dust bowl farmer might pull weeds angrily out of the earth and he floods the engine so he has to try it again. Jie slumps in the bottom of the boat once it gets started and calls directions up the river and into a few twists and turns while the river bank climbs on both sides into solid walls of ground. Finally the boat pulls in beside a rusty metal ladder and Jie says, "We have arrived."

Taggett's got a hand on his forty-five as he squints up the ladder. It goes up to a round hole in some kind of plank ceiling that juts out from the bank to block the sky that the hole at the ladder's top lets in the light from. "Just where have we arrived to?" he says. "This doesn't look like any way into the Prestige I've ever seen." He glances back at Jie and keeps his eyes narrowed and his hand near his holster.

Jie says, "Indeed not," and gracefully rises to his feet despite the swaying of the boat in the river. He starts to climb the ladder without waiting for his companions. Chen throws a look at Taggett and Taggett nods back and then the younger man starts up after Jie. The tough detective has to take his hand off his weapon so that he can grab the rough cold rungs of the ladder to climb it. That circle of brightness gets bigger as he gets closer. He slows down. He's listening for the scrape of shoes on wood or the thud of a fist into a human body or maybe even a gunshot. After a moment nothing happens. Jie's voice comes down from above. "Please allow me to assure you with all the sincerity at my admittedly modest command," it says, "that your safety and the safety of our younger colleague have always been at the forefront of each of my considerations. With that in mind, and with the added constraint connected to the short duration of the exposure my associates and I wish to endure in our perilous circumstances, I feel that I must state most emphatically my fervent hope that you can overcome the distrust to which your recent adventures have led you."

Then Chen's voice comes down through the hole and says, "Yeah, come on, Johnny. We don't want to be out in the daylight forever."

Taggett shrugs and nods to himself and pulls his body up the last few rungs until his head is sticking out of the hole. Still on the ladder, he looks around at Jie and Chen and a few tough-looking Chinese guys and then levers himself the rest of the way up until he's standing on a wooden deck and then hustling along with this crowd toward an old Ford that looks like someone picked it up and crumpled it into a jagged ball of metal and then straightened it out a bit and not too gently put it back down again. Chen lets out a whistle and says, "I see you've arranged for us to keep riding in style, Jie. Are those bullet holes in the side just decoration, or does this flivver just need a lot of ventilation?"

Jie makes a noise that's either a low chuckle or a discreet cough. "Indeed. I must admit to having taken the liberty of procuring a mode of transportation less ostentatious and thus indicative of our presence than the Silver Phantom has proven to be." He keeps explaining as the three of them shove into the back seat of the beat-up little heap and a couple of the tough guys pack themselves into the front. "I have instructed these men," he says, "to convey us to a destination suitable to our purposes of concealment from which we may in more comfort than such afforded by a swampland shack design a plan of action through which we might not only survive the gang war occasioned by Wing's abrupt disappearance but also discover solutions to the bizarre set of difficulties that has vexed you with such persistence."

Wedged between Johnny and Jie Chen says, "Why don't we just take all this muscle to the Prestige Hotel and hold that frail witch down until she squeals out some answers?" He manages to crack his knuckles as the heap clatters its way into narrower and darker alleys.

Taggett turns his head away from the window and says, "That won't work." He takes the cigarette that Jie's offering across Chen and lights up and squints away from the smoke. "That old bird's tougher than you think, maybe tougher than me. I don't think any five of us could dish out anything she hasn't taken already," he says. The driver rolls down his window to let the smoke out of the car. Taggett grunts and says, "Your Skid Row looks a lot different in the daylight."

"The denizens of these quarters generally restrict their activities to the nocturnal hours," says Jie. He offers Chen a smoke and the younger man lights up. The goon in the passenger seat rolls down his window. "Thus, these preprandial moments take on a tranquility that can only by contrast amplify the orgiastic frenzies that accompany the setting of the sun."

The car makes a turn and Taggett catches himself in a yawn and says, "That's any minute now, I think."

Chen says, "You got that right," and gives up a big yawn of his own. "Crazy how riding around in a boats and cars all day can take it out of you." He finishes his smoke and flicks the butt out the open window past the goon in the passenger seat. The goon doesn't flinch as the car makes another few turns deeper into that network of alleys. "I see what you mean about the Silver Phantom," Chen says. "Driving a fancy number like that around here would be like waving a flag. Thanks for looking out for us, Jie."

Next to him the older man blinks and swallows and says, "The pleasure of accompanying you on your adventures completely obviates the compensation of such gratitude, however warmly received." Taggett rolls down his window and flicks out the end of his smoke. The car slows to a stop so close to the grey three-story pile of bricks next to it that Jie and the passenger goon can't open the doors. The driver and Taggett let the rest of them out and they all stand there in the alley watching the shadows get longer for a minute or two.

Finally Chen says, "All right, I give. What's the gimmick?" He glances around the empty space as the lowering sun flashes off the commuter traffic scurrying past one end of the alley a few buildings away. The alley's other end is already closing down into shadows. "Are we just gonna camp here like a bunch of hoboes?"

Taggett snorts a chuckle and points back to the car and the ladder it's parked under that ends about six feet above the roof. "Jie's got us sneaking up the back of a flophouse," he says. "We just climb up that fire escape and one of these guys drives the car away and then we're in a room no one saw us walk into." Jie smiles and gives Taggett a little bow. Taggett nods back and says, "All right then, let's get on with it." He steps onto the hood of the car and then onto the roof and then pulls himself up to the ladder and climbs up three floors to its end at a little balcony in front of a window. The window opens into a hallway with flaking wooden doors interrupting the peeling wallpaper on either side. Taggett steps into the hall and waits for the other two. Soon enough they show up and Jie shepherds them in through one of those flimsy doors to a little room with a cot on the floor and a bed next to the cot and a chamber pot under the bed. The three of them stand there crowding the furniture until Taggett says, "I guess this'll do. Thanks, Jie."

Jie bows and says, "I take pleasure in such services as I find it within my power to provide." He glances around the squalid little room as dust motes swirl in the rectangular slant of light the setting sun is pushing through the grime frosting the window. "The accommodations provided by this establishment, despite their clearly Spartan nature, should allow us at least a night's rest and a base from which we might formulate a plan of action against your Mrs. Foulsworth."

Taggett's already on the bed with his hat over his eyes. "Yeah," he says. "Depending on whether that's who we're up against." His voice is starting to slow and blur a little as he keeps thinking out loud. "Might be One-Eye's trying to mess around with our minds, maybe this weird cult is trying to get the Violet Diamond out of me, or some kind of drug thing," he says. The tough detective's body shifts as he slowly sinks into the creaking of the ropes stretched across the bed frame to hold up the greasy mat he's on. "Just need to get my hands on someone," he mumbles, and then he's just snoring.

Jie's mouth curls up into a smile as he glances over at the cot where Chen's passed out and twitching a little. The sun's gone past the window and the room's filling up with shadows creeping over the sleeping bodies to cover them with imaginary blankets. "Rest well, my friends," he murmurs. "Tomorrow we face our opposition, the better to vanquish it." He steps through the door and closes it and tries the knob. It's locked. The older man turns and unlocks the door across the hall from Taggett's and steps in and closes it behind him as the evening blooms into night.

Some time later Jie's eyes open into darkness. The thick air in his crappy little room is clinging to every inch of his skin as he unfolds his legs from their lotus position and sniffs almost silently. Nothing's on fire. He places his feet in their thick black socks carefully onto the floor and rises from the chair and stands absolutely still for one entire minute. The tinny blare of jazz a few miles away creeps through the cracks in the flophouse's walls just beyond the range of most ears. Jie listens to it for another thirty seconds and then glides over the floor to the door of his room. With his hand on the knob he freezes again.

He turns the knob slowly but pulls the door open fast so that it just gives out a sharp creak that might be a cricket letting out a chirp and then he stands there looking into the deeper darkness of the hallway. He can't hear anyone breathing and the window at the end of the hall isn't letting in a draft from outside. After another moment he takes two big steps to cross the hall and plaster himself against the door of Taggett's room. With his ear against the door he can hear the two detectives in there snoring and grunting a little as they fight with their dreams. He wraps his hand around the doorknob and twists. Still locked. His throat gets tight as he swallows a growl. He steps back from the door into the center of the hall and lets his hands open and drift at about the level of his waist. His knees bend sharply as he creeps down the hall and avoids the creaky patches as he approaches the black rectangle that opens into the stairwell.

After another minute of waiting at the top of the stairs he starts down and drops silently to a crouch when he gets to the second-floor landing. He peers down the length of a hall just as dark as the one upstairs. The air's just as still. The window at the far end hasn't been opened and there's no one lurking in the shadows and breathing. Jie stays low as he steps into the rest of the stairwell toward the lobby on the ground floor.

The steps end in a doorway that frames a big room dotted with some random couches and chairs. Jie can see their dark shapes in the light that flickers and buzzes out of a breaking-down lamp on the desk against the building's back wall and to Jie's right. Behind the desk a withered old guy slumps in a chair with his feet up. Behind the guy a rack of keys glistens weakly in that flicker the way a warning sign might ghost in and out of vision through a midnight thunderstorm. Jie slips into the room along the wall from shadow to shadow until he makes it around to the desk and starts to reach past the scrawny senior citizen for the key to Taggett's room and then quits moving before his hand can get quite to the key rack as he looks down at the dried-up old night desk man. The guy isn't sleeping. He's not breathing and a slow drop of blood oozes out of his nose to thicken the line across his cheek and make a tiny splash on the floor as it hits the puddle that's collected there under the cooling body. Jie stifles a gasp. The antique bulb in the desk lamp flares white and pops and then the room is nothing but darkness and silence.

At the pop of the bulb Jie's ducked behind the desk. He stays there for a straight minute and a half of not breathing to listen for what else might be in the room. Then a cracked voice that might be coming from a very old woman or from a radio not quite on the right station says, "Come now, boy. Had I desired your end, I could have accomplished it as easily as I had that silly clerk's. My purpose here is merely conversation."

Jie straightens up and moves silently away from the desk before he says, "Mrs. Foulsworth, I presume."

"The same." Her voice comes back from a new spot in the room even though Jie didn't hear the movement. "And you are Jie, the elder henchman of that insufferable Johnny Taggett."

Jie says, "I have the good fortune to be associated with that worthy gentleman, yes," as he keeps drifting around in the dark. His extended hand brushes the wood of an invisible chair. "Indeed, I might be so bold as to claim friendship," he says, "with such an illustrious personage."

The voice makes a sound like a dry mockery of laughter from somewhere a little bit closer. "Boy, you might be so bold indeed," it says. "To claim true friendship with a white man, even one as debased as Johnny Taggett, demonstrates how far above your station you reach." Jie keeps moving away from the voice until it stops and he freezes again. "Nevertheless," it goes on, "I have a use for you, hence this conversation." The scrape of a chair leg over the floor sends Jie hopping in the other direction and almost bumping into a couch himself. His hands sink for a second into a cushion and then he pushes himself back up and freezes again. A thick moment crawls past in the silence. A hint of perfume drifts into Jie's nose with a corrupt scent of decaying jungle flowers. He flinches. That weird laugh comes again a little closer still.

He's moving away again as he says, "And of what activity might this potential employment consist," and then drops to all fours to scuttle away from the sound of his own voice. His hands find the back of another sofa and brace against the rough fabric as he crouches to keep listening.

That buzz of a laugh comes from where Jie was standing a second ago. "What an ostentatious vocabulary," says the voice, "for a savage. You jumped-up animals try so hard to stand on your hind legs and impress the real people, but you must know that you cannot fool your superiors." Jie keeps scrambling away as the voice drones on. He's staying on all fours and aiming for the nearest wall but the darkness has expanded the room to trick him. He bumps into a chair and throws himself away from the sound and then freezes up again. The voice stops for a second and then starts again in the neighborhood of that chair. "However, I cannot ignore the influence you have over that miserable detective," it says as it seems to get closer. It tells him, "You may be aware that he stubbornly insists on clinging to a property he does not in fact own, and I will have that property returned to me." As the voice advances on Jie he skitters back from it. "You will exert your influence over your master to achieve this goal," it says. Finally his back hits a wall and he slides along toward where the stairwell door should be. He extends a hand to grope for that emptiness. "In return I will allow you to continue your business without molestation from the authorities or your rivals," says the voice. It's echoing flatly back from the same wall Jie's pushing himself along. "Consider if you can in the depths of your pitiful native mind the benefits of obedience to your betters," the voice states flatly, "and the penalty for resistance."

The outstretched fingers finally curve around the edge of the doorway that frames the stairwell. He pulls himself into the recess and starts to creep back up the stairs without saying a word. Behind him he can vaguely hear, "I look forward to our next meeting and the results you bring me," and then a door opening and closing. As he's eventually inching along the third-floor hallways a drop of sweat hits the floor with a soft wet smack.

CHAPTER TWENTY SEVEN

Taggett's on his feet in that crappy little room clutching his forty-five and listening to some kind of crashing and banging from across the hall. Behind him in the bed the blonde rolls over and lets out a little disappointed kitten noise. "Come back to me, Johnny," she says. "That's not your problem out there." He looks back and there she is pouting back up at him with those lips and fluttering her eyelashes over those clear blue eyes. She says, "You've got better things to do over here," and moves her body in a way that almost turns him the rest of the way around. Then she lets out a sigh that finishes the job. The moonlight drifting in through the window silvers her curves and catches the little beads of sweat on her skin to give her the sparkle of a jewel as she lets her hands caress over the warmth of that half-shadowed body of hers. "Let it go," she says.

A thump and a grunt of pain from the other side of the door he's turned his back on almost make him flinch but her eyes are already pulling him forward the way a baited fish hook pulls a fish. He takes a shuffling step toward the bed. The softness of the carpet on the floor makes him stumble a little as he keeps falling forward and catching himself and getting closer to her. His fingers open and the forty-five barely makes a sound as it hits that lush softness that seems to be up to his ankles by now. She's propped herself up on the headboard to watch him drag himself closer. She's still trailing her hands over those luscious curves as he drops to his knees. "Yes," she says.

From back there behind the door someone yells his name. That makes him blink and force himself back to his feet. "What the hell," he says. "Who are you? Where the hell did you come from?" Her eyes go from blue to black as her face turns to ice. Someone back there starts screaming his name. "What the hell are you trying to do to me?" he says. The moonlight fades out of the room but she's still glowing somehow as she starts to hiss. The screaming of his name from outside gets louder as she coils to strike and he wakes up in a pitch-dark flophouse in Tsingtao.

Chen's kneeling next to the bed whispering his name in his ear. The blackness of the shabby room fades in around him as he grabs at his holster for his forty-five. It's right there where it should be and that lets him notice the rest of the noise from beyond the room's door. Someone out there is smashing a room to bits. Chen says, "Where's Jie?"

"Holy hell," says Taggett and starts to throw himself out of the bed when the racket shuts itself off abruptly as a radio when you tear the plug out of the wall. The two detectives look at each other across the bed in the sudden silence. Nothing happens for a moment. Taggett's keeping a hand on his forty-five and Chen's coiling back into himself the way he does before he starts breaking bodies. Another moment oozes past in the heavy silence. Taggett nods at Chen and the two of them take a step forward and then a new sound comes through the door and turns them into statues.

A voice that might come from an ancient rich woman or a badly tuned receiver bellows, "Incompetents! Just as I might have expected from such a race of monkeys!" Another voice mumbles something in Chinese. "Speak English!" comes the reply. "I have no patience for your gibbering. What excuse do you intend to present for your utter failure to locate my property?" The mumble comes through again in such a heavy accent it might as well still be Chinese. It lasts maybe half a sentence before the first voice cuts it off again. "And you found no sign of where that abominable Taggett could have gone to? No hint of my diamond?" it says.

Only Taggett's free hand spread out on Chen's chest is keeping the younger man from leaping through the door. The older detective grunts a little with the strain as he's reaching across the bed to hold back his partner. He takes his other hand off his forty-five to hold a finger to his lips. "We don't know how big a mob she's got," he whispers. Chen grits his teeth and nods slowly and lets his body relax a little.

That mumbling's been going on all this time and it's finally gotten loud enough for the two of them to recognize words. "So sorry," it's saying. "This Jie, he too smart, too careful. He hide too good."

"Perhaps, then, I should have employed his services in preference to yours," says that weird voice. "Aside from his pretensions to a race he cannot attain, he certainly outranks apes such as you in terms of cognition." Something made of glass shatters beyond the door and the voice says, "Clearly it is time that I relieve myself of the burden your so-called assistance presents." The mumble gets louder and lapses back into Chinese. "Damn you!" The voice bellows. "Plead for your useless life in English!" The mumbler's too busy screaming now to follow orders and then he suddenly stops and then there's the sound you hear in a butcher shop when the steak slaps onto the counter. A door squeaks open across the hall and slams shut on a noise that almost makes it to a shriek before it collapses into a wet gurgle. For a while there's some kind of crunching and cracking along with a mechanical buzz that might also be a wild animal growling deep in its throat. That stops and the door opens again. In the silence following that ghastly noise the detectives can hear muffled footsteps grazing over the floor of the hall the way clots of dirt might faintly hit a coffin lid. The top step of the stairs lets out a creak. Taggett and Chen let out the breath they've been holding all this time.

After another moment Taggett gives Chen a nod and they step toward the door and Chen reaches out to put his hand on the knob. Taggett pulls out his forty-five and gives Chen another nod and aims the weapon forward as Chen turns the knob. The door flings open and Taggett's finger tenses and then stops. Little smeared streaks of moonlight through the fire escape window show an empty hall and Jie's door hanging open to frame a deeper darkness. The older detective takes a step and leans down to whisper in Chen's ear, "Ready?" Chen nods and Johnny takes another step out through the door and a quick one to the side to get his back against the wall. After a second Chen slips into a position on the other side of the door. Nothing comes out of Jie's room at them as they stand there taking quiet shallow breaths and then Chen rolls across the hall and slams Jie's door the rest of the way open as he tumbles into the room. Taggett looks up and down the hall for reaction to all this noise. Nothing happens. The tough detective cocks his forty-five and steps into Jie's room and closes the door and turns on a light and can't keep himself from muttering, "Hell."

The bed's leaning up against the wall opposite the door. The window's smashed open and letting in the stink of the city to mingle with the stink of the crime scene they've stepped into. Jagged fragments of a chair lie on the floor along with the corpses of a couple of thugs pulled apart the same way the chair was. One of the bodies has a head. The other head's rolled into a corner where it would stare up at the ceiling if it still had eyes. Chen's looking back down at it while Taggett steps around the puddles of blood and little piles of meat to get to the wrecked bed and bend over to peer into the shadow behind it. Chen pulls out a smoke and lights up and says, "Where's Jie?"

Taggett straightens up and shrugs. "I've got a better question," he says. "Where's everyone else? All that racket should've brought a bigger crowd in here than just us." He slides his forty-five back into its holster and looks around at the mess and lights up a smoke of his own.

Chen says, "You think she killed everyone in the building?" He cracks his knuckles and leans toward the window to suck in a breath. "Jesus, I knew she was crazy but I didn't know she was trying for some kind of prize," he says.

Taggett shakes his head and says, "No, that doesn't make sense. Why would she leave just before she gets to us?" He steps away from the bed and slips a little on a dead goon's severed hand and says, "We need to check this place out, see what Jie's got us into here." Chen nods and pulls the door back open without turning the light off. The two of them step out into the yellow rectangle the light makes on the floor. Taggett glances up the hall at the fire escape window to see the sky between buildings turning grey as the sun teases its way into view. He takes a couple of steps in that direction until he's in front of the door next to Jie's and then he looks back down the hall at Chen in front of the door on the other side of the wide stripe of light. The two of them nod at each other and kick both doors in. Taggett pulls out his forty-five as he's diving through the door he's just opened and rolls and comes up in a room full of nothing but shadows and the smell of old beer and dried sweat. He presses on the bed with his free hand. The sheet's so stiff it almost cracks. "Damn," he says to himself and puts his forty-five away again and steps back out into the hall. Chen's coming out of the room on the other side of Jie's. He catches Taggett's eye and shakes his head. "Weird," says Taggett.

"Where's Jie?" says Chen.

Taggett shrugs and says, "I guess we better start looking for him."

So they spend the next few hours breaking into every room in the building. The dead guy they find in the lobby is the only other person they see in all that time. One of the rooms has a pile of canned pork and beans from the War on its bed and another of the rooms has one of those "Clan of the Violet Diamond" flyers in it. Finding that flyer makes Taggett tear the room apart the way those goons demolished Jie's but he doesn't find anything else. By the time they get to the dead guy in the lobby the morning sun's blasting light all over the place. Jie's nowhere.

The two of them stand there for a moment across from each other over the body. Chen's black turtleneck is smeared with dust and Taggett's got a rip in the shoulder of his jacket. Both of them are blinking and swaying a little. Finally Taggett bends down to take the corpse out of its chair and lay it on the floor. He grunts a little as he works to unbend the stiff so that it's lying flat. Chen's moved over to the flophouse's front door to make sure it's locked tight. Once they're done with their jobs they find their way to a couch in the middle of the lobby and sink into it. Chen says, "What now?"

"I've been thinking about that," says Taggett as he lights up a couple of smokes and hands one to Chen. "I figure this is the one building in Shanghai that whatever's after us won't look for us in."

Chen cracks his knuckles and says, "You mean that Mrs. Foulsworth." He jumps up from the sofa and paces around the floor for a minute and then stops to face Taggett. "You heard that voice," he says. "You saw that mess she left. Who else does that?"

Taggett looks up at his partner and takes another drag off his smoke and says, "I know what I heard. And you know as well as I do anyone can leave a mess like that." He smirks. "I think we've left a few of our own. But that's not the point." He glances around the room at the way the light that shafts in from the windows flanking the door makes such deep shadows out of the furniture. "Whether it's Foulsworth or One-Eye pretending he's Foulsworth or some kind of weird cult figurehead it doesn't know we're here," he says.

"How do you know?" says Chen.

"Because we'd be dead," says Taggett. "This whatever that's after us did that stuff upstairs with its bare hands." He taps out his ash on the floor. "Worse," he says, "without Jie we've got no friends in this town." Chen's started wandering around the lobby the way a panther does in a cage. Taggett keeps talking. "We don't even speak the language. Outside that door might as well be the moon as far as living through it goes." He finishes his smoke and drops the butt on the floor and grinds it out.

Chen's made it all the way over to the desk with the dead guy behind it when he stops and turns and says across the room, "So what do we do? I'm so sick of just getting pushed around like a chess piece." He punches one fist into his other hand. "I don't even care what's pushing me, I just want to do something about it." His voice gets a little strained as he slams that fist down on the desk. "What the hell do we do?"

Taggett says, "We wait." He gets up and steps through those thick bands of shadow to get to his partner at the desk. "Jie set us up in this place with no one in it," he says. "No one knows we're here. We've got enough smokes and food for at least a couple of days." He puts a hand on Chen's shoulder and looks him right in the eye and says, "We can afford to figure out what he's got in mind." The younger man clenches his jaw and nods.

So the two of them drag the corpse in the lobby up to the third floor and throw it in the room with the rest of the carnage. Taggett wrestles the mattress over to cover the window and try to keep some of the stink from getting out into the street and then the two of them move down to the second floor and shift from room to room. After that time blurs. They wake up and fall asleep and wake up again and eat canned franks and beans with their fingers and fall asleep again. After the first couple of days or so they stop talking. Chen gets into the habit of tracing the walls of the lobby in short careful steps as if he's measuring a tomb for occupancy. Taggett spends the daylight staring out the fire escape window on the second floor at the alley and the traffic beyond. He doesn't see anyone lurking out there but he doesn't stop looking.

After a while the sound of a motor pulls him out of some weird kind of blank dream where he's thrashing around in a big bowl of oatmeal into the darkness of a room on the second floor. He rolls out of bed and grabs his forty-five and takes a position just to the right of the front door and waits while the motor gets louder and closer and stops. Something metallic rattles for a split second and then a board creaks out in the hall. Taggett sucks in a breath and pulls back the hammer of his forty-five. He can hear his pulse pushing against the inside of his skull.

"Mr. Taggett. Mr. Chen." The voice of Jie drifts quietly through the door with the polite elegance of a highly accomplished butler. "Please accept my sincerest apologies for the abrupt nature both of my absence and of this reappearance." Taggett puts away his forty-five and opens the door to see his older friend standing in the middle of the hallway. Chen's framed in a door that opens across the hall. Jie says, "Gentlemen, I must encourage you both to proceed with all the dispatch at your command. We have urgent business." The two detectives join him and then the three of them clamber down the fire escape to the street. Jie says, "Have the two of you sufficiently prepared yourselves?"

Taggett says, "I guess we'll find out."

CHAPTER TWENTY EIGHT

The roads go to hell once you get out of the city. That beat-up Ford jalopy is rattling along a barely smoothed-out patch between fields and jolting through the holes it can't swerve around. Chen's grappling with the wheel and the gear shift and grinning wild. "Damn," he says, "I can't remember the last time I got to drive." The wind whistles through the bullet holes in the doors as he mashes down on the pedal and the car smashes through another set of ruts and grooves on its way further out into the country. "Where are we going, anyways?" the young detective says.

In the passenger seat next to him Jie says nothing. The breath flows calmly from his nose and back in through his loosely-closed lips as he meditates with the blank look of someone waiting patiently for an appointment with an accountant. He hasn't made a peep since he handed the Ford's key to Chen back in the city and said, "I have arranged sanctuary in a more bucolic setting, to which I shall rely on your talents as a chauffeur for transportation," and listed the rights and lefts to get them onto the road out of Tsingtao. As the car hits a bump that nearly bounces him through the heap's excuse for ceiling the older man keeps breathing and not saying anything.

From the back seat Taggett lets out a low growl and tries to shift his body to a different stress position. The car that was big enough a week ago for him and Chen and Jie and two goons got smaller when he dropped from the fire escape ladder onto its roof and crushed it a little so he's had to wedge himself in and hope that Chen doesn't smash into anything. The way out of Tsingtao didn't cause a lot of trouble but this country lane has turned the whole car into some kind of exotic torture device as it slams the tough detective around from one hard metal surface to another as if it's trying to powder his bones inside his skin. The landscape blurs for a while as he slips into some kind of trance. The weird silence of that flophouse in his memory almost blots out the sputtering noise of the coughing motor and the creaks of the car's frame and the smell of the corpses starting to turn still hovers in a cloud around his head. He just keeps staring out the blasted-out back side window at the flat green and blue color blocks of fields and sky streaking past. The jalopy swerves around one big hole in the ground only to bounce into and out of another. Taggett's head hits the ceiling and he curses again.

All this goes on as the sun gets higher in the sky until around the middle of the day Chen says, "I gotta piss" and pulls the car into the shade of some kind of ruined shack growing like a mushroom out here in the middle of nowhere. He gets out and yawns and stretches and looks at the sky and then back along the way they came. "I'd say we're making good time," he says, "if I had any idea what we're doing."

Jie's voice floats out of the passenger side window to say, "Perhaps you will allow me to offer my sincere apologies for having generated the tenebrous state of ignorance from which you currently suffer." He shoves the door open and rises from the car into the quiet this far outside the city. "An overabundance of caution has necessitated my discretion with the intent of defraying our inevitable pursuit by obfuscating our destination," he says and glides over the bending grass to water the other side of the shack.

"Damn, I thought I was figuring him out," says Chen as he starts to unbutton his fly and step to his own side of the little abandoned building. A yell from the car stops him.

From where he's jammed behind the front seats Taggett's hollering, "Let me the hell out of here!" Chen turns back to the car and tugs the door open and folds down the driver's seat in front to let the tough detective clamber out and fall to his knees in the soft earth. "I don't know how much more of that back seat I can take," the tough detective says.

Chen snickers and says, "Not my fault you don't look like you belong here, boss." He turns around and starts to water the shack in front of him. Over his shoulder he says, "Two Oriental guys driving around some little country burg won't pull a lot of attention, but an Oriental and a big white guy like you." He chuckles. "That'd get the whole jungle hotline going off like a fire alarm."

"Yeah, yeah," says Taggett as he pulls himself to his feet and then does a few knee bends. "Just because you're right doesn't mean I have to like it." He limps out into the middle of what they've been calling a road and looks back toward the boxy profile of the city in the distance. "Looks like we're ahead of them so far," he says.

Chen says, "Yeah," as he shakes himself off and puts himself away. As he wipes a hand on his pants he moves to join Johnny and says, "I guess whatever Jie's talking about is working."

"So far," says Taggett. He pulls a wrinkled pack of smokes from his pocket and hands one to Chen and lights up. The two of them stand there for a moment as the noise of insects and breeze fades back in and then Taggett says, "I can't believe how tired I am."

The younger man reaches up to pat Taggett on the shoulder. "Yeah," he says. "I get it."

A discreet throat-clearing comes from much closer than you'd expect. They spin to face it and there's Jie smiling serenely at them. "Gentlemen," he says, "although my confidence in the wisdom of my stratagem remains unabated, I have no desire to underestimate the tenacity of the forces from which we flee. Thus, perhaps I may suggest that we continue our flight in the most efficacious manner available to us."

To Chen's puzzled look Taggett says, "He says they're still chasing us and we should get going."

"Sure," says Chen. "You know, one of these days I'm gonna eat a dictionary so I can keep up with you geniuses." He chuckles and goes back to the car to wrestle open the door and fold down the seat for his partner.

The tough detective drops the last of his smoke into the packed dirt of the road and looks around and sighs and walks over to the car. As he crams his big body back into the little space he says, "I'm gonna have dreams about this car ride."

Chen pushes the back of the seat back into position and says, "I think we're better off not dreaming for a while." He's not chuckling at all as he gets into the car and slams the door shut. Jie's in front of the car giving the crank some hard turns until the engine comes to life with the sound of a tuberculosis patient waking up in the middle of the night. The older man gets into the passenger seat and gets that blank look on his face as Chen yanks the gear shift and works the pedals. The heap's wheels spin to kick up little bits of the road before the tires catch and the old jalopy shoots forward. Before too long Chen's grinning again. Taggett jams one foot against a vibrating metal surface and his shoulder against another so that he doesn't get bounced around too much and then he just fades into the blur of half-seen landscape and the drone of the motor.

When a hitch in that drone pulls him out of it the shadows have gotten longer and the road's getting smoother. The engine hacks again and the car has a spasm that shoves Taggett's face into the back of the driver's seat and Chen says, "I think we're running out of gas."

"Fortunately," says Jie, "I can claim to have anticipated such an occurrence and thus, I hope, to have ameliorated its intensity. Perhaps you will have ascertained the fueling station to our left as we approach it." The old heap is rattling along a thinly paved stretch of the road and getting close to an old barn that someone painted green and installed some gas pumps in front of. Wires for electricity and telephone stretch from the barn's roof to the poles that have started to sprout by the roadside. A sign on the barn says something in Chinese. As Chen's guiding the car to a shaky stop alongside the pump Jie says, "With your permission, I shall assume the role of interlocutor between our party and the proprietor of this establishment."

In the silence that follows as Chen turns off the engine and just sits there goggling at the older man Taggett says, "He means he'll do the talking."

"Makes sense," Chen says. "I don't think too many of the bumpkins out here talk much English, and I sure don't speak bumpkin." A door opens in the front of the barn and a little man starts walking toward the car and leaving dainty footprints in the crusty soil. Chen puts on the bored scowl of your standard goon. Taggett pulls his hat down over his face and tries to act like a load of old laundry.

The little guy makes it to the driver's side of the old heap. His scrawny face has a grin plastered on it so convincingly that it looks like a cardboard cutout of a crescent moon hanging by its points from his cheekbones. He says something in Chinese to Chen and Chen jerks his head to point over at Jie. The older man turns to stare across Chen for a moment at the little guy in the green jumpsuit until the guy walks around the car to stand at the passenger side. Then Jie rolls down his window and says something in Chinese and hands the guy a little stack of coins. That grin gets even happier as the guy trots back around to unhook the nozzle from the pump and feed it into the Ford's tank. Taggett can't tell whether the guy can see him wedged into the back seat. The pump rings a little bell and the guy pulls the nozzle back out of the Ford and hangs it up. Then he wipes off the windshield and trots back around to get another couple of coins from Jie and another brief conversation. Then the little guy gives the crank a few hard turns and the motor kicks in and Chen steers the jalopy back onto the road. After a second the young detective says, "Oh hell."

"What?" says Taggett.

Chen says, "Might be nothing, but that weaselly character just broke into a sprint to get back to his barn." He pauses for a minute to work the clutch and the gear shift and get the heap moving a little faster. "You saw that phone wire, right?"

Taggett says, "Yeah," and squirms around in that little space to get his hand up to his holster and grab his forty-five. He says, "Jie, where do you think he's calling?"

Jie's got his sleeves rolled up and even as the jalopy's bouncing all over the place he's steadily sliding flat knives into the spring-loaded scabbards on his wrists. "The necessarily limited knowledge in my possession suggests that my intended resort, a small city of my acquaintance located some miles ahead of our present position, has been infiltrated not only by telephonic technology but also by the forces of our adversaries," he calmly replies as he rolls his sleeves back down. "Alternately," he continues, "the functionary at the refueling station, having identified us as outsiders with money, may be working to alert bandits in that same small city of the prospect of oncoming prey."

Taggett barks out a laugh and says, "So either way we're driving into an ambush. Great." He manages to writhe around so he's on his knees looking out through the heap's narrow slit of a back window. "Oh, come on," he says. "This is just too damn much." The green barn's shrinking as they get away from it but a line of cars is closing that distance. Light from the afternoon sun ricochets from the purple coupe in front as the roar from all those engines slips into the jalopy and bounces around the walls. Taggett groans a little and says, "I thought we got rid of those creeps back at the leprosy hospital."

Jie says, "Persistence stands as the watchword of the truly successful criminal enterprise. Just as does the fabled Hydra, forces such as those we fly from earn their immortality through the easy replacement of constituent organs." The older man lets his palms rest on his thighs and looks forward through the windshield the way you might look at a movie you're just watching to keep out of the rain.

"Yeah," says Taggett. "You can always get new thugs." He cocks his forty-five and aims through the back of the Ford. "Too bad these won't last long." Chen yanks the wheel to get around a big pothole and Taggett almost falls over and yells, "Jesus! Slow down so I can get a bead!"

Chen shouts back, "No way!" He swerves the car around another hole and keeps hollering, "I'm not stopping this heap till we get where we're ditch these creeps!" The sides of the road have started to grow buildings. Little roadside shacks like tumors bulge out of the ground. Their doors fly open and guys with pitchforks spill out screaming as the Ford shoots past. "And I don't like the looks of the local welcome wagon ladies," Chen says.

Taggett squeezes off a shot but the coupes chasing them are still out of range. A rock someone threw from the roadside bounces off the door next to Jie. "The probability of attaining our goal seems to recede with the unavoidable resistance we appear to be approaching intensifies," says the older man. "Confrontation, perhaps with lethal consequences, presents itself as an inevitability." The buildings racing along beside them are getting bigger and side streets are starting to branch out into the city as it grows around them. Chen yanks the wheel and makes a right and swerves around a fruit vendor pushing a cart across the darkening street and then takes the next left.

Taggett lets out a breath. He uncocks the forty-five and keeps watching through the back at the empty street stretching behind the car that keeps roaring forward. "Looks like you ditched those," he says and then has to swallow the rest of the sentence as that purple coupe squeals around the corner. Taggett swears and cocks the forty-five again and pulls another shot that he can see make a spark as the bullet bounces off the coupe's fender. Then Chen takes another right and another right and a left and a left and a left. The jalopy shakes and rattles as he pushes it to its limit and gets deeper into this little city. The line of coupes keeps following the way greyhounds at the track chase that mechanical rabbit. Chen's almost standing on the accelerator. The car shoots across the main highway and makes another left and a right and a right and doesn't lose the tail. Taggett takes a shot that smashes the purple coupe's headlight and then he ducks as a shot from the coupe rings off the back of the car just above that little slit of a window. Chen wrestles with the wheel and the tires scream as they grab the road. He throws the car into another right and aims it back at the highway and skids left when he reaches it. Taggett throws another shot that smashes the coupe's windshield on the passenger side.

"Brace yourself!" Chen yells. "Something in the road!" Taggett throws a hand behind him as he blasts out one more shot that punches through the coupe's windshield on the driver's side and into the driver's forehead. The coupe jerks around to hit a rut in the road and spin itself onto its ceiling and block the thugs behind it. Taggett falls back as his hand presses hard into the back of the seat behind him. The jalopy's tires make shrieks like you'd hear from a woman getting her hair torn out as the heap shudders to a stop. The tough detective twists his body around.

A wall of junk is stretched across the road in front of the still shaking jalopy. The sun behind the tractors glows red as little sparks of light glint off the piles of old tractor parts and barbed wire and scythe blades spread over the flattened-out highway. Behind the garbage stand five men silhouetted with their rifles in the bloody dying sunlight. Behind him Taggett hears car doors open. The shadowy bandits behind their barricade raise their guns.

Chen says, "I guess we made it to the party," as the jalopy's engine cuts off. The thickening dusk fills itself with the mechanical clicks of cocking weapons. Chen cracks his knuckles and snorts a little laugh and says, "Shall we dance?"

"Yeah," says Taggett. "Let's get this over with."

CHAPTER TWENTY NINE

The headlights from the coupes behind them throw a big shadow on the mounds of trash blocking the road in front of them. Taggett hears a bunch of car doors slamming as goons get out and start to click heels over the pavement toward the old jalopy. At the same time figures are coming out from behind the barricade carrying pitchforks and looking like skeletons that don't know they're dead because they're too hungry. Taggett takes a peek through the slit of a rear window and says, "They're throwing a whole army at us."

From the front seat Chen says, "Yeah, these bumpkins in front of us look ready for an army. I don't know whether they want to fight these guys or eat them." The raggedy crowd of villagers doesn't give out a sound as those dozens of bare feet hit the pavement. The creeps coming up from the back are coughing and whispering and making all kinds of nervous little noises. "Or maybe we're the ones on the menu," Chen says as both groups get closer.

"I think I have an idea," Taggett says and pulls out his forty-five. "Get ready to dive." He uses his gunsight to find the nearest coupe's gas tank and squeezes the trigger to send a bullet through the metal and make the spark that turns the little car into a big ball of fire. Some of the creeps spin around to stare at the explosion while the rest of them hit the ground and Chen and Jie fling open their doors and spill out of the jalopy. The freaks with the pitchforks don't move. Taggett puts another bullet into another coupe and makes another fireball while

Chen yanks down the driver's seat to let him roll out onto the pavement. The two of them skin their hands and knees crawling to the side of the road and into the darkness of the shadows the burning cars are tattering over the ground.

One of the leathery villagers raises his pitchfork and yells something at the gangsters who are just now rising to their feet and turning away from the fires to hunt for the men they've been chasing. A few seconds of silence pass and then the guy yells it again. One of the gangsters wheels around and yells something back and raises a pistol and shoots the villager in the head. The clap of the shot echoes away toward the little town starting to tuck itself into bed while the body hitting the ground makes that usual wet thud and the car fires crackle. For a lingering moment no one moves. Then three of the guys with pitchforks drop to their knees to reveal three guys with rifles cocked and already swinging to point at the crowd of goons. Thunder comes out of the barrels and three creeps go down and the guys with pitchforks yell and charge.

Taggett tears his eyes away from this just in time to see Chen looking back at him. They nod at each other and start running up the highway toward the coupes. He throws a glance across the road through the knot of bodies getting stabbed and shot to see that Jie's got the same idea. The three of them get to one of the two-seaters behind the dying fires. They stand around it for a second while the battle rages until Jie says, "This bellicose distraction cannot maintain itself indefinitely. For that reason I propose that I leave this conveyance to the two of you to create an opportunity for your swiftest and most efficacious withdrawal from this increasingly hazardous circumstance." He ducks as a stray bullet flies past to prove his point.

"Great," says Taggett and tears open the passenger side door and crams himself into the little car. "Meet us outside the Prestige Hotel." Jie nods and scampers off into the night. Chen plants himself behind the wheel and thumbs the ignition and tears a squeal out of the tires as he backs away from the skirmish. Once he gets some distance he throws the car into a screeching U-turn and starts racing down the highway back to Shanghai.

With the little car rattling around them as it screams through the sleeping little city Chen darts a glance at his partner and says, "So what's the new plan, boss?" He starts to slow as the filing station approaches but Taggett shakes his head so Chen puts his foot back on the pedal and shoots the coupe further along the track. The darkness closes in around them. The world shrinks to the glimpses of beat-up road the flashlights can pick out rushing under the car. The growl of the motor and the rattle of the car's body as it jolts over the terrain fill the silence until Chen tries again. "Boss?" he says. "What's next?"

"I don't know," says Taggett. He reaches into his jacket for a smoke and comes up empty and says, "I don't know what's next or what's past or what's happening now. I just guess I'm tired." He runs a big hand over his face and flinches a little as his scar flares. "I don't know," he says. "I don't know what I am. Something about this Violet Diamond. I think it's doing something to me." He turns to Chen and starts to say, "I just feel," but the sound of his voice echoing in the little car stops him. He looks at Chen through the purple fog thickening the air between them. "I just," he says but now the fog's in his mouth and pressing down on his tongue with a taste of ether-soaked cotton and pushing into his brain through his eyes so he screws down his eyelids like a little kid pretending to cry.

He opens them and he's sitting in a wooden chair in a big opulent room that might be part of a luxury suite. He sits there for a moment trying to blink the world back into focus. The scar on his face is etching pain into his skin as he sits there breathing in a heavy stench of lavender from someone's teapot boiling over somewhere. Maybe he's in a ballroom. He twists his head around to try to track the fancy-dress types walking past without noticing him in the middle of the floor in his chair. He swallows and tries to call out and just gets a kind of strangled growl for his effort. After a few minutes of this a bony customer with slicked-back blond hair and the kind of sneer on his face that can only come from generations of wealth strolls up and stops in front of him and stoops down to talk in his face the way you talk to a toddler. "Well, Mr. Taggett," he says, "You've fallen into some trouble, haven't you?"

"Huh?" says Taggett. The room spins for a second until he shakes his head again. He takes a deep breath through his mouth and comes up with, "Wha?"

The slick customer gives a chuckle. "What a pity you're not at your best," he says. "I was rather looking forward to some of that witty badinage you specialize in. Ah, well." He straightens up and fusses with his tail-coat and white bow-tie for a moment grinning down at the tough detective. "That befuddled expression you're sporting tells me you don't remember me, even though we met with such ceremony," he says and takes out a smoke for himself and lights up and lets the grin curdle into a smirk. "You were such a help to my bride and me. Ah, but I guess you're not at your best, so I'll introduce myself again. I'm Edgar Foulsworth, old sport."

Taggett's eyes bulge as he stares at the guy. "The hell," he says. "Edgar Foulsworth's an old mummy in a wheelchair."

"Perhaps I was that," says the man calling himself Foulsworth, "but I've recently had a burden lifted from me." He takes another drag of his smoke and lets it out with a sigh. "I've missed this," he says. "At any rate, I just wanted to stop by and offer my sincere appreciation for your gullibility. Keep what you have, old sport." The blue eyes that have been twinkling down into Taggett's turn to ice. "Keep it far away from that vulture I married," says Foulsworth. "Don't let her get those claws into you." Then those thin lips curl back into the smirk they came in with and he says with a chuckle at the back of his tone, "Or do what you like. Soon enough you won't have much choice."

Taggett snarls and says, "What the hell are you talking about?" and tries to get up from the chair to give this jerk the sock in the jaw he's asking for. But Taggett can't move. He glances wildly down at his arms as they lie straight along the arms of the chair. They're not tied down and there's nothing around his ankles but the cuffs of what he's just now noticing are flimsy pajama pants. His lips come back from his teeth as he growls up at Foulsworth.

"Too late, I guess. So sorry, old sport, but better you than me," Foulsworth says and starts to whistle an old waltz tune as he drops his burnt-out stub on the floor and strides away into the ballroom that fades away as he leaves it into some kind of shadowy ward room in what Taggett somehow knows is a nuthouse.

The tough detective growls deeper in his throat. He keeps wrestling with his body. He can't even make a finger twitch. He whips his head around and sees Chen walking past and yells his partner's name so hard he feels something snap in his throat. The younger man keeps walking. He pushes open a double door into a square of light and the door swings shut and he's entirely gone. Soon enough Taggett's the only one in this big silent room. Something clicks behind him and he braces himself.

A cloud of swirling purple glitter comes in from the edges of his vision and takes over and when the sparkles finally fade out they take his body with them. He's part of the still air in a room that looks like an office. The room's bare walls make flat echoes out of the sobs leaking out from the little grinning freak from the gas station hunched on a stool and cradling in his right hand a left hand that's still oozing blood from around where the bones are sticking out. He's not grinning now. On the other side of an empty desk from the freak sits yet another smooth gangster in a black suit and tie with a shirt so white it gleams. He sits there watching the freak flinch as tears get into the fresh wounds and then finally says, "So you've failed."

"I—no—I don't—" The freak sobs and chokes and tries to start again. "I called, just like you told me," he whines. His spindly body twitches on the creaking stool.

The gangster casually opens a desk drawer and pulls out a revolver and puts it on the table between them. He says, "But too late. You called your bandits first, didn't you?" While the freak on the stool stutters and drools the gangster opens the cylinder and lets the bullets clatter on the wooden desktop. The freak on the stool sucks in a breath and shuts up as the gangster takes one bullet off the desk and puts it back in the gun and spins the barrel and snaps it into place. In the casual tone of a debt collector checking a form he says, "You called your bandits hoping they'd just leave some bodies for us to pick up so you could take whatever you thought we were looking for. Isn't that right?" The freak mumbles some kind of protest and shakes his head back and forth as if he's trying to get a stuck wig off. The gangster smirks again and points the revolver at the little victim. He pulls the trigger and the hammer goes click and the freak falls off the stool. The shock of his wrecked left hand hitting the floor pushes a deep moan out of the little sucker. The gangster sits there watching like a husband at the opera as the freak pulls himself up the stool with his right hand and finally perches on it again. The gangster says, "I've read that in America they say that the biggest dog eats first. Can you guess what that means?" While the freak is trying to come up with a response and getting only bubbles of spit seeping between his cracked lips the gangster pulls the trigger again. The hammer clicks and the freak somehow stays on the stool shaking his head and just letting out a low moan. The gangster's smirk goes away and he says, "It means you give us what we want when we tell you to. You don't decide what we get. We decide what you get. Understand?" He pulls the trigger and the bullet exploding from the barrel pushes the little freak's body off the stool and into the wall behind him where his body slumps to the floor. A red stain spreads on the rag of a shirt he's wearing and then the blood starts to run down onto the floor. The gangster leans back and cracks his knuckles and looks at the mess.

Then the door next to the corpse swings open and Mrs. Foulsworth passes through it the way a ghost might drift up through a coffin lid. The black figure pauses and turns to look down at the dead thing on the floor and then turns back to face the gangster at the desk. He's sitting up very straight by now. That weird mechanical insect of a voice filters through the veil to say, "The slovenly nature of your housekeeping goes without saying. However, even such a lowly specimen of a backwards race as yourself must have been trained in the simple propriety of rising from your seat when a lady enters the room." The gangster goes pale and scrambles to his feet so fast his chair makes a little screech as it scrapes back over the floor. "Better," says Mrs. Foulsworth as she glides around the desk. The gangster backs away as she gets closer until he's standing in front of the freak's stool and she's seating herself behind the desk. "So," she says, "you've failed."

The gangster curls his lips into a sad try at a confident smile and says, "Well, uh, you could say, you see—"

She cuts him off. "I see a great deal, Mr. Fang," she says, "and I'm sure you'll believe me when I inform you that I employ the honorific simply as evidence of the upbringing and manners which you so egregiously lack. I see the way you rely on inferior labor as recompense for the trust which I have placed on you personally to pursue my interests in your filthy sphere." She takes a moment to reach into a hidden pocket for one of those gnarled brown cigarettes and holds it against a spot on her veil where a regular face's lips would be. After a moment Fang figures it out and lights the cigarette for her. Its end glows red for a moment and then a thick sheet of smoke carries from under the veil the smell of a field of flowers withering in a firestorm. "The question becomes one of how I should honor such laziness and dereliction," she says. Fang's glance darts down to the gun on the table and the little pile of bullets next to it. A dry chuckle comes out of Mrs. Foulsworth as she says, "I suppose you're regretting your playful nature now." She takes another drag and stubs the smoke out on the desk. "Perhaps," she says, "had you simply had the ability to restrain for a moment your native propensity for showmanship, you could have interrogated this instrument of your incompetence"--she flicks her gloved hand at the corpse behind Fang—"to discover the location of my property or of that damnable Taggett." The black figure bends forward for a moment as if out of breath and then straightens again to face Fang. "But the question remains. How shall I reward your efforts in service to me?" Fang just stands there and sweats. Then he flinches back and knocks the stool over as the chair under Mrs. Foulsworth smashes into the wall. The old woman's crouched on the desk. Fang's staring straight into the empty space of that veil as she growls like a panther at him. "Do you wish to continue your miserable life," she snarls. He nods. "Then step closer," she says. His body twitches a little and then a foot lifts from the floor and lands a little closer. His face has gone completely blank. His other foot lifts and lands and he's another step closer. A thick drop falls from his slack lower lip to stain the top of his shoe as that foot lifts and falls and brings him closer and then he's standing right in front of her. He's close enough to see the motion of the veil as she breathes. Her hands rise and cradle his face and then her thumbs are in his eye sockets pressing.

His body spasms and he starts to scream but she lets go and pushes him back a few steps to fall over the stool. He's whimpering something about his eyes and blindness and his mommy and she says, "You haven't been blinded, you hysterical fool. I merely wanted to impart to you the sensation that your next failure will surely bring. Now blink the blood out of your eyes." She's still crouched on the desk as he pushes himself to his feet. He has to plant his hand in the cooling corpse and he retches a little and has to spoil his suit by wiping the filth and blood over his shirt. By the time he can see anything again Mrs. Foulsworth is back in the chair. "Now get back to operating your sordid affairs, Mr. Fang, and never let it slip your mind that I can replace you in just the same way that I replaced your predecessor and the one who died before him." Fang bows as well as his trembling body will let him and turns and gets his hand on the doorknob when she says, "And have someone clear away your refuse. Act as if you have some respect for yourself despite your mongrel nature." The gangster mutters something and closes the door behind him as he slinks off.

Mrs. Foulsworth sits in silence for a moment and then says to the empty room, "I can feel your presence, Taggett. Your possession of the diamond has formed an inextricable link between us. Soon either the diamond or you will be mine. You may choose while you still can." The silence returns and congeals the air in that little room. Taggett starts to notice again that he exists as the light starts to tint purple and Mrs. Foulsworth says, "Or perhaps your arrogance and stupidity have cause you to miss your chance after all," and starts to let that insect laugh buzz from under the veil to fill up the whole room and push that little particle of consciousness turning into Johnny out of the scene and back into a featureless purple void.

He opens his eyes in the passenger seat of a coupe idling by the side of the road to Shanghai and says to Chen, "I know what to do next."

CHAPTER THIRTY

By dawn they're back in the city. Jie's met them in the Silver Phantom with fresh packs of smokes and now they're all sitting and smoking and looking at the Prestige Hotel. Delivery trucks rattle and growl past the parked car. Inside the silence is thickening along with that blue cloud of smoke until Chen finally says, "Really? Visions? What the hell is this rock?"

"Yeah," says Taggett. "Visions. Or something. It's been happening for a while." He takes another drag and keeps staring at the hotel. "Worse lately," he says. "At least since we got to Shanghai. It's like I'm having some kind of crazy dream that's got me running around in circles." He sucks one last glow into the end of his smoke and then cracks the window to throw the butt out onto the sidewalk and says, "So it's time to wake up."

Chen turns around to look at his partner over the back of the front bench. His lips pull back from his teeth so he can grin while he snickers. "So this is where we wake up?" he says. "Looks like more of the same to me. I don't see why you don't just let that trinket drop off the side of the boat we get the hell out of here in."

"And go where?" Taggett says. His voice cracks a little at the end of his question as he lights up another smoke. "Home?" he says. "New York? Africa? That weird hag's got an army that won't quit chasing us, diamond or no diamond." He clamps his lips around the smoke and takes out his forty-five. "Anyway, I don't think it works like that." With fingers a little shaky he works the action and jacks out the clip. With the forty-five in one hand and the clip in the other he watches the traffic for a moment. Then he says, "I get this feeling like the diamond's leeching on to me, like I'm some kind of host," and slams the clip back home. "So I'm gonna get rid of it by putting it back where I got it."

This brings a gasp out of Jie and turns him around in the driver's seat to stare at Taggett all wide-eyed. He clears his throat and swallows and coughs again and says, "Despite my characteristic reluctance to present myself as an obstacle in any of our mutual endeavors, I find myself irresistibly compelled to object to the course of action to which you seem to allude." He's got himself so turned around that his hands are gripping the back of the bench. "Our adversary's demonstrable malevolence clearly disqualifies her from possession of an artifact with the undeniable power associated with the Violet Diamond," he says and blinks for a moment before he takes a breath and keeps going. "The mere contemplation of uniting such a monstrously evil personage with such a powerful weapon," he says, "seems to inaugurate a journey on a path whose terminus lies in the realm of cataclysm."

"I don't think so," says Taggett as he puts the forty-five back in its holster. "I think it needs a host. I mean, look at what happened to old Edgar Foulsworth. He finds the thing and before you know it he's some kind of mummy to wheel around like a wagon full of rocks. Who can live like that?" His voice cracks again and his eyes blaze into the faces of the other two men. "Maybe Mrs. Foulsworth doesn't want to go down the road her husband did." He flicks his butt out the window and starts a third smoke. "I don't want to go down that road either," he says.

Chen says, "Okay," and laces his fingers together to pull them back and crack the knuckles. "So we stop it here. But why here?"

"Two things," Taggett says. "One's a hunch just based on what I know about how that weird frail operates. She's gotta have the best of everything, right?" Chen nods. "But she thinks of this city as some kind of dung heap full of slimy bugs," Taggett goes on, "so she's not gonna buy herself any kind of permanent station." He throws out that third butt. "She's gonna rent and she's gotta do it as close to the action as she can with as much Western-style luxury as she can get. You know she's not staying in any kind of flop house. Plus, she's got enough cash to whore out this whole city. To me that adds up to the Prestige Hotel."

Chen lets out a whistle and says, "That's one hell of a hunch. Did you just come up with all of that?"

Taggett shrugs. "I guess I've been working on it for a while," he says. "And then there's that other thing. Have you noticed these delivery trucks?" Jie and Chen both nod and Taggett says, "Did you notice that not one of them is headed for the Prestige? What kind of hotel doesn't take deliveries every day?" Jie's brow furrows as the older man glances down in thought for a second and then looks back up into Taggett's eyes and nods. "Whoever's in there," says Taggett, "they're trying pretty hard to keep to themselves."

"Then let's bring them a little sunshine," Chen says and cracks his knuckles again. "It's not healthy being cooped up all on your own like that." He takes a last drag on his smoke and opens the passenger door. Taggett chuckles and opens his own door. As the two of them step to the sidewalk the tough detective puts out his hand and shoves Chen back into the shadow of the wall behind them. The younger man draws in a breath and then clamps his lips over whatever he was going to say. A discreet tap to Chen's hand lets him know that Jie has slipped into the shadow next to him. Chen glances at the older man and Jie replies with a questioning look so Chen points with his head across the street to the hotel's entrance and murmurs, "Stuart."

That big white guy who looks so weirdly like Taggett is striding through the thickening crowd of natives on the sidewalk like a schooner cutting through waves. The big man has a scowl on his face that looks like someone carved it there as he shoves his way along without looking left or right. He gets to the hotel's front door and pushes his way in while Jie stands there looking puzzled. "Stuart?" he says.

The other two men turn right around to goggle at their older friend for a moment. "Yeah," Taggett says. "Didn't you see him?" Jie just keeps giving that blank stare so Taggett says, "Seriously, big white guy like that, almost as big as me, how could you miss him?" Traffic rolls along behind Johnny and Chen as they wait for Jie to quit working his jaw and start making words.

"White?" he finally says and then blinks for a few seconds more. "I must with reluctance confess my inability to reconcile this characterization of Stuart as any kind of Caucasian with my knowledge of him as a Negro of, insofar as I can trust my memory under these peculiar circumstances, Ethiopian origin." Taggett glances over at Chen and sees the same dumb look that he must be sporting on his own face. "Thus," says Jie, "I find myself led irresistibly to the conclusion that the man you seem just to have indicated, the man you recognize as Stuart, merely represented himself in that capacity in order to lure you to the watery death from which I had the good fortune to rescue you.."

The three of them stand there like dopes until Taggett growls and says "Holy Hell! Enough!" and starts across the street in a straight line through the morning traffic. Tires shriek like scared girls as drivers try not to dent their grilles on him. He doesn't seem to notice. The other two men dodge and weave behind him around the horn honks and curses. They catch up to him just as he's ramming himself though the front door of the Prestige Hotel.

The lobby they step into spreads itself around them like a Venus flytrap around a struggling bug. Its crimson walls just about match its scarlet carpet which just about matches the plush burgundy chairs and sofas that keep a tasteful distance from each other. Each of the chairs has a guy in it and each of the sofas has two guys and the lobby hums low with dozens of male conversations that just growl like the background noise in the lion's den in the Bronx Zoo. Opposite the door and far across the floor that carpet turns into a vast lake of blood a little fellow with a smile pasted to the front of his big round head stands behind a counter with an ornate phone on it and fiddles around with some kind of paperwork. As the front door clicks shut he looks up and so do all the other hard-looking men in the lobby. Taggett keeps striding forward through the sudden silence until he gets to the counter. The little guy's pasted-on smile opens up and says in the voice of a radio announcer, "Welcome to the Prestige Hotel, gentlemen. I regret to inform you that we cannot accommodate guests without reservations and, further, that we have accepted no reservations for today's date. Regrettably, then, I must insist that you seek lodging elsewhere. Thank you." The smile seals itself shut again and the fellow goes back to his paperwork until Taggett reaches out and grabs the fellow's shirt and pulls him halfway over the counter.

"Listen," says Taggett. "I'm here to see your boss." He pulls the guy close enough to smell the breakfast fish on his breath. "So pick up your pretty little phone here," he snarls, "and get that freaky black bat down here or get me up there or get ready for more trouble than you want so early in the morning." He curls his fingers tighter and feels the starch crack in his shirt.

The smile on the little dude's face shifts into a smirk and that radio voice goes all nasal as he says, "Mister, I think you're in the wrong place. But don't worry. You won't be here long." Behind him Taggett hears the creak all that tasteful furniture makes when a big crowd of muscle stands up all at once. Chen and Jie on either side of him have turned around to face the mob and crouch slightly and sway back and forth a bit and get ready. Taggett just grins in that fat round face.

"You go first," says Taggett and pulls back a fist and pops the little guy right between his eyes. The guy's nose dribbles blood down over his lips. Taggett drops him back down behind his counter and whirls around to see the riot starting. A couple of the creeps have started running forward and Jie and Chen have dropped down and launched themselves forward in a pair of kicks that cripples one punk each. Then they tumble back up to their feet matching each other so exactly that they look like one guy in a mirror as they smash the heels of their palms into a couple of faces and knock down a couple more enforcers. A guy off to Chen's left is pulling out a gun so Taggett turns and grabs a pen off the desk and throws it into the goon's hand. The creep drops the gun and roars and charges at Taggett and Chen's foot flies in from the side and pushes the creep's face around to the side of his head and spins him to the floor. The two detectives nod at each other before Chen goes back to mowing down the muscle boys.

Then Taggett sees that fake Stuart's head over the grunting and writhing mob. The big white guy's ducking through a side door so Taggett steps after him into the mess. He almost trips over one of the bodies Jie knocks down and then he has to duck around a haymaker some goon's throwing. He takes a moment to dislocate the goon's jaw and throw an elbow back into some other creep's big sweaty face and then keeps heading for that side door. Finally he gets his hand on the knob. He turns his head to get a glimpse of his partners laying waste to the little army in there. Then he takes a breath and pulls out his forty-five and turns the knob and steps through the door.

The sound of the fight blurs down to angry mutters and thumps as the door clicks shut behind him. He stands there for a moment in a dim light that he can't see the source of. Stubby hallways stretch to his left and right behind the walls of the Prestige Hotel as he stands there listening. A wide staircase yawns down in front of him and he can see landings that lead to parallel hallways as the stairs sink into darkness. His heart throbs in his chest and sets his scar on fire as the sound of the fight fades further away. From down those wide stairs someone chuckles. A gruff voice comes floating up saying, "Fear ye not, Missus. I snuck in nimble as a barge rat amidst the scuffle." Taggett feels his lips pull back from his teeth as he recognizes Stuart's weird cartoonish brogue and starts down the staircase.

He can feel the wood creaking under his shoes as much as he can hear it. That crazy sourceless glow surrounds him like a dim fog so that the staircase seems to spread out into shadows with no end. Taggett finds a wall with his left hand and grips his forty-five in his right and creeps down step by step. After a while he loses count. The stairway just stretches down to keep up with him.

Then his left hand pushes forward into empty space and he's on the first landing. He turns and drops to a squat to peer along a hallway that seems to get lighter as it goes until it dead-ends in a big mural of a naked woman with her mouth open. After ten yards or so doors start to appear on either side. He starts to hear the moans of lust and satisfaction about the same time he notices the doors. "Whorehouse," he says to himself a second before he hears the click of a door opening behind him. He whirls around to see a big naked ape of a Chinese guy barreling toward him so he sets himself and lets the creep come on until the tough detective lashes out a kick and plants a foot right between the ape's meaty thighs. The guy makes a little squeak and goes right down so Taggett can put a heel to his head and knock him out. He stands there for a minute over the sleeping side of beef but no one else comes for him. Another of Stuart's raspy chuckles oozes up from the bottom of the staircase. Taggett steps around the ape and reaches out his left hand to find wall again and keeps going down.

The cool tile under his hand starts bleeding little droplets of water that slick up under his fingertips and then the smoothness gives way to some kind of rough rock just as wet. Taggett shivers a little. That unhelpful foggy glow is starting to go purple around the edges. He shakes his head the way a worn-down suspect might to deny his crime and the light goes back to that greasy yellow-grey as he makes it down to the next landing. As much as he can see reveals hallways that look much older than the ones upstairs. The doors are a little crooked on their hinges and from behind at least one of them comes the thud of fist on flesh and the whispered grunt a professional girl makes when takes one shot too many. "Aye, Missus," Stuart says a little more distinctly from below, "these catacombs be a smuggler's dream, best meeting place ye could conjure." Another one of those rusty chortles and Taggett's got his hand back on the wall scraping his palm on the ancient rock. He takes a step down and then another step and then another.

Before he's quite ready his shoes are clacking on some kind of rock. He's at the bottom. A wind is moaning somewhere and water drips and splashes and echoes. Taggett stands there for a moment facing a wall that someone must have painted glossy red but the dark makes it just look like a frozen slick of blood. Then he looks left and looks right and waits. Finally that crazy "Har!" comes from somewhere to his left so he turns that way and starts walking down what looks like a tunnel with a thin walkway at its bottom and nothing but black rock with purple veins on either side. He inches along. The mud at the bottom of the tunnel seems to come up a little over the edges of the walkway as if someone about as heavy as Taggett had pressed it down a few minutes ago. Johnny's face twitches a little as his scar blazes up and he makes out a sliver of light ahead of him. He freezes and crouches. The mud that narrow board is pressing into sends up fumes of sulphur. He stays down and squints and waits and gets a glimpse of shadow interrupting the light. "Someone pacing," he mutters to himself. "Just one?" He keeps waiting and breathing in that stink but the pattern doesn't break up in the right way. "Just one," he says to himself. Then he growls and says "Ah, Hell," and clambers to his feet and runs straight forward and smashes through a flimsy old door into a little room with a square table in its middle and a cheap electric lamp on the table. Standing next to the table in full Kaiser regalia is Otto.

"Greetings, Herr Taggett," he says in that weird Chinese German accent. "I have for some time been seeking this private audience." Taggett's frozen in place and framed by the doorway he's standing in. His grip tightens on his forty-five.

"What the hell?" says Taggett. "What the hell are you doing here? Where the hell are Stuart and Mrs. Foulsworth?" He brings the forty-five down to point it straight between Otto's eyes and says, "God help me, I'm gonna get some answers if I have to take you apart with my bare hands."

Otto smirks and his head makes a little tremor that must be a laugh. "For Mrs. Foulsworth I cannot speak. However," and here his voice turns into Stuart's, "if ye be seekin yer trusty scalawag from the dark part of town, why here I be." He reaches up as he's saying this and takes off a putty nose while Taggett actually takes a step back in shock.

Johnny says, "No way. It can't be. I saw you die."

"Surprise," says One-Eye.

CHAPTER THIRTY ONE

Somehow Taggett keeps himself from putting a bullet into the ninja out of reflex. Instead he swallows a tremble out of his voice and says, "Yeah, surprise is right. I could swear I saw you die."

A rough chuckle claws its way out of One-Eye's chest as he keeps taking off Otto's face. "But I stand here with you now," he says. "And now you know I have been in your life." He finishes peeling off the front of his head to reveal a knotted mass of scars with a piercing black eye glaring from inside it and starts to strip out of Otto's weird Hun outfit down to a tight black jumpsuit. His lipless mouth twists to a smirk as he says in a voice Taggett recognizes from the *Flower Song*, "You wonder now how many times you have seen me." The stiff suit crumples to the ground as the ninja sheds it.

"I wonder a lot of things," says Taggett. He hasn't moved an inch into One-Eye's little room but he also hasn't holstered his forty-five. He makes a smirk of his own and says, "But I guess this little strip tease you're doing means you're about to throw some answers."

One-Eye grates out another of those rusty chuckles and says, "No. I will give you no answers. There are no answers." He moves behind the lamp. Its deep shadow swallows him up. His voice comes out of the blackness like a thrown handful of pebbles. "Maybe the man you saw die was a paid duplicate," it says. "Or maybe a passing boat rescued me." That single eye seems to swallow up the light from the lamp and leave just a flicker that Taggett can barely look into. "Or maybe the

Violet Diamond has taken your mind and this is some kind of dream," says the voice.

"No," says Taggett. "I know what's real. I know where I am." A drop of sweat crawls down his face over his flaming scar. His finger curls on the trigger until he makes the effort to straighten it back out. He stands there staring into the shadow.

The voice says, "I also know where you are. You are deep underground. You are alone in a small room with your enemy. You are far away from your friends." That shadow spreads wings along the walls to either side of the back wall it's covering. Taggett watches as the darkness eats the room. "And I know that you have let me distract you from them for many minutes now," the voice says in a near-whisper that Taggett has to strain to hear. He catches himself leaning forward slightly as it says, "Think of what useful hostages they will make." A hand emerges from the shadow into the little yellow halo coming down from the lamp. Fingers close to switch it off. Everything turns into darkness.

Taggett turns and runs. His shoes slide over the board slimed with mud but he keeps his feet and makes it to the stone floor that clicks under his heels and runs until he sees the glow from the stairway and turns and starts climbing up two steps at a time. He's breathing hard as he sprints past the hall with the rough walls and the sounds of beatings but he can't stop. He barely notices as he crosses the whorehouse level that the naked Chinese creep has crawled a little way down that hall and collapsed again. He can feel the strength going out of his legs and the pulse throbbing around his field of vision as he pushes himself up those stairs. Finally he gets to the top and smashes through the door into the lobby.

The splintered remains of what used to be chairs and benches make a stunted forest on that blood-colored carpet as if someone gave up in the middle of putting together a bonfire. Taggett can see the furrows of bent pile where someone dragged a bunch of bodies through the double doors across the room from the door he's standing in front of. Then a kind of gurgling laugh pulls his attention to the door back out to the street and he growls deep in his throat. "Holy hell," he mutters.

The guy standing in front of the door takes up enough space for two or three regular-sized creeps to hide behind. His thick lips are shiny with drool and projecting a little from his baby-smooth head as he sways a little on his feet and chuckles again. A bubble of spit pops in the big freak's mouth while Taggett watches that massive stump of a head turn his way like the gun turret on a tank. The glassy black eyes light up and the lips curl up to expose a set of teeth filed to points and the guy says, "Taggett. You die now." Then he charges.

He's too fast for Taggett to shoot before a pair of thick arms wraps around the detective's torso and squeezes tight. He feels his ribs shift and his legs flap as the giant ragdolls him around and Taggett tightens his trigger finger and fires point-blank into the meat of the freak's hip. This gets a roar out of the weirdo that drenches Taggett's ear in acid-smelling spit and then the giant tosses him into a little pile of sticks and nails that reach out to rip a furrow in his jacket and shirt and skin. He raises his gun but the freak is on him again. A fist bigger than a cannonball slams into his shoulder and turns his arm numb but he manages to roll out of the way before it can smash his face in. He keeps rolling through the sharp rubble and pushes himself to his knees and uses his left hand to lift his right arm and aim. Through the pins and needles he manages to pull the trigger and shoot the charging freak in his knee. The giant roars again and goes down but momentum lets him push the detective down to his back and get a meaty grip on Taggett's ankles and start trying to climb up his body. Taggett pulls a leg back and kicks the big creep in the face and just gets another one of those wet giggles for his trouble. He kicks again and catches that silly face right in the middle with the heel of his shoe to mask the guy's face with blood. The freak keeps laughing and gurgling as Taggett manages to push him far enough away to put a bullet between his eyes and shut him up. In the sudden silence Taggett lets his head fall back to the carpet and lies there looking up at the red ceiling for a moment to let his breath come back. Finally he makes it back to his feet. "Jesus," he mutters to himself. "What next?" The pile of meat bleeding into the blood-red carpet doesn't answer.

In the sudden quiet of the lobby he looks around at the double doors the drag marks lead to. As he gets closer to those doors he notices a page of Prestige Hotel stationery stuck to them with Mrs. Foulsworth's spidery scribble on it. "Elevator out of order," it says. "Take stairs to penthouse or bear the shame of having abandoned your companions to my ministrations." The tough detective growls and glances to the side to see a single door almost completely masked by the wallpaper. He checks the clip in his forty-five to make sure he's got a few rounds left before he grabs the stub of a doorknob and twists and pushes the door open into new darkness and steps through.

The doorway behind him makes a rectangle of light on the stairs leading up as Taggett walks into his own shadow. Soon enough he gets to a landing with a bulb flickering in a sconce above a sign that says "ONE" next to a door. He has to turn around to get up the next flight and then the next and then the next and then the next. Sweat itches along his scar. He climbs more stairs from dim light to dim light as his legs slowly turn to wood. Somewhere in there he's started muttering to himself.

"Enough," he's saying. "This has to end. I'm sick of all this bouncing around." His low growl echoes with a flat slap from the nondescript walls that hem in the narrow stairway. "Like a god damn toy, like a rubber ball in some kid's game. Waste of time," says the detective and keeps climbing. He passes a sign that says "TEN" and then a sign that says "ELEVEN" and then stops on that landing for a moment to breathe. "One of us is gonna die today," he tells himself and pushes his body up to the final landing. The sign says "PENTHOUSE ACCESS" but a smudge of blood about the size of someone's face still damp and shiny under the sconced bulb covers the end of the second word. "Guess I'll find out who," says Taggett. He checks his forty-five one more time and faces the door and kicks it open.

The hallway that stretches between the stairway entrance and the gilded door at its other end that must lead to the penthouse has the same relentless crimson shade that the lobby does. It has the same deep red carpet and the same violently scarlet wallpaper with a few rips in it revealing grey plaster. Some yellow chairs line the walls about four feet apart. Closer to the penthouse door they've turned into yellow-painted sticks of wood where someone smashed a couple of them. Taggett keeps his forty-five up as he steps carefully along the center of the hall. The carpet swallows his feet. Each step turns into a little struggle with a bloody swamp. Finally he gets to the door and stops and listens.

He hears nothing. "Maybe the door's too thick," he tells himself. He slides the action back on his forty-five and steps back to shift his balance so he can kick the door down but a click like something he heard once in a bad dream freezes him. He swivels his head back down the hall and sees nothing but his tracks. He peers back around to the door. It doesn't have any obvious peepholes to poke a heater through. Another click snaps his head to a loudspeaker painted to blend in with the garish hallway.

"Such utterly inconsequential effort," it says in Mrs. Foulsworth's creaky buzz. The speaker's distortion makes her voice sound like a radio transmission from the other side of the world. "This violent solution you propose to the mundane task of opening a simple door serves exquisitely to ratify my prudence in determining the simple physical employments to which I will assign you once you have submitted to your destiny," says the box as Taggett keeps staring up at it. He keeps his lips buttoned and the box lets out a crackle and then says, "I shall endeavor to express myself in the most basic possible terms as befits one of your limited capacities. Reach for the doorknob with your hand, turn the doorknob, and push so that the door opens into the room. Then you may enter and truly begin your service to me." The speaker shuts off with a last click. Taggett turns the knob and opens the door.

The room beyond the gilded door makes Taggett blink for a second as he stands there. It looks like a sitting room with five jet black chairs arranged around an ebony coffee table in the middle of a snow-colored carpet that stretches between ivory walls. A black rectangle of a door breaks up the wall opposite the door where Taggett gawks. Chen and Jie occupy a couple of those chairs on the other side of the table with manacles binding them at wrists and ankles to the arms and legs. Jie's dripping a red puddle into the carpet while Chen growls and squirms and shoots glares at the two guys standing a few feet away and sighting down gun barrels at him. While Taggett takes all this in another creep in that weird gangster uniform of black suit and white shirt and skinny black tie steps up to him. This one's got shades on so as to stand out from the others. He makes a smirk and nods at the forty-five dangling in Taggett's right hand and says, "I'll have the heater, lawman."

Taggett snorts a chuckle and says, "Law, right," and gives the creep a straight left jab to the middle of his face. The creep goes down into that snowdrift of a carpet and Chen's head whips around to find his partner but the guys with the guns don't flinch. Taggett stands there and looks down at the mess he made of this guy's nose. The creep reaches up to straighten his shades and pushes himself up to his feet. Taggett takes a step into the room.

The creep takes another step toward the tough detective and says, "Listen, bulldog, no one comes in here holding any kind of weapon unless he gets the all clear from me, and I'm not giving you the all clear. Get me?" Blood drips out of his smashed up nose as he takes another step. He reaches out his hand with its palm up the way a tollbooth operator reaches for a dime. That smirk has somehow managed to screw itself back onto his face even as he snorts up a big plug of blood and swallows. He says again, "Do you get me?"

Taggett nods and socks him in the face again. The shades break into pieces under his knuckles and fall off either side of the creep's face as Taggett's left jab knocks him back down. He lies there staining the carpet for another moment and then turns back to stab at Taggett with a pair of red-rimmed eyes that look like pits leading to a night-black hell at the center of the earth. Taggett takes half a step back as the creep snarls something in Chinese and yanks a little pistol out of his jacket and points it up at the detective when a roar of "ENOUGH" stops everything in the room. "Fang, these theatrics have begun to bore me," continues the voice of Mrs. Foulsworth, "and I see no reason to deprive our Taggett of the security, erstwhile as it may be, of his weapon. Why take the blanket from the baby?" The creep keeps lying there with his arm stretched out and quivering a little as Mrs. Foulsworth finishes her mechanical chuckling and says, "Come in, Johnny. Your keen observational skills, if I may be permitted a brief sarcasm, must have ascertained by now that the contest between us has ended. I have demonstrated your inability to successfully contend against the unalterable fate I have chosen for you. Come in and surrender." The smell of one of those putrid little cigarettes wafts around a corner. "You have no other option," says the voice.

Taggett steps around Fang and turns to face Mrs. Foulsworth as she smokes behind a big mahogany desk. He steps between the chairs holding Chen and Jie but he's not looking at either of them. His face points directly at the void where Mrs. Foulsworth's face should be. "Actually, I think I have one more move," he says and raises his forty-five and sights down the barrel at the black shape behind the desk.

Instantly the goons on either side of him have their guns on him. One pokes into his ribs and the other knocks against his temple as that weird droning laugh comes out of Mrs. Foulsworth again. "Really," she says after a while of this. "You must pardon my reaction to the threat you imply so charmlessly. I simply cannot extend to you the seriousness you seem to expect from me." She stubs out the cigarette on the desk in front of her and places her hands flat in front of her. The black velvet of her gloves disappears into the dark wood. She says, "You must realize the infinitesimal chance of survival incumbent upon an attempt such as that at which you gesture."

"Yeah," says Taggett. "I've been thinking about that." He takes a step forward and the guns on either side track him. "And I think you don't want me dead," he says. "Otherwise I'd be in the ground by now. You've put too much work into me, making up a conspiracy and hiring someone to play One-Eye and screwing up your business in Shanghai at least twice." He takes another step forward. By this time he's about a foot away from the desk and a foot in front of the chairs. "Besides," he says, "if you kill me you'll have to spend extra time and energy finding the Diamond again, and who knows how long you've got for that kind of a hunt." He takes another step forward with his arm still extended with the forty-five at the end of it pointed right at the middle of Mrs. Foulsworth's head. He says, "So it looks like either I kill you and die or I just die. I don't care which at this point. You played me too hard." He takes another step forward. The guns on him go click as the goons cock them.

Some kind of growl's coming out of Mrs. Foulsworth along with the scratch of her nails as she claws into the desk. "Damn you," she says and then the growl cuts off as if someone flipped a switch. The room fills up with silence for a stretching moment and then that creepy chortling and she says, "But what of your companions, Taggett? My reluctance to allow your demise derives entirely from your usefulness, as you have so arrogantly explained to me. Your friends, however, possess no such utility." A kind of wheezing snicker comes out from behind the veil and she lights another of those twisted brown smokes and says, "Surrender or your beloved associates will pay the price of your recalcitrance."

From behind everyone but Mrs. Foulsworth Fang says, "They're gone."

Another of those roars comes out of the black shape behind the desk and then she's squatting on top of it like a panther ready to pounce. The cigarette tumbles down into the carpet and a black spot starts to spread and smoke around where it fell. Mrs. Foulsworth's standing on the desk and shaking and Taggett's arm rises a little to keep a bead on her as she just yells, "What? And you did nothing?"

"That's right," says Fang. "I watched the little one pick his cuffs and spring the old one and drag him out of here and I didn't do a thing at all. You must've gotten distracted or something." The creep's voice is getting a little louder and a little less squeaky as he keeps talking. "I guess you just need to hire better help," he says. "I hear the natives can't be trusted."

The sound coming out of Mrs. Foulsworth sounds like jammed gears battling each other to a standstill that will wreck the machine. The black spot next to the desk has started to sprout little flames. The noise she makes turns into words and she says, "You cannot exhibit such disobedience with impunity. I will destroy you and your family and your associates and this whole Godforsaken 239."

"Maybe," Fang says. "And then again maybe you'll just get the hell out of here while we let you." The squeak has completely left his voice as he snaps his fingers and the goons flanking Taggett turn their guns on Mrs. Foulsworth. Fang says, "Not everyone in Shanghai is ready to die for your little game, you hag." She starts to say something and Fang says, "Shut up. We're done. Come on, boys, we've got business to do."

The goons step back and after a moment Taggett hears the door open and shut. "I guess we're even, Taggett," says Fang and then the door opens and shuts again and the penthouse has no other sound but the rusty noise coming out of Mrs. Foulsworth.

Taggett says, "I guess you don't have all the resources you thought," as he puts away his forty-five and takes a step closer to the black figure shaking on the desk. "So let me tell you how this ends. You won't kill me and you won't kill my friends and you won't bother any of us ever again." He takes another step forward. She trembles there on the desk just inches away. He can almost smell her breath like the wind from a graveyard. He says, "If I ever hear from you again or if my friends ever hear from you again I will just kill you. I'll find you and kill you and then your story's over." He reaches up a little to put his hand on her throat. He can feel a pulse like a hummingbird beating against the velvet under his fingers as they curl to squeeze just enough. "Do you understand?" he says. The tendons tighten as she nods. He lets her go and turns around and walks out of the penthouse and down the silent hall and down the quiet stairs to the peace of that wrecked lobby and out through the front door like any other citizen.

He stops on the sidewalk and takes a long breath and lets it out. Cars hustle past on the street in both directions on vital missions that no one but their heroes particularly cares about. Tourists make their private ways along the sidewalks on either side and step around the three men standing there staring at each other while Chen finishes his smoke and Jie finishes bandaging himself with a few winds of gauze around his bleeding head. After a minute or so of this Chen says, "So did you kill her?"

"No," Taggett says. Chen's jaw actually drops as he stares at the tough detective. "Listen, says Taggett, "if I kill her, that just invites some new freak of nature to get interested in this rock and come after me and then we all get stuck in this ridiculous game some more." He lights up a smoke of his own and says, "But if I get her scared of me, she'll work hard to make sure that no one pesters us." Some guy in a white suit pushes by between the two of them as Taggett pulls out another smoke and offers it to Chen and glances at Jie. "Are you all right?" he says.

Chen takes the smoke and lights up and nods and Jie says, "Happily, I can report that although I seem to have absorbed what I must characterize as a significant number of abrasions and contusions, and even some cranial lacerations that, to my shame and dismay, seem to have momentarily incapacitated me, none of my injuries will to the level of an encumbrance on my habitual activities." Chen just goggles at him for a minute until he says, "In other words, my state of being can be considered, ah, copacetic." That gets a laugh out of all three of them as Jie slips behind the wheel and Chen opens the passenger door of the Silver Phantom.

Taggett looks up at the top window of the Hotel Prestige to see a puff of grey smoke drifting away without a sound. "Let's get out of here," he says, "before someone calls a cop."